Death
on the
Shelf

Also available by Allison Brook

The Haunted Library Mysteries

Checked Out for Murder

Buried in the Stacks

Read and Gone

Death Overdue

Death

on the

Shelf

A HAUNTED LIBRARY MYSTERY

Allison Brook

NEW YORK

Copyright © 2021 by Marilyn Levinson

Published in the United States by Crooked Lane Books, an imprint of The Quick Brown Fox & Company LLC.

Crooked Lane Books and its logo are trademarks of The Quick Brown Fox & Company LLC.

Library of Congress Catalog-in-Publication data available upon request.

ISBN (hardcover): 978-1-64385-780-0
ISBN (ebook): 978-1-64385-781-7

Cover illustration by Griesbach/Martucci

Printed in the United States.

www.crookedlanebooks.com

Crooked Lane Books
34 West 27th St., 10th Floor
New York, NY 10001

First Edition: November 2021

10 9 8 7 6 5 4 3 2 1

For my wonderful agent, Dawn Dowdle,
who's always only a phone call away.

Chapter One

"I can't believe it! This simply cannot be happening!" Angela Vecchio looked up from her cell phone and burst into tears.

"What's wrong?" I reached over to hug my best friend, aware that people, many of whom we knew, were staring. It was lunchtime, and the Cozy Corner Café was packed as usual.

Angela kept on sobbing. "Carrie, this wedding is cursed! Steve and I should have eloped."

"Who called you?" I handed Angela a tissue.

She blew her nose loudly. "That was the restaurant."

"What restaurant?"

"Where I was supposed to be having my bridal shower. There was a fire and—and extensive damage."

"Oh, no!" I patted Angela's back as a new burst of sobs threatened. I drew a deep breath, relieved that she was growing calmer and the spectators were returning to their meals and conversations. "But why did they call you and not me since I'm the one in charge?"

Angela sniffed. "The woman said her name was Brenda and apologized for calling me when she realized the shower was for me. She'll call you later this afternoon."

"I'm so sorry, Angela." I was horrified as well, but I bit my lip to stop myself from saying more.

Angela and I worked together at the Clover Ridge Library— she at the circulation desk and I as head of programs and events. Our director, Sally Prescott; Angela's boss, Fran Kessler; Marion Marshall, the children's librarian; and I had selected the restaurant because it offered a private room with enough choices on the menu for a group of close to forty women aged twenty to ninety.

Today was Monday. The bridal shower was scheduled to be on Saturday, a mere five days away. Where were we supposed to find a suitable replacement venue in such a short period of time?

Angela pushed the plate with her half-eaten sandwich to the center of the table. "Lately, nothing is going right with this wedding. My gown needs an adjustment, some cousins on my dad's side refuse to sit at the same table, there's a problem with the flowers we ordered for the table settings, and now this!"

Who are you and what have you done with my best friend? Angela was a cheerful person, a positive person, and the farthest thing from a drama queen. But this was her wedding. And so I found myself making a promise I wasn't sure I could keep.

"Angela, you'll have your shower. Once Fran, Sally, Marion, and I put our heads together, we'll come up with a new place even nicer than the restaurant we originally chose. We could even hold it at my cottage—"

"Except that's when Mrs. C is doing her spring cleaning," Angela reminded me.

I grimaced. "You're right. And Dylan finally arranged for the plumber to come on Saturday to fix the leak in the guest bathroom."

My boyfriend, Dylan Avery, owned the cottage, which was a quarter mile down the private road from the manor, as I secretly called the large white house where he lived.

"We'll think of something," I finished lamely.

"Can we leave now?" Angela asked.

I waved over our waitress and asked her to wrap the rest of my sandwich.

"Are you gals in a rush?" Jilly asked, eyeing our unfinished lunches.

"Kind of," I said.

"Do you want yours wrapped too?" she asked Angela.

Angela shook her head and got to her feet. "Meet you outside." She handed me a twenty and scooted off.

"Too much," I began, but Angela was gone.

I joined her minutes later. A gentle June breeze wafted past us, carrying the fragrance of flowers in bloom and newly cut grass; the sky above was a lovely shade of blue. But all this was lost on Angela.

We walked back to the library in silence, which was pretty unusual for us since we were both rather chatty and Angela loved to talk about her wedding—sometimes too much. But she was in an unusually negative mood. Maybe this was wedding jitters. I doubted she had any doubts about marrying Steve, whom she loved with all her heart. But a wedding and all that it involved was a major event.

"And he's flying here on Thursday," Angela said, as if we were in the middle of a conversation. "I really could do without his presence in the house."

Angela's brother, a movie producer of sorts, lived in California. Angela had confided to me that he'd tormented her when they were growing up, and she wanted to have as little to do with him as possible.

"Why don't you stay in your new condo? It's practically in move-in condition, isn't it?"

"It is," Angela said, "and I could, but Mom would be so disappointed. She keeps talking about how this is the last time we'll be together as a family."

I wrapped my arms around her. "Ange, all this anxiety will be over and done with in a few weeks' time."

She lowered her head to nestle in the crook of my neck. "I know, but I so wanted this to be a special time. One I will always remember."

"I'll round up the girls and we'll find a new place for your shower."

Angela smiled for the first time since she'd received that phone call. "If anyone can fix this, it's you, Carrie Singleton."

* * *

Smoky Joe, his bushy tail held high, was waiting for me as we entered the library's back entrance that opened from the parking lot. Smoky Joe was the library cat—technically, my cat since he'd lived with me ever since one autumn morning when he'd made his way to my cottage from the farm on the other side of the woods.

I bent down to pet his gray flank. "Hungry?"

He meowed and set off for my office, certain that I'd follow him.

I hugged Angela. "Try not to let this get you down. I promise we will find a new place for your bridal shower."

She answered me with a nod.

As the Clover Ridge Library's head of programs and events, I had my own office—large enough for my desk and the one shared by my two part-time assistants—Trish Templeton and Susan Roberts—who were never here at the same time.

Trish waved to me as I entered the office, barely looking up from her computer. She was short and round, with rosy cheeks, and was as efficient as anyone could wish for an assistant to be.

When she finished what she was doing, she said, "I was just shooting off program applications to two applicants that sounded promising. One is a craftsy person who would like to do a program on fall decorations. The other is a home decorator who wants to do a program on sprucing up your home without spending big bucks."

I fed Smoky Joe, sank back into my chair, and let out a big sigh. Which must have made Trish think I was disappointed in her, because she said, "Is there a problem? You told me to use my judgment when possible presenters call or email and you're not here."

I waved my hand. "Sorry, Trish. They sound fine. I'm upset. The restaurant where we were supposed to be holding Angela's bridal shower had a fire. We need to find a new place and fast."

"Oh, no! I'll start calling restaurants," Trish said.

"And I'm off to talk to Sally, Fran, and Marion. See if they have any ideas."

My first stop was Sally's office. Sally was our library's director and my boss. She was shocked to hear what had happened. Shocked, but unable to come up with a viable alternative.

"Sorry, Carrie. I can't offer our home. Bob invited a few of his friends over to swim in our pool on Saturday."

"Not to worry," I said. "We'll find something."

But Fran and Marion weren't able to offer their homes either.

Back at my office, I emailed my three co-hostesses: "No luck so far, but Trish is still calling restaurants. I think we have to notify the bridal shower guests re the cancellation and ask if they have any suggestions." Then I shot off an email to the shower guests and made a mental note to call those who didn't have email that evening. Having done all I could, I turned to my library duties that I'd sadly been neglecting.

Trish left at three o'clock, having had no success with any of the restaurants in a fifteen-mile radius of Clover Ridge. She'd no sooner closed the door when Evelyn Havers appeared. Today my ghostly friend was dressed in a pretty spring dress—tiny colorful flowers against a pale blue background—that set off her salt and pepper hair, which had been cut in a glamorous new way. One day I planned to pin down Evelyn and have her explain just where she kept her extensive wardrobe and had her hair styled, but getting Evelyn to talk about that which she didn't choose to talk about was tough going. She dodged questions as skillfully as a veteran spy.

Now she perched on the edge of Trish and Susan's desk, her usual position when she paid me a visit.

"Poor Angela," she tsk-tsked. "She's so upset about her bridal shower, she can't concentrate on what she's doing. She told one woman that the book she was about to take out was overdue and she owed three dollars. More than one patron has complained to Fran."

I frowned at Evelyn. "I would think you'd be more sympathetic. Angela's been so excited about her wedding plans, and now her bridal shower has been all but canceled. We're having a hard time finding another place on such short notice."

"I doubt that you will. Carrie, dear, I'm afraid the restaurant fire is a bad omen of things to come."

"That's not a very kind thing to say."

"I'm not trying to be mean. You know I'm fond of Angela, which is why I'm alerting you to the possibility that something major might go very wrong at her wedding."

"Is there something you know that you're not telling me?"

Evelyn shook her head. "Of course not. It's just a feeling I have."

I pursed my lips. "Well, I'm hoping that you're wrong. But I have to admit, it will take a miracle to fix this bridal shower problem, a miracle that better happen soon."

The miracle arrived less than an hour later in a text from Angela's cousin, Donna Harrington.

"Sorry about the fire. Angie must be so upset. I'm happy to host the bridal shower at my house. It's certainly large enough and a mere ten-minute drive from Clover Ridge. Please let me know how many guests to expect so I'll know how much food to order. There's a great caterer nearby that I often use for events. I'll send you their menu and you can tell me what to get."

How much food to order? I texted right back, thanking Donna for offering her home and making it clear that the shower's three other hosts and I would be paying for the food.

"If you insist. But I'm happy to provide several yummy desserts from a local bakery, along with coffee, tea, and soda and wine. Here's my address. Please let everyone know the change of venue."

Minutes later I had the caterer's information, directions to Donna's home, and an update from Donna that she'd contacted another cousin, Roxy, who was happy to help out any way she could. Delighted that the bridal shower problem had been solved in the most pleasant way possible, I strode over to the circulation desk where Fran was attending to patrons.

"I told Angela to take a walk around the Green and get some fresh air," she whispered to me between checking out books and CDs.

I briefly told Fran the good news and went outside to share it with Angela.

The Green had come into existence when Clover Ridge was first settled in the seventeenth century. Despite the town's continuing growth and development, this grassy, squarish piece of land remained its heart and center, the site where festivals, concerts, and other events were held throughout the year.

The library was situated on its northeastern corner. Like most of the other centuries-old white wooden-frame buildings bordering the Green, it was once a private residence. Some buildings on the opposite side of the Green had remained private homes—my great-uncle Bosco and great-aunt Harriet lived in one of them—but most had been converted into upscale shops, a gourmet market, an inn, galleries, and restaurants.

Angela must have taken Fran's suggestion literally because I caught sight of her walking toward me on one of the paths that crossed the Green.

I went to meet her, eager to put her mind at rest. "We have good news! Your cousin Donna offered to have the shower at her house, and your cousin Roxy is going to help her. Isn't that wonderful?"

But Angela was scowling. "You agreed to have my shower at Donna's house?"

"I just said—"

"And Roxy's involved?"

"Well, yes. But Fran, Sally, Marion, and I are still handling the food. I've gotten the menu from the place Donna recommended. You can choose—"

Angela grabbed my arm. "Carrie, in all the time you've known me, have I ever mentioned Donna or Roxy?"

"Well, no, but you invited them to the shower."

Angela rolled her eyes. "I *had* to, didn't I? They're my first cousins."

"What's wrong with them?"

"Let's see. Where shall I begin? They're both five years older than me, which is a big age difference when you're a kid. They're beautiful, savvy, and rich. They know where to buy the perfect outfit, eat in the hottest restaurant, buy tickets for the latest show on Broadway. I always felt like the poor little match girl when I was with them, so I've hardly spent any time with them in years."

"Maybe they've changed. I mean, why would Donna make such a generous offer if she didn't care about you?"

Angela sniffed. "So she could play Lady Bountiful. Roxy, too. They're close friends—when they aren't competing with each other."

We walked slowly back to the library. "I had no idea," I said. "I'll call Donna back and tell her thanks but no thanks."

Angela shook her head. "Don't do that, Carrie. I'm being silly. You've worked so hard to find a new place for my bridal shower, and Donna's house is beautiful—so my mother's told me." She gave me a little smile. "It's fine. Really it is."

"Then come to my office and tell me what selections you'd like us to order for lunch on Saturday."

Angela managed a smile. "I'm always happy to help when it comes to menus."

Chapter Two

Though the rest of the week went by without any further calamities, I was busy every waking minute. Running the programs and events at the library required constant attention, and now I had the revised plans of Angela's bridal shower to see to. Good thing I had efficient partners in Sally, Fran, and Marion. Between us, we contacted all the guests about the new locale and selected and ordered the food from the caterers Donna had recommended. Brenda, the woman from the restaurant, called to assure me that I'd be receiving our deposit back within the next two weeks.

Angela regained her usual good humor and seemed no longer upset that her cousins Donna and Roxy were now deeply involved in the arrangements for her bridal shower. Susan Roberts, my very creative assistant who worked late afternoons, had made decorations for the luncheon and offered to drop them off at Donna's house on Friday. Donna and I exchanged several phone calls. She was friendly and seemed eager to make Angela's bridal shower a happy experience.

"Angie's my baby cousin," she told me. "She's always been shy. I'm so happy that she's found someone to share her life with."

Angela shy? "She and Steve are very well suited," I said.

"I'm glad, because her mother, Aunt Rosemary, is my favorite aunt."

Because I worked some evenings and Dylan often returned late from his office, it was a rare treat when we managed to have dinner together during the week. Dylan was an investigator dealing with stolen artwork and jewels. Recently he had been made a full partner in the company and had opened his own office in New Haven. He had branched out into other types of investigations and was *finally* actively looking to hire another investigator to help with the work load.

Since we were both free on Wednesday evening, Dylan decided to barbecue lamb chops and potatoes on the little-used, expensive grill on the manor house's back terrace. At seven o'clock, I drove over with the dishes I'd prepared. I put the salad in the fridge and the asparagus in the large toaster oven to heat, then went outside to join my significant other.

Dylan kissed me and handed me a chilled glass of Chardonnay.

"Are we eating inside or out?" I asked.

"Inside, I think. It's getting chilly. Do you agree?"

"I do. I'll go in and set the table."

I placed cutlery and plates on the kitchen table, which was situated in a nook almost twice as large as the entire kitchen in my cottage. But all my appliances were new since Dylan had modernized the cottage kitchen just before I'd moved in. I couldn't help but compare them to the appliances in this kitchen, which looked to be about twenty years old.

I peered into the formal dining room and the living room. Clearly, Dylan hadn't changed anything in either room since his parents had lived here. The furniture was graceless and stodgy and had that unused appearance. Not very inviting, I thought. Then I felt a bit nervous, wondering if I would have to live here if we ever decided to move in together.

"Dinner's ready!" Dylan said, carrying the platter with the lamb chops and potatoes aloft.

I brought out the salad and asparagus, Dylan served the other hot food and grabbed the bottle of wine from the fridge, and we sat down to eat.

We chatted about our day's activities—Dylan's cases and his latest interview, the library scuttlebutt and the upcoming shower.

"It sounds like Angela's calmed down," Dylan said.

"She has, but that will only last until her brother arrives from California."

Dylan was grinning when he leaned over to kiss me. "Your life is a constant merry-go-round."

"Hey, this is about Angela, not me!" I protested.

"Your BFF. Whatever bothers her spills onto you—especially where her wedding's concerned."

"I'm sure things will settle down after the big event."

We had ice cream for dessert, and I left a few hours later. We both had to get up early the following morning. I kissed Dylan good-night and drove home wondering how it would feel if we had dinner together every evening.

* * *

Friday morning Angela was perturbed because her brother Tommy had arrived the night before.

"Is he planning to stay at your parents' house until after the wedding?" I asked. We were having a morning coffee break in the library's coffee shop.

"Hah! Tommy doesn't bother to let anyone in on his plans. I only know he came to the East Coast on business. He's looking for investors to back his latest movie."

"If it's business, then he won't be around much."

"I suppose not. And he was very civil last night when he arrived."

"Maybe he's changed, Ange."

"Leopards don't change their spots."

* * *

Saturday dawned, a lovely June day. I thought of Evelyn's dire prediction on Monday and decided it was nonsense. Because Sally, Marion, Fran, and I would be at the shower all afternoon, the three part-time aides were covering the circulation desk, children's room, and hospitality desk at the library from eleven until closing time at five. The reference desk and computer department weren't affected as the men in charge of those departments would not be attending the shower.

"Sorry you have to stay home today," I told Smoky Joe as I was about to set out for the library. Sally, Marion, Fran, and I had arranged to work from nine until eleven thirty, at which time I would drive us all to Donna's house.

Smoky Joe meowed as he gave me a woeful look.

"Sorry, boy, I left you plenty of food. Mrs. C will be here all day, and Dylan will stop by with the plumber later and give you some treats."

My furry feline turned his back on me and sauntered away. I reached for the beautifully wrapped nightgown I'd bought for Angela and headed for my car.

At work, I felt a sense of excitement about the upcoming party as I answered emails and checked on the programs in progress. After graduating from college, I'd never stayed long enough in any one place to make close friends until I'd settled down in Clover Ridge. Which was why I'd never even been to a bridal shower before, much less been in charge of one. Good thing the others had plenty of experience. Marion and Fran had planned a few games for everyone to play, and we were bringing along a few gifts for the winners.

At eleven thirty, the four of us headed for my car in the parking lot. I stowed their gifts in the trunk and, when we were all seated, I turned on my GPS.

"We're off!" I said as I drove onto the street.

Sally, who was sitting beside me in the passenger seat, glanced at the GPS. "According to this, it should take us eighteen minutes to reach Donna's house."

Marion laughed. "Not exactly the ten-minute trip she told you it would be."

"That's all right," Fran said. "It will be worth the extra time to get there. I looked up the house online. It's on the water and should be spectacular."

And spectacular it was! We were all oohing and ahing as I drove through two stone posts and onto a narrow lane that brought us to a semicircular driveway.

"Wow!" we exclaimed together as we gaped at the large sprawling house before us. It managed to blend spacious floor-to-ceiling windows with the typical white wooden exterior so popular in this area of Connecticut.

"Well, hubby is a surgeon," Fran said knowingly. "What else would you expect?"

As soon as I stopped in front of the double oak doors, a college-aged young man came dashing from the side of the house.

"I'll be happy to park your car," he said.

I handed him my key fob and we exited the car. We retrieved our presents and prizes from the trunk and walked up the three marble steps to the house. I rang the bell, then noticed that one of the doors stood open. As soon as I entered, a woman walked toward me, her arms outstretched in greeting. She was tall and slender, yet curvaceous. Her long auburn hair had the most stunning blonde highlights I'd ever seen and must have cost hundreds of dollars. She was beautiful, too, with perfect teeth and large blue eyes.

"You must be Carrie!" she said, enveloping me in a hug. I breathed in a very expensive perfume.

"And you're Donna," I said when she released me. I pointed to my friends. "This is Sally, Fran, and Marion. We so appreciate that you're opening your home to host Angela's bridal shower."

Donna smiled at each of them in turn. "Of course! I was happy to do it. I'm so touched that my little cousin Angie has endeared herself to her coworkers." She gestured to a small room. "Why don't you leave your gifts in there, then join the others in the den? Can't miss it. It's the room next to the kitchen."

She widened her smile and left us to drop off our gifts and leave our pocketbooks in a corner where five or six already sat in a pile.

"Little cousin Angie," Fran muttered as she set her gift on the long table. "The way she talks, you'd think Angela's five instead of twenty-nine."

"I think Donna and her cousin Roxy are both thirty-four." I lowered my voice. "An age difference like that means a lot when you're young. One reason Angela felt intimidated by Donna and Roxy when she was growing up."

"Angela's a good-looking gal, but let's face it—Donna's drop-dead gorgeous," Sally said in her usual no-nonsense manner. "That's intimidating enough."

The den was a large, airy room with sliding glass doors leading out to a terrace. Beyond the pool, the extensive lawn sloped down to the Long Island Sound. Angela and her mom were standing with a group of women near two long couches that faced each other over a coffee table laden with snacks. I hugged them both and said hi to Steve's sister, who was also named Donna. An attractive redhead with eyes as green as emeralds approached.

"Hello, I'm Roxy Forlano. So nice to meet you."

"Hi, I'm Carrie Singleton."

Roxy grinned as we shook hands. "Of course! Angie's BFF. Aunt Rosemary's told us so much about you."

I smiled and introduced Roxy to Sally, Marion, and Fran.

"Has the food arrived yet?" I asked.

"Yes. Come with me and see for yourself."

The four of us followed her into the largest kitchen I'd ever seen, done tastefully in white and black. The aroma of stuffed mushrooms, quiches, and other delectable foods wafted past me. Interesting, since we hadn't ordered any hot appetizers.

"Donna and I put the perishables in the fridge since we weren't sure when you guys wanted to serve lunch. And we added a few hot appetizers, which should be ready soon. We thought we'd start serving them when a few more people arrived. Meanwhile, have something to drink."

She gestured to the counter where coffee was going in a large urn and water was heating in an electric teakettle. There were also bottles of soda, seltzer, red and white wine. Nearby were good-quality disposable cups and utensils and a large ice bucket for the soda and seltzer.

"I think we've covered everything, but let me know if anything's missing. And check out the dining room. We've opened up the table and added several small tables in the living room where people can eat when we serve lunch."

"Thanks so much," Marion said. "I'd say you and Donna have seen to everything."

Roxy winked. "We're both used to feeding large crowds, though I'm happy to say my hostess days are over." And with that cryptic comment, she left us.

For a moment, the four of us stared at one another, too floored to speak.

"Looks to me like we lucked out," Fran said, pouring herself a glass of red wine.

"Looks that way," I agreed.

A timer went off, and Donna dashed into kitchen and began placing hot hors d'oeuvres on platters. We helped carry them out to the den, where several more guests were now milling around. The four of us made a quick decision to give everyone half an hour to nosh and chat while we set out the food we'd ordered, buffet style. We'd invite them into the kitchen to select what they liked, then take a seat in the dining room or the living room. After eating, we'd play a few games, and Angela would open her gifts.

The afternoon flew by. Angela was always on my radar. I was delighted to see her enjoying herself in the company of all the women who loved her. Fran, Sally, Marion, and I kept on top of everything, but there was little we had to do with Donna and Roxy on hand to see to our guests' needs. They were upbeat and helpful without taking over. Though once, when I went into the kitchen in search of napkins, I caught them squabbling over something. They both glanced up and smiled at me. I grabbed a handful of napkins and quickly retreated to the dining room.

Lunch was delicious, the games were fun, and Angela's array of gifts ran the gamut from a stand mixer, which she'd never use, to outrageous lingerie, which she might never use either. We were drinking coffee or tea and munching on the most scrumptious chocolate-filled cookies, pecan pie, and other delicious desserts, when two men in their thirties entered the house and stood watching us from the hall.

The taller of the two was smiling as he surveyed the forty or so women sitting around the living room and the dining room table. "Good afternoon, ladies. I hope you're all enjoying yourselves!"

"We sure are, Aiden," many responded with silly grins on their faces.

So this was Dr. Aiden Harrington, as handsome as he was charming, his broad shoulders and slender physique evident in his sky blue rugby shirt and white Bermuda shorts.

"A female patient's fantasy," Sally whispered to me.

"I'd say!"

Donna hurried over to them. "Aiden! Tommy! You're just in time for dessert." She kissed her husband square on the mouth. He gave a start, but quickly put an arm around her waist. When she tried to lead him to the dining room table, he pulled away.

"Be right there, soon as I say hello to everyone."

Donna pursed her lips as Aiden strode into the living room, a man comfortable among a roomful of women, and hugged

Donna's mother and Rosemary Vecchio. Donna tossed her perfectly coifed tresses over her shoulder and focused her attention on the man named Tommy, who looked like he wanted to run out of the house.

"Come with me, cousin dear, and have some coffee and cake."

Cousin? This had to be Tommy Vecchio, Angela's brother. I would never have guessed. Tommy had dark wavy hair like his sister, but that's where their resemblance ended. Tommy appeared to be five nine—Angela's height—but while she was thin and wiry, he was stocky and hunched his shoulders so that his neck all but disappeared. His gray T-shirt and jeans looked like they'd been through the washing machine too many times, giving him a slovenly appearance.

"Thanks, Donna, but I don't want to crash your hen party. I told Aiden we'd be in the way, but he—"

"Don't be silly," Donna trilled. "Sit down and have something to eat."

Tommy frowned but allowed her to lead him to the chair she'd been occupying a minute earlier.

"Coffee?" Donna asked.

"Thanks," Tommy said, reaching for the plate of cookies.

I turned to Angela, who was sitting on the other side of me. The joyous expression she'd worn earlier had changed to a scowl.

"Why did Aiden have to bring him here?" she mumbled.

"I had no idea Tommy and Aiden were friends," I said.

"They're not. Tommy's desperate to raise money for his movie. He called every relative and old friend he could think of. Aiden said he might be interested, so they arranged to meet for lunch."

I sensed someone behind me. I turned as Aiden stepped between us to give Angela a hug.

"And here's our guest of honor!" he said. "I hope you're enjoying your bridal shower. I know Donna and Roxy want you to have a day you will always remember."

Angela grinned, her good mood somewhat restored by his attention. "It's been a wonderful party. All thanks to Donna and Roxy and to my dear library friends." She gestured to us. "Aiden, this is Carrie, Sally, Fran, and Marion."

"Nice to meet you all," Aiden said, gifting us with a warm smile as he shook hands with each of us in turn.

It felt like receiving a blessing from a highly evolved person. Not because Aiden was gorgeous or a doctor, but because during our brief exchange he made me feel cherished. I turned to Sally and saw the same bemused expression that was probably on my face.

"Here you are!"

I blinked as Roxy came to claim Aiden, linking her arm in his.

"Hi, Roxy. Angela's been introducing me to her library colleagues."

"And now that you've met them, why don't you sit down and have some coffee and dessert? We made room for you at the other end of the table."

"All right." Aiden turned back to us. "I'm glad we had a chance to meet. See you at the wedding." He followed Roxy.

Sally nudged me. "Notice where his seat is. Next to hers."

I laughed. "So? What are you implying?"

"I'm not implying anything. I'm simply fascinated by the dynamics in Angela's family," was Sally's cryptic response.

Chapter Three

I was off on Sunday, the day after Angela's shower. After making pancakes for Dylan and me, we ran a few errands in town, then went our separate ways until dinner time—me to help Angela and Steve arrange furniture in their new condo and Dylan to his office to interview a prospective employee.

I arrived at Angela and Steve's new condo a little after two, in time to help settle a dispute over how to arrange their living room furniture, which had just been delivered. The room was rectangular. Angela wanted the sofa placed with its back against the glass sliding doors, while Steve thought it looked best against the adjacent wall facing the two wing chairs.

I let them carry on for a minute or two, doing my best not to smile. They were so perfectly suited for each other, both tall and slender, with dark, lustrous hair and passionate temperaments which, right now, were in danger of spilling out of proportion. Time to say something.

"Here's what I think." I waited till I had their attention. "I agree with Steve."

Angela shot me a baleful look. I was *her* best friend after all.

"The area in front of the sliding doors would be perfect for an array of plants to soak up the morning sun," I said. "Steve's suggestion has your sitting area in a narrower, more intimate arrangement. Easier for people to chat and reach for snacks off the coffee table between them."

"Hmm," Angela said, considering.

"And this way you won't catch a draft if you feel like reading on the sofa during the winter months," Steve said.

"The longer wall is better for the end tables," I added.

"I suppose so," Angela said.

Steve put his arm around her and kissed her. "You are so agreeable, my love. Why don't we put everything in place so we can see how it looks?"

Minutes later, we were puffing a bit from putting the chairs, sofa, and tables where we'd decided they should go. Angela set the lamps on the end tables, plugged them into the wall, and switched them on. "Voilà!" she announced, obviously pleased with the way the room looked.

I glanced at the pile of gifts on and around the table in the hall. "Do you want me to help you go through those?" I asked.

"No, thanks," Angela said. "I've already pulled out all the kitchen utensils and appliances. Next, I want to put the kitchen in order, so let's start lining the cabinet shelves and drawers in there." She sent a meaningful glance at Steve. "You *did* remember to bring over that cutting device, didn't you?"

"Of course, dear. How could I forget when you texted me three times?"

Angela opened her mouth to argue, but before she uttered one word, Steve went on. "I say we take a break and open a bottle of wine. Carrie, red or white?"

I grinned. "You know I always go for white."

Minutes later we were sitting on the new living room furniture, sipping Chardonnay and nibbling on peanuts.

I glanced around the sun-filled room from my seat in one the wing chairs. "I love your condo. It's so bright and cheerful. And you've got three bedrooms, so you can stay as long as you like."

On the sofa, Angela and Steve beamed at each other. "We think we made a good choice," she said, then turned to me. "Carrie, thanks again for the wonderful shower. I know how much work you guys put into it."

"So, having Donna and Roxy come to the rescue wasn't such a bad idea?" I teased.

"No, they were really nice. Like they really wanted me to have a shower I'd always remember."

"I would have stopped by if I'd known other males were crashing, but I was told not to show up under pain of death," Steve said.

"Sorry, sweetheart." Angela rubbed his arm. "It was supposed to be an all-female afternoon. I can't imagine why Aiden came by, much less with my brother."

"He didn't seem too happy to be there," I said.

"He wasn't, but since Aiden agreed to give him a substantial amount of money, he figured he'd better act agreeable," Angela said. "That's my brother."

"Are the two of you getting along any better?" I asked.

Angela scowled, then finished off her wine. She held out her glass and Steve refilled it.

Time to change the subject. "Aiden Harrington strikes me as every girl's dream husband: a drop-dead gorgeous doctor. Rich, kind, and personable."

Angela scoffed. "Carrie, you know nothing is ever as good as it seems."

"What do you mean? Aren't he and Donna getting along?"

Angela shrugged. "According to my cousin Frankie, things have been tense between Donna and Aiden. And lately Donna's been worried because Aiden seems stressed out about something."

Donna's younger sister, Frankie, and Angela were good friends. Like me, she was one of Angela's bridesmaids. Frankie lived in Manhattan, had a wonderful job and a boyfriend, and was in no hurry to get married.

"That's too bad," I said. "I didn't realize the two sisters were so close. They seem so different."

Angela laughed. "They are very different. Frankie's down to earth and Donna's—Donna. Frankie's a wonderful aunt. She often comes to Connecticut on weekends to spend time with Liam and little Emma."

I'd met Donna and Aiden's children yesterday when the au pair brought them home as we were leaving the bridal shower. "They are adorable." I sipped my wine. "Does Roxy have any children?"

"No," Angela said. "And I suppose that's a good thing, too, because Frankie said her divorce just went through. This must have been very recent because my mother never mentioned it."

"Or she didn't want to mention the word divorce to you," Steve said, "in case it gave you ideas."

Angela rolled her eyes.

"I thought it kind of odd that while Aiden was talking to us, Roxy came over and whisked him away," I said.

"Me, too," Angela said. "Frankie said that Aiden was very supportive of Roxy all through her divorce. I suppose he's still playing the good friend role."

"Really?" Steve said. "I thought Aiden and Miles were good buddies."

"They are," Angela said. "Best friends since medical school."

I nodded as I digested what I'd just heard. "Interesting family dynamics among your cousins."

Angela smiled. "They can do what they like, as long as my wedding goes as planned."

Chapter Four

A festive air spread throughout the library during the two weeks leading up to the wedding. Angela was a well-liked member of the library staff, and several patrons stopped by to congratulate her on her upcoming nuptials, often bringing gifts. I was filled with a sense of excitement as the wedding day drew closer. As one of Angela's maids of honor, I was part of the bridal party, and by now I'd met many of the invited guests. I saw firsthand how Angela and Steve were affected as their wedding drew near. Nervous, yes, but happy to be starting married life together.

It was also the first wedding I'd be attending with Dylan. At times I got swept up in wedding fever and occasionally found myself imagining how I would want our wedding to be—the setting, the service, even the menu. But as quickly as these thoughts came, I brushed them aside. Dylan and I weren't getting married— at least not anytime soon.

The early June weather ranged from the mid-seventies to the low eighties, with not a rain cloud in sight. The wedding celebration was being held at the Gilbert House, once a centuries-old private residence, just outside of town. When it was turned into a wedding venue and catering hall, they added a large bluestone terrace and a beautiful rose garden. Angela was hoping that the warm weather would continue so that the cocktail hour could be held outdoors.

The Tuesday afternoon after the bridal shower, I was in my office and had just finished responding to a bunch of emails when I received a surprise visit from Julia and her little daughter, Tacey. Julia was married to my cousin, Randy Singleton. We were very fond of each other, but our busy lives usually didn't allow us to spend much time together.

Tacey ran into my arms for a hug. "Cousin Carrie, Cousin Carrie, guess what! I just signed up for kindergarten!"

"That is a big, big step," I told her.

"The teacher said I wrote my name really well. And Singleton has lots of letters."

"Good job," I said and shot Julia a questioning glance. "The teacher asked her to write her name?"

"That was part of the interview."

Interview? "Now there are requirements to get into kindergarten?"

I was half-kidding, but Julia made a scoffing sound. "Your child is supposed to be able to write his or her name, be familiar with if not know how to write the letters of the alphabet in both upper and lower case, numbers one to twenty, *and* shapes and colors."

"Wow!" I exclaimed.

"I know them all—don't I, Mommy?"

Julia stroked her daughter's head. "You sure do, honey."

"And now Mommy and me are going to pick out some books to read, right Mommy?"

"Yes, we are, Tacey."

Tacey grinned at me. "And we want to invite you to a barbecue. You and your boyfriend."

"Well, thank you both."

"I know it's short notice," Julia said, "but I hope you guys can make it this Sunday afternoon. It's just family—you and Dylan and Aunt Harriet and Uncle Bosco. The good weather's expected to hold, and Randy can't wait to try out our new grill."

"Sounds great. I'm off Sunday and I'll check with Dylan."

Julia glanced at her watch. "And now, Tacey, we should get our books and start for home." She gave me the look of a harried mother. "Randy's coming home early so I can serve dinner at five and he can watch Mark and Tacey while I see a customer."

"Of course," I said. "I'll text you tonight about Sunday."

"Mommy, can I stay with Carrie while you choose some books for me?"

"Honey, Carrie has to work."

"I can spare a few minutes to spend with my favorite girl cousin," I said.

"Well . . ."

"You can pick out three books for me and I'll stay here with Carrie," Tacey said.

Julia and I exchanged glances. "Okay, Tacey. Ten minutes. Then we have to go home."

"Thank you, Mommy."

This child is four and a half! I marveled, because I knew why Tacey wanted to stay with me. She was the only other person I knew who could see and talk to Evelyn Havers. In fact, she and Evelyn were very fond of each other. Tacey used to try to offer Evelyn cookies, which upset Julia because she thought her daughter had an imaginary friend. I could only imagine how she'd react if she knew that Tacey had a relationship with a ghost.

"Have you seen Miss Evelyn?" she asked as soon as we were alone.

"Many times."

Tacey pursed her lips. "Is she all right?"

"I'm perfectly fine, my dear," Evelyn said as she manifested before our eyes.

"I'm so glad!" Tacey stretched out her arms before she remembered that she couldn't hug Evelyn.

"I heard you tell Cousin Carrie that you registered for kindergarten today," Evelyn said.

"I did, but school doesn't start until September."

"You're going to love kindergarten, Tacey," Evelyn said. "You'll have so much fun and make lots of new friends."

"I suppose." Tacey's voice fell. "It's such a big school, bigger than nursery school."

"Of course it's bigger. You'll be a big girl in September. Almost five."

They spoke softly, and I turned back to my computer to give them some privacy. I was the only person who knew of this unusual bond between my little cousin and Evelyn and how much they cared for each other.

Finally, I turned to them. "Tacey, time to say good-bye to Miss Evelyn."

When Evelyn left, Tacey hugged me. "I wish Miss Evelyn could come to the barbecue on Sunday."

"I know you do."

Chapter Five

I made a batch of my double chocolate brownies for Julia and Randy's barbecue, and Dylan picked out a red wine from his collection that he knew Uncle Bosco liked. I also bought a book for each of the kids—one about the planets for Mark and a humorous picture book for Tacey. Julia had said to come around two, so after feeding Smoky Joe an extra portion of treats, we set out at twenty to. Though the sun was shining, it was cooler than it had been all week.

Dylan had readily agreed to accompany me to my cousins' barbecue. He'd gotten to know them from the few family gatherings he'd attended and seemed to enjoy their company, including that of Tacey and her eight-year-old brother, Mark.

Besides, he was very fond of my great-uncle Bosco and great-aunt Harriet, whom he'd known all his life. As a boy, Dylan had often visited the Singleton Farm, where they'd lived before moving to one of the few remaining private residences on the far side of the Green from the library, to play with my brother Jordan during the summer months we came to visit.

When we stopped at a red light, I leaned over to kiss Dylan's cheek.

"What's that for?"

"I'm glad you don't mind going to my cousins' today?"

"Why should I mind? They're nice people and Julia's a great cook."

"And you know Aunt Harriet's bound to bring two homemade desserts."

"That, too, not to mention your brownies, which you only make for special occasions."

"Whatever's left after you swiped a handful of them."

"What can I say, babe? I've got no control when it comes to your brownies."

We both laughed, but I was suddenly aware of how important it was to me that Dylan got along well with the people I loved. He and my dad were great pals as well as work colleagues now that Jim was working for the company with Mac in the Atlanta office. Dylan's relationship with my family wasn't something I had ever given much thought to . . . until recently.

The barbecue was in full swing as we followed the path around the side of the house to the beautiful redwood deck off the kitchen that Julia and Randy had built last year. Dylan and I exchanged hugs with everyone and I handed Mark and Tacey their books. They thanked me and seemed to like what I'd chosen, then I went into the kitchen to drop off the brownies. Uncle Bosco was already uncorking the bottle of wine Dylan had brought.

When I rejoined the others on the deck, Mark asked, "Cousin Carrie, did Mom show you the photos we took the day we were in the movie?"

I shook my head. "No, I'd love to see them."

"They're on the iPad. I'll go get it." Mark dashed into the house and returned a minute later.

I looked at the pictures of Mark, Tacey, and Julia taken the day they were extras in *I Love You, I Do*, the movie that had recently been filmed in Clover Ridge.

"And here we are with Tom and your mother," Mark said. Tom Farrell, my mother's husband, had a major role in the movie.

"Have you heard from Linda since they went back to California?" Uncle Bosco asked, handing me a glass of white wine.

"Just a text to say they had arrived safely."

"Figures," Uncle Bosco said.

He was never fond of my mother when she'd been married to my father, and his opinion hadn't changed during her recent visit. My mother was a difficult woman—self-absorbed and manipulative—not the warm, maternal mother I'd yearned for growing up. But during the weeks she and Tom were here in Clover Ridge we'd grown a bit closer, and I was learning to accept her as she was.

Aunt Harriet and Julia wanted to hear all about Angela's shower, so I told them in detail as we made a large salad and attended to the side dishes in the kitchen.

"A friend of mine went to Dr. Harrington when she broke her arm," Julia said. "She was very pleased with the care she received and how well the break healed."

"I'm not surprised," I said. "Aiden struck me as a very caring person as well as a conscientious doctor."

We carried the dishes to the table outside, then I stopped to watch my cousin Randy skillfully turn chicken parts, hamburgers, and hot dogs on the grill.

"I see you're quite an expert at this," I said.

Randy grinned at his son and daughter, who were watching him too. "I have to be, with this crowd giving orders."

"I like to eat my chicken and my hot dog at the same time," Tacey explained.

Minutes later, the eight of us were seated around the large round table. Randy had tilted the umbrella so that it blocked the sun from everyone's eyes. I helped spoon out salads and beans while Randy went around with a huge platter of meat, asking everyone what they wanted.

Both Tacey and Mark were very decisive about what they would and would not eat. Tacey wanted lots of potato salad to go with her hot dog and chicken leg, while Mark only wanted baked beans and two hot dogs. Neither Julia nor Randy urged them to try other foods. I wondered if I would nag my children to eat salad or veggies because it was good for them.

But why was I wondering if and how I'd regulate my children's eating habits when I didn't have any and becoming a parent was the furthest thing from my mind?

"Looks like the library construction work will begin in early September as planned," Uncle Bosco said, interrupting my musings. He was a member of the library board and responsible for having suggested that they hire me to fill the position I now held. "You'll be hearing plenty of noise, especially when they break through the connecting wall to form the archway between the two buildings.

I grimaced. "I don't look forward to the commotion, but I'll be happy when it's all done."

"I thought it was brilliant of the library to buy the building next door and enlarge it that way," Julia said. "I bet the Clover Ridge Library turns out to be one of the most impressive libraries in the state."

"Since we're on the Green, buying the building next door was the only possible option," I said. "Unless we expanded upward."

"And that was too limiting, since the town rule is that buildings around the Green may be no more than two stories high," Uncle Bosco said. "The library board had been eyeing the building next door for years. Trouble was, its ownership was in dispute by three members of a family, each claiming it was his or hers by rights. The only thing they agreed on was setting up an account for minimum upkeep and taxes. The case was finally settled and, with the generous donations of some of our wealthier patrons, we managed to buy it. Now we have as much space as we need, and the parking lot will almost double the current size."

"Parking is always a problem," Aunt Harriet said.

"I can't wait to start planning events for our stadium-seating auditorium," I said. "Think of all the plays and concerts we'll present!"

Uncle Bosco reached across the table to pat my hand. "Your domain, my dear Carrie. Aren't you glad you stayed and took the job instead of leaving town like you were thinking of doing at one time?"

I squeezed his hand. "You have no idea how happy I am that I stayed."

"I'll second that," Dylan said.

When we finished eating, I helped Julia clear the table, which mostly involved dumping the paper plates and cups we'd used into a large plastic bag and refrigerating the leftovers.

Tacey took me upstairs to her room to show me her new doll. Then we sat down on her bed and talked about Evelyn.

"Miss Evelyn missed all the fun today," Tacey said.

"Honey, you know you can only see her in the library," I said, "and only when she decides to show up."

The sigh she let out was too large for a four-year-old. "I suppose. But where does she go when she's not in the library?"

I shrugged. "I haven't the slightest idea. We just have to accept that there are many things we will never know about Miss Evelyn."

"You mean, like accepting that it's cold in the winter and hot in the summer?"

I grinned. "Kind of like that."

We went downstairs, and I helped Julia set the table for dessert. She brewed a pot of coffee for the adults and brought out milk for Mark and Tacey. Aunt Harriet had made a pecan pie and an apple pie, two of my favorites. We placed them and my brownies, along with two containers of ice cream, out on the table.

For a few minutes, we were all too busy ingesting enough sugar to last us the week to speak. I caught Aunt Harriet and Uncle Bosco exchanging glances, then looking my way.

"All right. What are you two conspiring about?" I asked.

"Nothing," Uncle Bosco said. "Let's just enjoy our Sunday afternoon with our family."

"Tell her," Aunt Harriet said firmly. "You said you would."

"Only because Al was twisting my arm."

"Al? Are you talking about the mayor?"

Uncle Bosco exhaled loudly. "The one and only. I told him I'd think about bringing up the subject."

Aunt Harriet narrowed her eyes at him. "But then we discussed it . . ."

I threw up my hands in frustration. "Put me out of my misery and tell me what Al Tripp wants you to discuss with me. Please!"

Uncle Bosco pursed his lips. "Okay, Carrie. It's this—Al would like you to consider taking a position on the town council board."

"Oh. That."

Randy laughed. "That's a pretty big honor, cuz, but you don't sound the least bit surprised."

I turned to the cousin who used to tease me mercilessly when I came to spend summers on the farm. "That's because when Al was in the library a few weeks ago, he told me I should consider running for town council."

Now it was my aunt and uncle's turn to look surprised.

"You never said," Uncle Bosco said, sounding hurt.

"Why would I? I told Al that my job and my personal life keep me very busy."

"Not to mention solving all those mysteries," Randy added with a twinkle in his eye.

"That, too," Dylan said.

I watched Uncle Bosco fold and refold a paper napkin. There was more.

"The thing is, Carrie, Jeannette Rivers is planning to move in a few months. With her gone, that leaves two males besides Al and one female on the board. Al thinks it only fair to bring in another female. Someone young, someone who has her finger on the pulse of the community."

"And Al, knowing how I feel about this, presumed on your friendship and asked you to ask me," I finished, not hiding my displeasure.

Rebuked, Uncle Bosco nodded. "It would only be for a year. Jeannette's position is up a year from November."

"The board meets twice a month," Aunt Harriet said.

"And gets embroiled in all kinds of town issues," I said. "You can tell Al 'thanks but no thanks.'"

Aunt Harriet smiled as she placed her hand on my shoulder. "Carrie, do you remember how you reacted when Sally offered you the library position last October?"

Reluctantly, I nodded.

"You were all set to take off—to God knows where. Your uncle and I advised you to consider taking the job. And if you didn't like it after giving it a try, well, then you could always quit."

I squeezed my aunt's hand. "I remember."

"All Bosco and I want you to do is to think about Al's offer. Like Randy says, it is an honor."

"All right." I turned to Uncle Bosco. "When does Al want an answer?"

"You've got plenty of time. Till the end of July to decide."

* * *

Julia quickly changed the conversation to the Singleton family picnic that was coming up in August, but I couldn't shake my foul mood. I'd been blindsided by Uncle Bosco acting as Al Tripp's messenger. Our esteemed mayor had no right pressuring me to join the council. Not after I'd made it very plain that I didn't want the position.

Aunt Harriet caught on immediately that their little surprise had gone awry. When Dylan and I bid everyone good night some fifteen minutes later, she apologized.

"I'm so sorry, Carrie." She spoke low so no one could hear. "Your uncle wanted nothing to do with Al's proposal, but I urged him to sound you out. I thought you would see it as a compliment."

"I don't like being put in a position of having to explain myself after I've made my wishes very clear," I said.

"Of course, my dear. You know what's best."

Dylan and I left shortly after. We drove home in silence. I kept my hand in his so he'd know my mood had nothing to do with him.

When we stopped at a red light, he turned to me. "You know I'll go along with whatever you decide."

I nodded. "Thank you. I just don't like being pressured into doing something."

Dylan laughed. "I can understand that, but people ask you to do things all the time and I've never seen you react the way you did tonight."

I thought about it. "You're right," I said as we continued on our way. "I felt like I was being conned into doing something I don't want to do. My mother did it often enough—getting me to handle something she should have taken care of herself."

"I get that," Dylan said, "but this isn't Linda being manipulative. This is our mayor offering you a very prestigious position because he sees you as a concerned citizen capable of weighing in on important decisions."

"I suppose," I said grudgingly.

"You don't have to join the council, babe, but I wish you would give it some thought before you turn down the offer."

"Why, Dylan?"

"Because I think Al's right—you would make a wonderful addition to the council." He cleared his throat. "And if we're going to be living in Clover Ridge for the long haul, we might as well get involved where we can do some good."

Chapter Six

Having Dylan's support meant a lot to me, and I found myself humming as I went about my usual routine the following day. *The long haul.* I spoke the words aloud several times, trying not to place too much importance on them. Did that refer to us on a permanent basis? Each of us separately? I wasn't sure since Dylan rarely made comments about the future. Which was fine with me since talking about our future together was a scary topic for me, probably because my parents' marriage was far from harmonious for years before their divorce. And so I didn't try to analyze his words—just allowed them to shower me with good feelings.

But I was starting to realize that I'd allowed my mother's constant scheming to color my response to Al's offer. My cousin Randy was right. Al wanting to put my name up as a member of the town council was an honor. I had to view it in the right perspective. Only then could I decide if I wanted the position or not. The good thing was, I had a month and a half to make up my mind.

* * *

"Excited about Angela's wedding?" Evelyn asked.

It was Wednesday afternoon. Trish had gone for the day and Susan wouldn't be in for another hour or so. Evelyn was perched on the edge of my assistants' desk as usual. Today she wore a navy wrap-around dress and navy sling-back heels. A white cardigan draped from her shoulders.

"Very. And Angela's like a floating balloon ready to burst with joy."

"I might say the same about you," Evelyn observed. "There's something new in your life. Something that's making you happy."

"Well, Dylan and I are doing well."

"What exactly does that mean?"

"He went with me to Randy and Julia's barbecue on Sunday and said something about us being in it for the long haul."

Evelyn pursed her lips. "Not a very romantic way of putting it."

I smiled. "Actually, it *was* romantic the way he said it."

She eyed me carefully. "Anything else you care to share?"

"Al Tripp wants me to join the town council. Jeannette Rivers is moving soon, and they need a replacement."

Evelyn beamed at me. "I'm proud of you, Carrie! Being on the council means you'll have a vote on important issues. You can make a difference. Help bring Clover Ridge into the modern world."

"I didn't say I'd take the position."

Evelyn exhaled exceedingly loud for a ghost. "Here we go again. I hope you didn't say no."

"I have a while to think it over."

"You know what I think you should do."

"Of course. You just told me."

It was Evelyn who had advised me to tell Sally I needed time to decide about taking the position of head of programs and events when I was about to turn it down. And now Aunt Harriet, Uncle Bosco, and Evelyn—the same three people responsible for my still living in Clover Ridge—were urging me to think about going on the town council.

"I have until the end of July to make up my mind."

Evelyn eyed me firmly. "I trust you'll make the right decision." She drew back her shoulders and set one foot in front of the other as if she were about to embark on a quest. "I would like to ask a favor of you, Carrie."

Her serious demeanor made me uneasy. Evelyn's requests sometimes took me far out of my comfort zone. "What is it?"

"I'd like you to find my brother Harold."

My jaw fell open. "I had no idea you had a brother."

"Of course you didn't. How would you know that I have a brother?"

I scoffed at her haughty tone. "Why wouldn't I? You've talked about your sister often enough, even though she's dead. And I've had dealings with all three of her children." *None of which were pleasant.* "I find it very odd that you never mentioned you have a brother."

Evelyn had the grace to look sheepish. "I'm sorry, Carrie. Harold left town fifteen years ago. No one has heard from him since."

"Why did he leave?" I asked.

"Does that matter?" The waspish tone was back.

This time I met her gaze with a frown. Evelyn was hiding some vital information. She often did when it involved presenting her relatives in a less than favorable light. "If you want my help, you're going to have to come clean and tell me everything—why your brother left town and why you need him back so desperately."

"All right." She cleared her throat. "First of all, Harold was a wonderful brother, husband, and father. He had a good job as an accountant for a large firm in New Haven. His only problem was he liked to gamble."

"Is that why he left town?"

Evelyn pursed her lips. "Harold owed money to some rough people. And so he did something he had no business doing. He stole from a client to pay his debt. Shortly after, he learned that the feds were about to investigate his firm." She drew a deep breath. "So he took off, abandoning his wife Glenda and their teenaged son and daughter."

"How did they manage?"

"Glenda and the kids moved to Ohio to live near Glenda's sister. She died about ten years ago."

"You never mentioned —"

"I know!" Evelyn said. "I was so ashamed of what my brother had done, I didn't reach out to his family as I should have. And then they moved out of town. I'm sorry to say I lost touch with Glenda."

I waited for Evelyn to explain why she was suddenly interested in her brother after all these years.

"I'm worried about my niece, Michelle," she finally blurted out. "It turns out she's back here living in Clover Ridge."

"Have you seen her here in the library?"

Evelyn shook her head. "Not that I'm aware. I've been on the lookout for her, but Michelle was sixteen, going on seventeen, when Harold took off. I might not recognize her as a thirty-two-year-old woman."

"So why are you worried about her?"

"Yesterday I overheard two women talking about Michelle. One referred to her as Michelle Davis—her maiden name. Mine, too, of course. It sounded like the younger woman was Michelle's neighbor. She said Michelle was in a bad way because her husband left her and cleaned out their account. This on top of her losing her job because of downsizing. The poor thing's terrified she's about to be thrown out of her apartment."

"How awful!"

"That's not all." I felt a chill when Evelyn leaned closer, as if she didn't want to be overheard. "The neighbor said that Michelle suffers from depression. She was worried that Michelle might do something foolish."

"No wonder you're upset," I said. "Do you know Michelle's married name?"

"I wish I did. You have to help her, Carrie. You have to find my brother. I sense that he's still alive and somewhere on this plane. His full name is Harold Lester Davis—if he's still going by that name."

"Okay," I said. "I'll ask Dylan if his secretary can try to track him down. But I can't promise that she'll have any luck. It's been fifteen years since your brother left Clover Ridge. He might be anywhere in the world."

"Harold used to take his family on vacations in Mexico, if that's any help."

"Could be. I'll mention it."

"Thank you, Carrie. I know you'll do your best," Evelyn said and faded from sight.

*   *   *

As soon as Evelyn left, I called Dylan's office. Rosalind put me through to him. I quickly told him what Evelyn wanted and why.

"Sure, babe. I'll have Rosalind get on this ASAP."

Rosalind Feratti was in her forties, married, and a mother of three, who, in the six months since Dylan had opened the New

Haven office, had proven herself to be indispensable. A short while ago with not much information to go on, she'd unearthed the identity and whereabouts of a woman who had been missing even longer than Evelyn's brother. I knew that if anyone could locate Harold Lester Davis, or whatever he was calling himself these days, it was Rosalind. Whether he was in a position to help out his daughter financially was another matter entirely.

I gave Rosalind every piece of information I had that might help her find him—Michelle's maiden name, her parents' names, the name of Harold's old firm, and the fact that he had absconded with a client's money. Rosalind said she'd look into it.

* * *

"Two more days, and I'll be Mrs. Steven Prisco," Angela said, downing a healthy gulp of her Moscow mule.

"I'll drink to that," Fran said, sipping her wine.

The rest of us—Sally, Marion, and I—drank to Angela's future.

It was Thursday evening and the five of us were in the bar of the Inn on the Green. Angela had insisted on treating us to drinks to thank us for her bridal shower. Knowing how restless she was with pre-wedding jitters, I figured she needed to be surrounded by the people who loved her until the moment she said "I do." Whatever the reason, we were all happy to oblige her.

"There's nothing wrong with going by Angela Vecchio," I said. "Women often keep their maiden name as their professional name."

"Is that what you plan to do, Ms. Singleton?"

My face grew warm as four pairs of eyes studied me. "What are you talking about, Ange? I'm simply pointing out—"

Angela finished off her drink. "I heard what you said, but I plan to go by Angela Prisco after Saturday night. I'm simply wondering what you want to be called when you and Dylan finally make things official."

I shrugged. "Since the subject has never come up, I haven't given it any thought."

"Right," Sally said.

Why are they all laughing?

"Avery will put your kids at the start of the alphabet," Sally teased.

"Way ahead of S for Singleton," Angela chimed in. "I'm not doing as well, but at least I'm moving up from V to P."

Kids? How did kids enter this conversation?

Angela waved to our bartender and ordered another Moscow mule. "Anyone else?"

We all shook our heads. Everyone but Angela was working the following day. It was a good thing I'd driven her to the Inn because she was three sheets to the wind.

To change the subject, I said, "It's too bad your cousins couldn't join us tonight."

"I agree," Angela said. "I'm forever grateful to them for saving my bridal shower, but Donna said Aiden was working late and their au pair was off and she couldn't get anyone to babysit. As for Roxy . . ." She shrugged. "She gave me some vague excuse. I think she didn't want to come without Donna."

"They must be very close," Marion said. "I saw how well they worked together at the shower."

Sally laughed. "I caught them squabbling in the kitchen over some food issue."

"They're like sisters," Angela said. "More like twins, since they're only three months apart and grew up a few blocks from each other. I don't know how close they are now. Donna's very busy with her two little ones, and Roxy's divorce just came through."

"You'll get a chance to spend time with them at the rehearsal dinner tomorrow night," I said.

"I plan to buy each of them something nice on our honeymoon. They deserve it."

Our waiter brought Angela's drink, and we sat around chatting until she finished it and asked for the check. As soon as it arrived and Angela handed him her credit card, we stood to leave. It was close to eleven o'clock and I, for one, was getting sleepy.

Fran, Marion, and Sally took turns hugging Angela and wishing her well. We all loved Angela and wanted the very best for her. Soon she and I were following the others out the Inn's rear door that led to the parking area.

"That was lovely, Ange," I said as we walked to my car. "So very sweet of you to treat us tonight. It certainly wasn't necessary."

Angela waved away my thanks. "Are you kidding? You ladies are the best! I love each and every one of you. I'm lucky to work with the best people in the world."

We climbed into my car. Angela yawned. "My out-of-town relatives will start arriving tomorrow in time to make the rehearsal dinner."

"Dylan and I are looking forward to seeing everyone," I said. "And you know that Due Amici is one of our favorite restaurants."

I drove, heading for Angela's parents' house. "Is Tommy still staying with your parents?"

"No. Lucky me. He picked up Zoe—that's his latest girlfriend—at Kennedy this afternoon in his rented car. They're staying at the motel, though I don't know what Zoe did tonight. Knowing Tommy, he probably dropped her off at my parents'."

"Why? What was he doing this evening?" I asked.

"Having dinner with Aiden to talk about firming up their arrangement."

"And he couldn't bring his girlfriend along?"

Angela shrugged. She was falling asleep.

I turned into the Vecchios' development. "I thought Donna told you Aiden was working late tonight."

"Did I?" Was that a snore?

"Hmmm," I mused, but Angela was too zonked to pick up on it.

She awoke with a start as I pulled into the driveway. "Shall I walk you to the door?" I asked, only half kidding. She had drunk much more than her usual amount.

"No. Not necessary." She smiled at me. "I'll sleep in tomorrow and get up in time to make my salon appointment at noon."

"In that case, good night. See you at the church at four for the rehearsal."

Angela surprised me by grabbing me in a bear hug. "Thanks for being my BFF, Carrie. I'm so lucky to have you in my life."

"Exactly how I feel about you," I said, hugging her back.

I smiled all the way home.

Chapter Seven

As soon as I returned from lunch on Friday, I called Rosalind to ask if she'd made any headway finding Harold Lester Davis.

"Sorry, Carrie. It's a madhouse here. Believe it or not, three new cases have come in today. Three! Dylan had to reschedule an interview."

"Wow! That's wonderful."

"I promise to get on your missing person as soon as things settle down," Rosalind said. "Want to say hi to Dylan?"

"Not if you guys are busy."

"He's right here and wants to talk to you. I'll put you through."

I bit my lip, hoping that Dylan wasn't about to tell me that he'd be getting home too late to make the rehearsal dinner.

"Hi, babe," Dylan said. "Three new cases! Business is picking up."

"It's a good thing you're about to hire an investigator."

"Just a few more interviews to go and I'll decide on my man." Dylan laughed. "I may have to insist that he stay at this office to work on current cases instead of going to Atlanta for training with Mac."

"Will you still be able to make the rehearsal dinner tonight? We're supposed to be at the restaurant at seven o'clock."

"Of course. I'll pick you up no later than twenty to. Gotta go."

I put down the phone, pleased that Dylan had wanted to tell me the news about his new cases himself.

The next two hours I read and responded to emails, then looked in on the programs in progress. Getting through my pile of paperwork took longer than usual because I was too excited to concentrate properly. Angela was getting married tomorrow!

I hadn't brought Smoky Joe to the library today because the wedding rehearsal was scheduled for four o'clock and I'd be going there directly from work. Trish had arranged to work from one till six and Susan would work from four until closing time. They would cover tomorrow as well and attend the wedding reception at night. I was scheduled to work on Sunday, after the big event was over.

At three forty-five I said goodbye to Trish and drove to St. Stephen's, which was a few minutes' drive from the center of town. St. Stephen's was a white wooden-framed church with a steeple, typical of the architecture in the area. I pulled into the side lot, where eight or nine cars were parked.

As soon as I entered the church, Angela dashed over and enveloped me in a fierce hug. "I'm so glad you're here, Carrie!"

"What's wrong?" I asked.

"Nothing. Everything!"

Her cousins Frankie and Tina, both bridesmaids, were going to be late. And Steve hadn't arrived.

"Calm down," I said as we entered the nave. Further down the aisle, family members stood around chatting while the organist ran through chords. "We have plenty of time."

"Actually, we don't," Angela said. "The priest has an emergency appointment at five o'clock."

"Why did he cut it so close?" I asked.

"You tell me!" Angela said. She was close to tears.

The young priest came over and said a few comforting words to Angela as the three of us joined the family group. The priest greeted everyone with a warm smile and invited us to call him Father Dan. I had no idea how he managed to establish calm and order, but in minutes we were lined up in the vestibule, ready to begin, when Steve and Frankie appeared.

We were four bridesmaids—Steve's sister Donna, Frankie, Tina, and me—four groomsmen, Steve's best man Jake Borelli, the small ring bearer—Liam—and even smaller flower girl—Emma. The organist began to play for real when Tina came huffing through the front door.

Marie, a pleasant woman in her sixties, told us she was the parish's unofficial wedding coordinator. Her job was to let each of us know when it was our turn to start down the aisle and where we were to stand during the ceremony. All went according to plan, and the rehearsal was over at ten to five.

I hugged Angela's mother, Steve, and various other people, then drove home to change for dinner.

Smoky Joe greeted me with loud meows to make sure I knew how unhappy he was that I'd left him cooped up all day on his lonesome instead of spending time with his library pals. I picked him up for a cuddle, then fed him his dinner, along with a generous handful of treats. That taken care of, I showered, then put on the dress I'd recently bought for the occasion along with my favorite pieces of jewelry—a gold heart pendant with diamonds that Dylan had bought me for Christmas and gold hoop earrings with a sprinkling of diamonds from my father. My two favorite men, I thought, as I reached for my blue eye shadow and got to work on my makeup.

* * *

"Don't you look stunning," Dylan said as I stepped into the BMW.

I leaned over to kiss him, breathing in the subtle woodsy fragrance of his cologne. "And you smell delicious."

Dylan reached for my hand and we drove through the Avery property in companionable silence. "How did the rehearsal go?" he asked, turning onto the main road that led back to Clover Ridge.

"Oh. The usual hysteria when a few people were late, but the young priest calmed everyone down and the rehearsal went smoothly from there."

"I'm sure everything will go according to schedule tomorrow," Dylan said.

I laughed. "If Liam doesn't drop the rings and Emma remembers to scatter the flowers instead of running to her mommy. Tell me about your new cases."

"Well, two involve small businesses whose owners believe an employee is stealing from the company."

"And the third?"

"Jewelry taken from a home. There's no sign of a break-in, and the only person outside of the family with free access to the house is the housekeeper. The homeowner can't believe the housekeeper took it. But someone did. I have to find out who."

I grinned. "You will! You or your new investigator."

"I've set up two interviews tomorrow. After that, I'll make my decision."

"The wedding ceremony starts at five, but I'm supposed to be at the church at four—for photos of the wedding party." I thought a minute. "You could meet me there then—"

Dylan stopped me in midsentence. "No way, my love. This is the first wedding we're going to and we'll go there together. Don't worry. I'll be home in plenty of time to get you to the church on time."

To get me to the church on time. I squeezed Dylan's arm. "Thank you."

When we arrived at Due Amici, the main dining room was set with about a dozen round tables for dinner. Some of the tables were already occupied, while other guests stood in groups, chatting and laughing.

Angela and Steve held hands as they came to greet us. Tonight my best friend was a vision in a purple floor-length halter-neck dress that set off her slender figure. I was happy to see she looked relaxed. We hugged and Dylan and I extended our best wishes.

I looked around, surveying the large room that was quickly filling up. "Did you invite the entire wedding?"

Steve laughed. "At least half of the wedding guests are expected here tonight."

"The dinner is for everyone in the bridal party plus the out-of-towners," Angela said.

Steve frowned. "As well as most of your relatives."

"*Close* relatives," Angela said. "Since Frankie's a bridesmaid, my mother felt her parents should be invited, along with Donna and Aiden. And if Donna was coming, it would be rude to leave Roxy off the list. Or her father. Poor Uncle Dominic is still grieving for Aunt Terri."

Steve rolled his eyes. "Who died two years ago."

"It's three years, and for your information, everyone grieves differently," Angela said.

"Carrie! How nice to see you!"

I turned as Donna in a gold-colored mini-dress joined our group. "Hello, Donna. Nice to see you, too. This is my boyfriend, Dylan."

Donna and Dylan shook hands. Roxy appeared a minute later, her red hair piled high, and I introduced her to Dylan. Dylan went off to get us drinks and Angela and Steve left to mingle.

"Where's Aiden?" I asked Donna.

Donna waved her hand. "He's around here somewhere."

"Right . . . over there," Roxy pointed.

Aiden and Tommy stood in a corner of the room deep in conversation. That is, Tommy appeared to be speaking with a great show of hand gestures while Aiden looked desperate to get away but didn't know how.

"I wonder what the problem is," I said.

Donna shrugged. "I have no idea. Aiden's been acting strange lately. Nick called earlier this evening to tell me he's worried about him."

"Who's Nick?" I asked.

"Aiden's partner in the practice."

"Do you think Aiden's having second thoughts about investing in Tommy's next movie?" I asked.

Donna shook her head. "I have no idea. I leave all money decisions to Aiden. If he thinks Tommy's next film is a good investment, then he'll put money in it. If he's changed his mind, then Tommy will have to find someone else to back his movie."

I thought it odd that Donna had so little interest in her husband's financial decisions. But maybe Aiden's income was large enough that the occasional investment had little impact on their budget.

"The place is filling up. I think we'd better find a table," Roxy said.

I looked around and felt a stab of panic when I saw that most of the tables were occupied with people I didn't know.

"There's one with enough places for all of us."

Donna dashed over to the table near the corner where her husband and Tommy had been talking earlier. Roxy and I followed after her.

Two older couples were already seated at the table. We exchanged introductions and learned that they were Steve's relatives from Chicago. Dylan joined us, carrying our drinks, and Aiden came over a few minutes later. I introduced him to Dylan. The two men struck up a conversation, which became more animated when they discovered they knew some people in common.

The cuisine at Due Amici was always delicious and tonight was no exception. We were served salad and offered a choice of three entrees—I chose eggplant rollatini and had a few forkfuls of Dylan's sausage and peppers. Later on, we'd have tiramisu or cannoli cake for dessert with our coffee.

It was an enjoyable evening. Donna and Roxy regaled us with amusing family anecdotes. At times it seemed that they were trying to outdo each other, and once they came very close to arguing over an incident each remembered somewhat differently. Perhaps rivalry was a natural result and to be expected of two strong-minded, outgoing female cousins who were the same age and had grown up living close to each other. I could understand why Angela felt intimidated when she was with either Donna or Roxy or with both of them.

The servers had just cleared the table of our main course when Angela and Steve stopped by our table.

"Having fun?" Angela asked while Steve chatted with his relatives.

"I am," I said. "The food's wonderful and your cousins are entertaining us with family stories."

"I'm glad." Angela lowered her voice. "It would be a perfect evening except for someone causing trouble as usual."

I shot her a questioning glance, which she returned with a jerk of her head. Noting that everyone at the table was engrossed in conversation, I followed her out into the hall.

"What's wrong?" I asked, though I had a pretty good idea.

"Tommy's in a snit and grousing about it to everyone at our table. He claims Aiden's reneging on his promise to put money into his movie."

"I saw them talking before dinner," I said. "Aiden looked like he wanted to escape but was too polite to make his move."

Angela rubbed her eyes. She was on the verge of tears. "Once again my brother makes himself the center of attention. And this is *my* rehearsal dinner for *my* wedding."

I wrapped my arms around her. "Oh, Ange. Don't let Tommy upset you tonight. Can't your parents stop him?"

"My father tried, but Tommy just shouted louder." She scoffed. "Mom tried to smooth everything over. Tommy's girlfriend, who seems like a nice person, was mortified. Steve saw how upset I was and said it was time for us to circulate."

"Would you like to sit at our table for the rest of the evening? We can ask them to bring over two more chairs."

Angela sniffed. "No, I'll be all right. Thanks for letting me unload on you."

I smiled. "Of course. What are best friends for?"

We walked back into the dining room as our waitress was setting out cups for coffee and tea at our table. Donna and Roxy were laughing over something and Dylan and Steve were conversing quietly. Both men stopped to watch Angela and me as we joined them.

"Ready to move on?" Steve asked Angela softly.

She nodded and winked at me to let me know she was okay.

"Trouble?" Dylan murmured.

"Tell you later."

The two older couples must have left while Angela and I were in the hall, and Aiden's seat was empty. I figured he'd gone to the men's room. But when dessert was served and he still hadn't returned, I turned to Donna.

"Where's Aiden?"

"He said he wasn't feeling so great, so he left early. Roxy will drive me home."

After his animated discussion with Dylan, Aiden had been quiet during dinner, but I'd figured that was because Donna and Roxy had monopolized the conversation, rarely letting anyone else get a word in. "I hope he'll be all right for the wedding tomorrow," I said.

"It's probably just his grass pollen allergies acting up after playing outside with the kids." She rolled her eyes. "I told him to start taking allergy shots but he insists that over-the-counter medicine works the few times he needs anything."

I took a spoonful of my cannoli cake and was in heaven. Minutes later, after conferring with Roxy quietly, Donna stood and bestowed a big smile on Dylan and me. "Well, we're off! See you guys tomorrow."

"Good night," Roxy said.

"See you tomorrow," we answered.

As soon as she and Donna were out of earshot, Dylan turned to me. "Those two have the weirdest relationship."

"What do you mean?" I asked.

"While you were in the hall talking to Angela, Aiden said he wasn't feeling well and wanted to leave. He asked Roxy to drive Donna home. Instead, Roxy offered to drive *him* home. She said she needed to talk to him."

"That's odd," I said.

"You can say that again. Donna was livid. She accused Roxy of making a play for her husband."

I remembered how Roxy had arranged for Aiden to sit beside her at the bridal shower. "Why didn't Donna drive Aiden home?"

"Good question. She didn't offer, and I could tell he didn't want to cut her evening short. Anyway, Roxy did a complete turnabout and said she'd drive Donna home as he had originally asked her to."

"And Donna was okay with that?" I asked.

"Yep. She acted like nothing happened. You saw for yourself."

So I had. Weird, as Dylan said.

We joined the crowd saying good night to Angela and Steve and their parents. Angela was back to being her usual brash and bouncy self, probably because her brother was nowhere in sight. Tommy was a pain in the butt, but I hoped she'd soon realize he no longer had an impact on her life.

In the car I leaned back into my seat and sighed contentedly. "I think I've just eaten enough for the next three days."

"Buck up. Tomorrow's an even bigger eating marathon."

"That's not till the evening. I don't intend to eat even a crumb until then."

We both laughed, knowing that wasn't true.

"What was Angela upset about?" Dylan asked.

"Tommy was causing a fuss at their table, angry because Aiden doesn't plan to invest in his movie after all. Angela gets bent out of shape whenever her brother acts up. He was awful to her when they were kids, and her parents—especially Rosemary—never would acknowledge how bad it was. It especially bothered her tonight, this being the rehearsal dinner for her wedding."

When Dylan didn't say anything, I studied his profile. He looked pensive.

"What is it?" I asked. "Did Aiden tell you he'd reconsidered investing in Tommy's movie?"

Dylan shook his head. "He didn't mention Tommy or the movie."

"But?" I said, knowing there was something he wasn't saying.

"I never brought it up with him, but he already knew I was an investigator."

My pulse quickened. "I never mentioned it either."

"Aiden said he'd be calling me next week. I said I'd be happy to talk to him and gave him my card."

Chapter Eight

S aturday dawned bright and sunny—a perfect day for a June wedding. I fed Smoky Joe, then made scrambled eggs and toast for Dylan and me. He left an hour later to interview job candidates. Angela's original plan to have her four bridesmaids get ready with her the day of her wedding began to fall apart when she learned that the room in the church where we'd be getting dressed was closed due to water damage. Her future sister-in-law took this as a cue to insist on having her hair done at her own beauty salon. Angela's cousin Donna followed suit. Angela had thrown up her hands and said she'd see us an hour before the ceremony. And so I showered, then drove to nearby Merrivale to have my hair washed and blown out, then went for a mani-pedi a block away.

I drove home in a state of excitement. Jeez! You'd think I was getting married. I was even too nervous to eat lunch. Instead, I answered emails and played with Smoky Joe, aware of the minutes passing by. Dylan texted to say he was leaving the office and sent along a smiley face because he'd finally made his decision about who to hire.

"Tell you about it in the car. I'll pick you up at three thirty."

"I'll be ready," I texted back.

Finally, I slipped my bridesmaid's dress over my head and zipped up the back. I smiled as I remembered choosing it when Angela and I had gone shopping one winter evening. Her wedding color scheme was yellow, silver, and cornflower blue, and we'd agreed that blue would look most flattering on her future sister-in-law, her cousins Frankie and Tina, and me. Finding the right style was much harder since the four of us varied in shape, height, and weight. I'd tried on several before Angela and I decided that the knee-length cornflower blue sateen dress with a sweetheart neckline and petal sleeves would suit us all.

*　*　*

Dylan whistled when I opened the front door of the cottage. "You are a vision in blue," he said before he kissed me.

"My makeup," I protested feebly before being swooped up in his arms.

I drew back a minute later to study him. "I didn't realize you'd be wearing a tux."

"The invitation said 'black tie, optional' so I thought I'd give the old tux an airing."

"It looks great on you. Why do you own a tux?" I asked, suddenly aware of all the things I didn't know about Dylan.

"Attending galas hosted by our wealthy clients as well as my share of friends' weddings. I figured it was better to be fitted for a tux once than having to rent one each time I needed one."

When we arrived at the church, I was surprised at the number of cars already in the parking lot. As soon as we entered, someone called my name.

"Carrie, hurry! They want you for some photos."

"Donna! Roxy! What are you doing here so early?"

"What do you think? We're here to help," Donna said.

My gaze went from one to the other. Both slender and elegant, they looked like models about to strut down a runway. Or movie stars dressed for a red-carpet event. Donna wore a slinky black gown with a thigh-high slit and a cutout at the waist. Her long hair was pulled back and artfully arranged to fall in a cascade of curls, her only jewelry long dangling earrings studded with glittering diamonds. Roxy, meanwhile, had on an iridescent green gown that set off her green eyes and red hair, which she wore over one shoulder. Both wore spiked heels.

"You both look awesome," I finally said, barely able to keep from poking Dylan to make him stop staring.

"You look lovely, too." Roxy patted my arm, and I knew exactly how Angela had felt growing up with her older cousins. "And now it's time for you to go inside, Carrie. Dylan, some of the guys are down in the basement."

"I'll find them," Dylan said. He opened the door to the nave and I hurried to join Angela and the others in the bridal party.

* * *

After all the pictures had been taken and guests had been seated, it was time for the ceremony to begin. Once again, Marie, the friendly church parishioner who helped out at weddings, stood with us in the vestibule to tell each of us when to start down the aisle. "Remember. Walk slowly," she whispered more than once.

So many people! I thought when it was my turn, noting the sea of faces on both sides of the aisle. Dylan caught my eye and I returned his smile. We four bridesmaids continued on to the front of the church, where we would stand near Angela as she took her vows.

How stunning she looked floating down the aisle on her father's arm! How radiant with joy! I noticed a flutter of handkerchiefs and tissues and realized I wasn't the only one moved by this special occasion.

The ceremony began. Angela had warned me it would be long, and it was. Finally, the part that we were waiting for began as Angela and Steve proclaimed their vows. The little ring bearer delivered the rings and they were declared man and wife. Cheering broke out when they kissed.

Slowly, everyone gathered outside the church. Dylan found me and clasped my hand. "Beautiful ceremony, but so long." His voice was softer when he added, "And I missed you."

I missed you. I kissed his cheek, reveling in his words.

We congratulated the new couple and their parents while the photographer snapped more photos.

"Didn't she look like an angel?" Fran asked as she, Sally, Marion, and their plus ones joined us.

"Absolutely!" I agreed.

We hugged one another. Dylan exchanged greetings with the women and Sally's husband Bob, whom he knew, and I introduced him to Matt, Fran's husband, and Nelson, Marion's significant other. It felt good being included in a group of friends and colleagues as though I belonged. I *did* belong, I reminded myself. Angela was my best friend and I'd just taken part in her wedding. Hard to believe how much my life had changed since October when I'd become head of programs and events at the library.

Dylan glanced at his watch, then at me. "I think we'd better leave."

I turned to the others. "Angela wants photos taken in the beautiful rose garden before it gets dark. We'll see you at the Gilbert House."

Dylan and I made our way through the crowd en route to the parking lot. We'd just about reached it when I noticed Angela's brother, Tommy, and his girlfriend Zoe a few feet ahead of us. He was in a foul mood, shouting at the top of his lungs.

"So suddenly Dr. Big Shot can't afford to invest in my movie! That's bullshit and he knows it."

"Tommy, you have to stop pressuring him. It won't make him change his mind."

Tommy balled his fist and pounded the roof of a car. "He's gonna be sorry he screwed me over this way. People don't renege on a promise made to Tommy Vecchio!"

Zoe tugged at his sleeve. "Please! Your sister just got married. Let's get through the reception in a peaceful manner."

"Peaceful? I'm not feeling very peaceful today."

They walked to their rental car in silence. A minute later, Tommy slammed his car door shut, then zoomed out of the lot.

"I hope Angela didn't hear Tommy harassing Aiden," I said when we were inside Dylan's BMW. "She doesn't need aggravation on her wedding day."

Dylan shook his head. "That guy's a nut job. I was talking to Aiden before the ceremony while you were taking photos. He said he never promised to invest in Tommy's movie. Only that he was thinking about it. Tommy went berserk when Aiden told him he'd decided not to."

"Tommy's telling everyone that Aiden promised to put up money and then backed out. He must be desperate," I said.

Dylan scoffed. "His pleasant disposition certainly won't bring him any backers."

"Angela's parents always told her she was exaggerating about her brother's behavior. It sounds like Tommy's only gotten worse over the years."

Dylan pursed his lips. "I've seen guys like this lose control and do some real bad stuff."

I shivered. "I hope nothing like that happens tonight."

* * *

The Gilbert House was a large white wooden-framed building that dated back to the early 1800s. Built as a private residence, it was eventually converted into an inn, and about twenty years ago turned into a highly praised restaurant and catering hall. As much as I looked forward to visiting every room and experiencing their renowned cuisine, I couldn't wait to explore the rose garden, which had been featured in many magazines.

Rienzo, Angela and Steve's scarecrow-skinny photographer, knew what he was doing. He shepherded the wedding party to the garden, where he took shot after shot of Angela and Steve, Angela and her four bridesmaids, then a few of the entire wedding party. By seven o'clock, the garden was crowded with wedding guests.

I found Dylan on the terrace that ran the length of the house and featured a bar and several small tables. He was chatting with Roxy.

"For you," he said, handing me a glass of white wine.

"Thank you." I took a sip.

Roxy gulped down a swallow of what looked like straight vodka or gin. Her words slurred when she spoke. *Sloshed already?* "Dylan was telling me he's a private investigator."

"He is."

"Such a fascinating career." Roxy winked and finished off her drink. "And so sexy."

Dylan and I stared at her. Roxy burst out laughing as though she'd said something amusing.

"Well, time to mingle," she said, wiggling her fingers. "See you guys later."

We watched her join Donna and Aiden. She slipped her arm through Aiden's and practically glued herself to his side.

"Now that's interesting," Dylan commented.

"Come on. They're cousins."

"By marriage. Which makes them kissing cousins."

I grinned. "You just made that up."

Dylan grinned back. "Maybe I did."

The wait staff walked around with trays of delicious hot hors d'oeuvres for us to sample—mini-meatballs, tiny shrimp quiches, mini-pizzas. In between bites, Dylan and I chatted with Angela's parents. When Steve and Angela joined us, she couldn't stop grinning. I hugged her tight, taking delight in her happiness.

"So, how does it feel to be married?" I asked when the others were conversing and couldn't hear us.

"Like I'm floating on a cloud and haven't touched the ground."

"You picked the perfect place for your wedding reception," I said.

"We did."

"And the perfect mate."

Angela gazed fondly at Steve, who was talking to her dad. "I did."

She placed her hand on my arm. "You and Dylan should get married here."

"Ange! Just because you got hitched doesn't mean everyone else should."

"Just sayin'."

Angela's words stayed in my head through the rest of the cocktail hour. I loved Dylan, but marriage was a huge step, especially for someone like me who was just starting to get her life together. Still, I loved having him at my side as we chatted with various guests, sipped wine, and devoured more hors d'oeuvres. And I *loved* the Gilbert House—at least what I'd seen of it so far.

I caught sight of Tommy a few times during the cocktail hour, always with a glass of hard liquor in his hand. But he seemed to have his anger under control. Aiden came into my line of vision as well. I saw him smile and nod but not say very much. And he seemed to blink his eyes frequently and even stumbled once, like he was having difficulty staying awake.

Eventually, we were asked to find our seats in the main dining room. Dylan and I joined the crowd filing through the double doors.

Our library table of eight was situated near the dance floor. We chatted as we waited for the newlyweds to make their appearance, which they did with a flourish. How glamorous they looked, both tall, dark, and slender, and grinning with happiness. The seven-piece band played "Can't Help Falling in Love" as they swayed to the music, their arms around each other. Then Angela danced with her father and Steve with his mother. The emcee invited everyone to join in, and Dylan escorted me to the dance floor. I felt a bit nervous. Despite how close we'd become, this was our very first dance.

But I had nothing to fear. We moved well together. Even when the beat sped up and our steps became more creative. Dylan was a wonderful dancer. He had a sense of rhythm and moved gracefully to the music. I had always loved to dance and could follow anyone around the dance floor.

The evening flew by. Dylan and I danced, we ate, we drank wine, and chatted with the library crowd, with Angela's cousins, with Angela and Steve. I kept an eye out for Tommy, but he didn't act differently than any other guest. He ate, he danced with Zoe, he chatted with the other guests at his table. He never approached Aiden, though I caught him glaring at his cousin-in-law a few times.

Aiden and Donna and Roxy sat with Frankie and her boyfriend, Tina and her husband, and another male cousin on the other side of the dance floor. I noticed Aiden and Donna dancing together a few times. He also danced with Roxy. One slow dance, Roxy seemed to drape her body over his like a cloak. Even over the music I could hear her drunken laughter while Aiden moved slowly, shuffling his feet.

Dylan caught sight of them and nudged me. "Do you think Aiden's on drugs?"

"I hope not."

And then it was time for the speeches. The dance floor cleared and voices grew silent.

Jake Borelli, Steve's best man, got up to toast the new couple. He told a few stories at Steve's expense that brought on good-natured laughter. After Angela's dad said a few words, I walked to the front of the dance floor to address the newlyweds and their guests.

"I came to Clover Ridge last fall, a place I used to visit when I was small and my relatives owned a farm outside of town. Angela befriended me when I started working in the library. We grew close and soon were best friends. I got to know Steve, of course, and saw what a perfect couple they made. And now they're married. They're Mr. and Mrs. Prisco. I know they will have a wonderful life together because they are both wonderful people. Let's raise our glasses and toast Angela and Steve!"

Dylan gave me a thumbs up when I sat down. As the tables were being cleared for cake and coffee, Sally and Bob got up to leave because Bob had an early tennis game. I hugged them both, suddenly feeling sad. The party would soon be over and I didn't want it to end.

The wedding cake cart was rolled out to the sounds of oohs and ahs. The newlyweds came to the center of the room. Steve cut the first piece and fed it to Angela. Then Angela did the same. Guests cheered and stamped their feet as Rienzo shot photos. Several cell phone cameras videoed the scene as well.

The wedding cake was moved to a corner of the room where pieces were cut and placed on trays. Out came a much larger table laden with several varieties of desserts. An impressive chocolate fountain with three tiers of flowing chocolate had the place of honor.

"Yum! That's my favorite!" Marion exclaimed. "Chocolate-covered strawberries."

While the wait staff served pieces of wedding cake to each guest, most of us dashed up to the dessert table. I had my eye on the Italian desserts. Though I had no room for another morsel of food, I couldn't resist eating a miniature cannoli, a mini-tiramisu trifle, and of course a few pieces of chocolate-covered fruit.

Dylan followed me as I worked my way up to the very popular chocolate fountain. I studied the dipping items available to dunk: strawberries, pieces of banana and melon, marshmallows, and a variety of cookies. *Choose two*, I told myself. Aiden, Donna, and Roxy were in front of me. When Aiden noticed me, he smiled and invited me to go ahead of him.

His words slurred together. Had he had too much to drink? But it wasn't any of my business, so I returned his smile.

"No thank you. I'm still trying to decide."

Roxy and Donna chatted together as they selected pieces of fruit, which they held under the chocolate fountain. They left and Aiden moved closer. He was spearing a strawberry when he suddenly fell forward. His face landed on the second tier of the fountain. I watched in horror as it slowly slid down to the first tier. Aiden made a gurgling sound as he crumpled to the floor.

Dylan was the first to move into action. He knelt beside Aiden and placed his fingers to his neck. His head shook ever so slightly as he felt for a pulse on Aiden's wrist.

"Is he . . . ?" I asked.

Dylan nodded. Aiden was gone.

Chapter Nine

There was turmoil all around me. People shouted, scarcely able to take in what had just happened, as they pressed closer to see for themselves that Aiden was dead. I was feeling claustrophobic when Dylan leaped to his feet and spread out his arms. "Everyone step back!" he bellowed.

Steve and Jake joined him to keep the guests at bay. I pushed through the crowd to reach our table where I'd left my phone and speed-dialed John Mathers's cell. Our police chief picked up on the third ring.

"Carrie, what's wrong?"

"I'm at Angela's wedding. Her cousin's husband, Aiden Harrington, just died."

"The doctor? Are you sure he's dead? I'll send an ambulance."

"Dylan checked his pulse." My voice quivered. "I watched him keel over and die."

"I'll be there ASAP. Dylan knows to keep everyone away from the body."

When I turned back to the crowd, Aiden and Steve were restraining a hysterical Donna from throwing herself on Aiden's body. Finally, her father succeeded in leading her away. A weeping

Roxy tried to embrace her, but Donna shoved her so hard, only a chair saved her from landing on the floor.

I walked over to Angela's parents' table, where Rosemary was consoling Angela. I sank into the empty chair beside my best friend and put my arm around her. "I'm so sorry this happened, Ange. Aiden was a great guy."

Angela rubbed her face with a cloth napkin. When she looked up, her eyes blazed with anger. "He couldn't stand to see me have my day."

"Aiden?"

"Of course not Aiden!" She pointed at her brother, who was talking to their father, his girlfriend standing meekly behind him.

". . . so, goodnight. Zoe's flying home tomorrow but I'm staying a while longer. My friend Kevin's set up a few meetings with friends who might be interested in backing my movie." Tommy came over to kiss his mother, then turned to Angela.

She pushed him away. "Go on, leave! Your dirty work is done!"

Tommy stared at her. "What the hell are you talking about?"

"You poisoned Aiden! I saw how he could barely stand all evening."

He curled his lip. "You're crazy. I never should have bothered flying all this way to be at your wedding."

"You only came east to wheedle money out of Aiden. And when he didn't give it to you, you murdered him!"

Poor Rosemary Vecchio was beside herself. "Angela! Tommy! Stop this crazy talk. You're family."

"Aiden's family, too," Angela said, "and your darling son just murdered him!"

Tommy stalked off, dragging a bewildered Zoe behind him.

* * *

"So, based on what you've been telling me, I'd better order an extensive tox screen," John said.

Dylan and I both nodded. I yawned, which made them both yawn. And no wonder. It was past two a.m. and we were drinking coffee in my kitchen. John had spent the last three hours interviewing wedding guests who had known Aiden or had witnessed his death, and had asked Dylan and me if he could come over and have us run through the scene of Aiden's death once again.

"Did either of you see anyone tamper with Aiden's food or drink during the wedding reception?" he asked.

"Nope," Dylan said.

"He claimed he wasn't feeling well last night at the rehearsal dinner, and seemed unsteady on his feet the few times I noticed him tonight."

"And there's the business between him and Tommy Vecchio," John said.

Dylan and I nodded.

"We'll find out soon enough if the good doctor died of natural causes or if he ingested something toxic," John said. "I've questioned the people closest to him. His wife Donna noticed he hadn't been himself lately." He cocked his head. "I know you didn't know the guy well, but was there anything about his behavior that struck you as odd?"

"He was planning to call me at the office after the weekend, which means there was something on his mind," Dylan said.

"Yes, you mentioned that," John said.

I giggled because Dylan had already mentioned it a few times. One of John's interrogation methods was to ask the same question again and again. But for it to cause me to laugh must mean I was overtired.

Both men looked at me and Dylan reached over to rub my back. "You're exhausted."

"I am."

John raked his fingers through his hair. "I'm almost done." He turned to me. "And you think Dr. Harrington might have been having an affair with his wife's cousin, Roxy Forlano."

"Possibly. Roxy had just gone through a difficult divorce and, according to Donna's sister Frankie, Aiden had been very supportive of her. Also, Roxy's ex—Miles Forlano—is Aiden's best friend," I said.

"Roxy was all over Aiden tonight," Dylan said. "During the cocktail hour; when they danced together."

"Sounds very incestuous," John said.

"Donna and Roxy have a tempestuous relationship as well," I said. "They argue and make up quickly, though after Aiden died, Donna pushed Roxy away—literally."

John had us run through the same questions one last time. Finally, he sighed, drew himself to his feet, and called it a night.

"Do you think this is a homicide?" I asked.

"Could be. We'll have to see what the tests show. Right now it's considered a suspicious death. I plan to talk again to everyone closely related to Aiden and anyone who had a reason to want him dead."

"Like Tommy Vecchio," I said.

"Like Tommy Vecchio and others. Good morning to you both."

I saw John to the door, then put out some food for Smoky Joe, hoping he would let me sleep in tomorrow morning. I was scheduled to work, but Sunday's library hours began at noon, at least till next week when the library would be closed Sundays until Labor Day weekend.

Dylan was already asleep when I slipped into bed. I hoped the image of Aiden crashing into the chocolate fountain then sliding to the ground wouldn't keep me awake. This was the second time someone had died before my eyes. Poor Aiden. Poor Donna and little Emma and Liam. Poor Angela and Steve, who would always remember that someone had died at their wedding reception.

Smoky Joe jumped onto the bed and nestled against me. With Dylan snoring gently beside me and my furry feline purring contentedly, I felt protected and loved. Within minutes I too drifted into a deep sleep.

* * *

Though Sunday proved to be a perfect June day, warm enough for boating and sitting on a beach if not swimming, a pall reigned over the library. Angela was popular with her colleagues as well as with patrons, and news that someone had died while dessert was being served at her wedding reception was the topic of conversation throughout the day. Sally, Marion, Fran, and I commiserated with one another via email, texting, and in the library's coffee shop, expressing our concern for Angela. I'd texted her earlier that morning, and she'd texted back, saying she was as good as could be expected and she'd call when she got a free moment.

When my office phone rang at three o'clock, I thought finally! Angela's calling. To my surprise, her mother Rosemary was on the other end of the line.

"Carrie, I'm so glad I managed to catch you!"

"Rosemary, how is everyone? I'm so sorry about Aiden and that it happened at Angela's wedding. How is she?"

Rosemary drew a deep breath. "That's why I called. I'm worried about her, Carrie."

A chill ran up my back.

"Angela's beside herself. She's got it into her head that Aiden was murdered and that . . . her brother killed him somehow."

I hesitated, then went ahead with what was on my mind. "Rosemary, there's a good possibility that Aiden was poisoned. We won't know until the tests come back."

"I know that," Rosemary said dryly. "Lieutenant Mathers questioned Tommy for quite some time. He advised Tommy to remain in Clover Ridge for the next few days."

So John had warned Tommy that he might be a suspect in a murder investigation. "Tommy was seen arguing with Aiden at the rehearsal dinner. I heard him tell his girlfriend that Aiden was going to pay for disrespecting him."

"My son's a hothead, but he wouldn't murder his cousin's husband."

"Angela told me how he treated her when they were growing up," I said.

Silence. Was Rosemary going to keep on denying that Tommy had tormented Angela both physically and psychologically when they were younger?

"I've apologized again and again for not listening to her when I should have. Angela keeps saying it's too late. The damage has been done. And now she refuses to leave their condo to go on their honeymoon."

I drew in breath. "I'm so sorry, Rosemary. I know how much she was looking forward to going to California."

"Angela said now isn't the time to leave us and go on vacation." Rosemary lowered her voice. "She's planning to go in to work tomorrow like always. Steve's tried to get her to see reason. That she's not doing herself or anyone any good by refusing to go on their honeymoon, but she won't listen."

"This doesn't sound like Angela," I said.

Rosemary began to cry. "Would you please talk to her, Carrie? This was supposed to be the most wonderful time of her life and now it's just about the worst."

"They're scheduled to fly to California tomorrow. Has she canceled all their reservations?"

"I don't know. But Steve's cousin arranged everything—the flight and the two different resorts where they'd planned to stay. Hopefully, she can make everything right if you can get Angela to leave as planned."

"When the library closes, I'll go over to the condo to talk to her."

"Thank you, Carrie. I'll tell Steve to expect you."

I hung up the phone and was mulling over my conversation with Rosemary when Evelyn appeared.

"I heard the sad news about what happened at Angela and Steve's wedding," she said.

"It was awful. Poor Aiden keeled over and died right in front of Dylan and me."

Evelyn perched on the corner of my assistants' desk and raised her eyebrows. "A heart attack or was he murdered?"

"We'll know that after the autopsy and the results of the tox screen come back. There's a good chance Aiden was poisoned. Slow-acting poison. Aiden complained that he wasn't feeling well at the rehearsal dinner, and he appeared slow-moving and unsteady at the wedding reception."

"Any suspects?"

"The spouse is always a suspect," I said. "Then there's Roxy, his wife's cousin. She was very fond of Aiden."

"Oh?" The one syllable was rich with suggestion.

"Roxy has just gone through a painful divorce from Aiden's best friend. Either Aiden was being an especially kind and helpful friend or . . ."

"Or they were having an affair. In which case, his wife had a motive to kill him," Evelyn finished for me.

I nodded. "And there's Tommy Vecchio, Angela's short-fused brother. Angela thinks *he* killed Aiden because Tommy was furious because he believed Aiden reneged on a promise to put money into his next film when Aiden might have only said he'd think about investing and decided not to."

"Three suspects."

"That we know of," I said.

Evelyn cleared her throat. "With all this going on, I don't suppose you've had a chance to do any research into finding my lost brother."

"Sorry, I haven't, other than to ask Dylan's secretary Rosalind to work on it. And she's been swamped at the office. But Rosalind will let me know as soon as she finds out something."

"Thanks, Carrie."

"And I'll do what I can, but right now Angela is my main concern. It's like the trauma of her brother's behavior during their childhood has returned with a vengeance. She was upset because Friday night at the rehearsal dinner Tommy monopolized the conversation at their table, ranting how Aiden didn't do what he'd promised. And now she's convinced that Tommy killed Aiden."

"Do you think he did?"

"I have no idea. It's possible. Dylan and I overheard him telling his girlfriend that Aiden was going to be sorry he'd reneged on his promise. Of course, that could be all talk, but Tommy looks and acts like a thug. You'd never believe he was Angela's brother. Then, of course, Aiden might have died of an aneurysm or a coronary."

After Evelyn left, I called Dylan to tell him I couldn't see him for dinner as planned because I needed to visit Angela and talk some sense into her.

"Go to it, babe. If anyone can get her out of her funk, it's you."

Chapter Ten

I was glad I had Smoky Joe with me when I went to Angela and Steve's condo. Angela was one of his biggest fans, and I hoped that a visit from him would help cheer her up. I rang the bell and Steve let me in.

I set the cat carrier down and released Smoky Joe, then I hugged Steve. He let out a deep sigh.

"Does she know I'm stopping by?"

"I just told her. She's making a pot of coffee."

Smoky Joe must have headed straight for the kitchen because we heard a squeal of delight, then, "What are *you* doing here?" Steve and I grinned at each other before I went in to see Angela.

"Hello, Mrs. Prisco. How are you today?"

She shrugged. "About how'd you'd expect a bride to be whose wedding was cut short when a guest dropped dead, probably murdered by her brother."

"Oh, Ange." I wrapped her in a bear hug, which wasn't that easy since Angela was several inches taller than me. She burst into tears. I patted her back, waiting for her to sob herself out. I felt helpless, not knowing how to help my dearest friend. Angela, who was always bubbly and cheerful, was clearly going through an emotional crisis.

Steve joined us in the kitchen. "The coffee's ready by the smell of it."

Angela looked up and I let her go. "Aroma," she said. "I keep telling you aroma. Smell sounds smelly."

"Sorry, dear," Steve said. Turning to me, he added, "Married one day and you see I'm henpecked already."

That brought a slight smile to Angela's lips that didn't quite reach her eyes. We sat down at the table and Angela poured three mugs of coffee from the carafe. Time for me to bring up the subject I'd come to discuss. But how to begin?

By being honest and forthright, I decided. "Ange, your mom called me today. She told me you don't want to go on your honeymoon."

"I think it's better if we postpone it for now," Angela said. "Steve's cousin, Brenda, said she could rebook it and we wouldn't lose more than a few hundred dollars."

"What do you think, Steve?" I asked.

He answered with a shrug and a frown. "Of course I want to go tomorrow as planned, but I'm tired of arguing. Our flight leaves tomorrow afternoon. We have to call Brenda by eight tonight if we're canceling." He shook his head. "I've got no idea if I can reschedule my vacation time."

I put my hand on Angela's arm. "What's keeping you from going off on your honeymoon as planned?"

Her face twisted in anger. "I'm surprised you have to ask me that. Aiden died at our wedding. I hate to fly off into the sunset, leaving my grieving family at a time like this."

"But your parents want you to go," I said.

Angela shrugged.

"Do you think Aiden would be happy to see you upset?" Steve asked.

"Of course not! Aiden was a good person. A kind person." Smoky Joe rubbed against Angela's legs. She reached down to pet him. "He didn't deserve to die like that."

Like that. Again I thought it best to speak my mind. "You think Aiden was murdered."

"Don't you?"

"Not necessarily. We'll know soon enough when the test results come back. That won't be for at least a week."

"I know Tommy was furious at Aiden. Friday night he went on and on how he was going to make Aiden pay. He must have poisoned him somehow."

"So—Tommy ruined your rehearsal dinner and now you're going to let him ruin your honeymoon?"

Angela stared at me as she absorbed what I'd just said. "I never looked at it that way," she finally admitted.

The discussion didn't end there, but I knew it was pretty much a done deal after that. Fifteen minutes later I was hugging them goodbye.

"Thanks, Carrie," Steve said. "You're a miracle worker."

"And what am I?" Angela said, giving him a light punch on the arm.

"My one true love."

"Smart man."

I grinned at them, happy to see they were back on an even keel. I'd helped Angela decide to go on her honeymoon, but Tommy Vecchio remained a problem. He may or may not have murdered Aiden Harrington, but he was causing his sister deep psychological pain that could only be addressed by a professional. Something I'd advise Angela to consider when she was back from her honeymoon.

"Have a wonderful time, you two." I lifted Smoky Joe's carrier. "Ange, I'll text you the minute I hear anything about the ME's report."

"You'd better," she said.

* * *

Rosemary called me that evening to thank me for convincing Angela to go on her honeymoon.

"I was glad I could help."

"Angela sounded like herself when she called to give me the news. Aiden's tragic death has upset all of us in the family. At least the question of how he died will soon be put to rest. Lieutenant Mathers told Donna he expects to get the medical examiner's report by Wednesday."

"Good. Then Donna can go ahead with the funeral. I would like to pay my respects. I hardly knew Aiden, but he struck me as a caring person and doctor."

"That he was. My sister is distraught, worrying how Donna and the little ones will manage without him. Hold on a minute while I get the funeral arrangements."

Rosemary returned to the phone a minute later. "The wake is Friday afternoon and evening at the Ryan Funeral Home outside of town. The funeral is Saturday morning at St. Stephen's, but I'm afraid it's for family only."

St. Stephens, where Angela and Steve just got married. "In that case, I'll come to the wake."

"Thank you, Carrie, for being such a good friend to my Angela. She's lucky to have you in her life."

"And I'm lucky to have her in mine."

* * *

Monday turned out to be a busy day at the library. The computer system stopped working in the morning, and all entries had to be done the old-fashioned way—by hand. I was helping out at the hospitality desk, signing up patrons for programs and events, when Angela called from the airport to say they were going to start boarding in a few minutes.

"I'm going to miss my lunch companion," I told her.

"I'll be back before you know it."

"As an old married woman," I teased. "Have a wonderful time in California."

"I plan to," Angela said. "And keep me informed like you promised."

"I will."

By midafternoon, the computers were fixed. I worked on reports, then ran through the growing list of possible new presenters. Trish left and Susan arrived, all excited because the mugs and tote bags she had designed for Gallery on the Green had all sold out.

After work, I stopped at the Gourmet Delight to pick up dinner for Dylan and me. I selected gazpacho, a strawberry-pistachio nut salad of baby greens, and cold poached salmon with an array of veggies. When Dylan arrived, it was obvious he was excited about something.

"Well, I've made my decision! I've asked Gary Winton to join our company."

"That's great," I said. "You seemed to be favoring him all along."

"I have. Gary's smart, curious, a bit brash—but that's to be expected—and eager to work with Mac and me. I had a long chat with Mac before saying anything to Gary and he gave his okay. Said he trusts my judgment on this."

"So he'll be working with you in the New Haven office?" I said.

"Starting next Monday. We're getting the paperwork done tomorrow and Wednesday. He'll start out with me, since I've got a few cases that require an investigator. He'll go down to Atlanta for training when things here ease up."

I chuckled. "I suppose that means he'll be learning a few things from my father."

"No doubt. By the way, Jim called today to ask me something about an old case. Sends you his love."

"You'd think he would bother to call and tell me that himself," I groused.

But inside I was smiling. My father had given up his criminal career when Mac hired him to work on the other side of the fence and use what he knew to catch thieves. He and Dylan had developed a friendship that went far beyond their working relationship.

"Gary's going to be spending the next few days looking for an apartment," Dylan said, "probably in or near New Haven. I was thinking, when he's settled, let's invite him over to dinner. I'd like you guys to meet."

"Sure. I'd like that."

Our conversation moved on to Aiden's death. "John told Donna that he should have the ME's report by Wednesday."

"That's a pretty fast turnaround," Dylan said. "It looks like John suspects foul play and convinced them to get the autopsy done ASAP. Especially since one of the suspects lives out of state."

"You mean Tommy Vecchio? I overheard him tell his father he was spending a few more days here—to try to convince some potential backers to put money into his movie."

I cleared the table, and since neither of us wanted coffee or dessert, we moved into the living room to watch the news. Dylan left shortly after that. I hummed as I got ready for bed. My life was very full and Dylan was a major part of it. Actually, we were important in each other's life. I was touched that he wanted me to meet his new employee. Things were going great for us. If only they continued this way.

* * *

Rosalind called me late Tuesday morning sounding exasperated. "Carrie, I finally got a block of time to search for that person you asked me to trace—Harold Lester Davis—but I'm sorry to say I came up with zilch."

"Really? Did you check out Mexico as well as the U.S.?"

"Of course, since you said he used to vacation there."

"Maybe he changed his name. Or died."

"Could be. Who is this for?"

"A friend from the library."

"I'll expand the search. See what I can find, but I'm not hopeful."

"Thanks, Rosalind. Much appreciated."

When Evelyn appeared a short while later, I gave her Rosalind's news. Evelyn sighed. "I've been hovering around the library, hoping to find out more about Michelle. Then earlier in the coffee shop I heard that same young woman—my niece's neighbor, apparently—tell her friend she felt sorry for Michelle Forbes. She said, 'The poor girl's desperate. She has no one to turn to. She's talking about ending it all.'"

"And you think she was talking about your niece?"

"I do."

"If Forbes is Michelle's last name, it should be easy enough to find her."

I turned to my computer and clicked on Facebook. I shivered. The chill running down my spine informed me that Evelyn was peering over my shoulder.

"Sorry," she muttered and backed away.

"And here she is," I said when I got to Michelle's page. I studied the photo of the pretty woman in her early thirties. She had long brown hair, brown eyes, and her smile lit up her face. Meanwhile, her companion, who I imagined was her ex-husband, wore a bored expression on his handsome face.

Evelyn sighed. "Such a lovely girl."

"Yes. And from the looks of him, he doesn't appreciate her."

I scrolled down to check out the latest entries and wasn't surprised that the last one was several months old. The name Brad appeared in two of the comments. Probably her husband.

"Michelle hasn't bothered to post anything in quite some time."

I clicked on other sections of her page to see what information I might gather. Michelle had indicated she lived in Clover Ridge and that she worked in an insurance office in a nearby town. She listed only a handful of Clover Ridge people as friends. I jotted down their names, then googled Michelle's name. Sure enough, there was a Clover Ridge address for a Michelle and Bradley Forbes.

"Now I know where she lives and the names of some of her friends," I told Evelyn.

Instead of looking pleased, she seemed more worried than before. "But even if you contact Michelle, I doubt that she knows where her father is."

I glanced at her sharply. "It seems to me Michelle needs our immediate attention, not finding your brother."

"Of course," she quickly agreed. "But I dearly wish you could locate Harold so he could help her. I'm certain he would. After all, Michelle is his daughter."

The daughter he abandoned, I thought but didn't say. "One step at a time, Evelyn. One step at a time."

*   *   *

Since I was working late on Wednesday, I decided to spend the morning visiting Michelle. The address I had was for a garden apartment complex a half mile or so outside of town. I drove there and glanced up at the second-floor unit. The curtains were drawn and I didn't see any light coming through to indicate that someone was home. Still, I climbed the stairs and rang the bell. No one answered. I decided to ring the bell of the apartment next door.

A young woman cracked opened the door. "Yes?"

"Does Michelle Forbes live in the apartment next to you?" I asked.

"And you are?"

"A friend of the family."

"Oh." The door opened a bit wider.

"I heard things were difficult for Michelle and I wanted to help."

That did the trick. The neighbor's tone softened. "Are they ever. Michelle can use all the help she can get. That SOB cleaned out their savings account just when her office decided to downsize and let her go. She can't afford to pay the rent here much longer."

"Won't she be getting unemployment insurance?"

"No, because she only worked there five months. She's fallen into a funk, and who can blame her?" The young woman eyed me appreciatively. "But you're here to help her, right? My name's Bobbie, by the way."

"Mine's Carrie. Bobbie, would you happen to have Michelle's cell number? I'd like to call her."

We both turned at the sound of an infant's cry. Bobbie disappeared inside her apartment and returned a few minutes later holding a baby. She handed me a paper.

"Here's Michelle's cell number. She wanted to start a family, but good old Bradley didn't want any little ones taking attention away from him. And then he decided he'd be happier with someone else. Poor girl didn't see it coming."

"Thanks. I'll call Michelle," I said. "Please don't mention I was here. I'd rather explain everything myself." *And come up with a story other than the truth, which would drive the poor girl to the psych ward.*

"Well, okay, if that's how you want to do it. But call her ASAP, okay? She's really in a bad way."

I trotted back down the stairs, wishing I would accidentally run into Michelle, who would then magically tell me where her father was. That would certainly please Evelyn, but it wasn't about to happen. Once again, Evelyn had bestowed on me an almost impossible assignment.

Chapter Eleven

The following day, I'd just returned to my office after checking on the late afternoon movie being shown in the meeting room, when Susan told me I had a phone call.

"Carrie, it's John. We have the ME's report. Aiden was poisoned by a slow-acting toxin."

I exhaled a deep sigh. "So he was murdered."

"Yep. They're thinking thallium, but they're doing further testing to nail down the specific poison. Meanwhile, I'm interviewing everyone who had a motive to kill the good doctor or who witnessed his death. Since you and Dylan fall into the second group, I'll be talking to you again."

"I'll text Angela with the news. I promised to keep her informed."

"As of now, we don't know when he ingested the poison since it could have been administered days before the actual death. This widens the list of suspects. I know you didn't know Dr. Harrington well, but you did see him the evening before the wedding. It would be helpful if you could recall his behavior, appearance, and demeanor at the rehearsal dinner."

"Will do," I said.

I disconnected, thinking about John's request. Friday evening, Aiden had left the dinner early because he wasn't feeling well.

Which meant anyone at the rehearsal dinner could have slipped something into his drink or food. Though if it was a slow-acting poison, someone had probably administered it a day or two before. That opened the suspect field to include people in his medical office. And Donna. Of course, the spouse was always Suspect Number One. I remembered Donna's emotional reaction to his death on Saturday night. Had she been exhibiting her genuine feelings or was she a supreme actress?

I googled thallium and read that it was a chemical element found in several ores as well in some vegetables like kale. It was very toxic and was used in rat poison and some insecticides until 1975, when it was banned in the U.S. and some other countries. However, there were many uses for thallium, among them manufacturing electronic devices and the optical industry. Fascinated, I checked out a few more sites about thallium and was amazed to see it could be ordered online. Who knew?

And who had bought it? I grimaced, hating how a homicide always put one in the position of suspecting everyone. Thank goodness Angela and Steve were in California because they were among the few I knew to be totally innocent.

I texted Angela to let her know that Aiden had been poisoned. She texted back immediately.

"Not surprised. And won't be surprised when Tommy is charged."

"We'll leave that to John to find out."

"LOL" was Angela's reply.

"R U having fun?"

"A wonderful time. Steve sends love. Me 2."

*   *   *

Since I was working Friday during the day, I decided to attend Aiden's wake that evening. The hours were from six to eight.

Instead of bringing Smoky Joe home after work and then driving back to town, I called Aunt Harriet to ask if I could drop him off while I attended the wake.

"Of course you can. And stay for dinner," was her answer.

"Are you sure? I wasn't trying to wangle a meal."

"Nonsense, you have to eat dinner, don't you? And since when do you stand on ceremony with your uncle and me?"

"Sorry. I don't want you to feel I'm taking advantage of you and Uncle Bosco."

Aunt Harriet chuckled. "As if you could ever do that. And tonight you're in luck. Your uncle is making lamp chops on the grill and I'm trying out an orange-strawberry salad."

"Sounds yummy," I said.

I smiled as I thought of my great-aunt and uncle. They had nurtured me the seven months I'd lived with them when I had first moved to town, giving me a sense of security and belonging, something I'd never received growing up. It was safe to say that my current stable and productive lifestyle was mainly due to them.

After work, I stopped by the Gourmet Delight for two quarts of gelato—pistachio and orange-chocolate—my aunt and uncle's favorites. Then I drove around the Green and parked in their driveway.

Uncle Bosco opened the front door just as I'd climbed the outdoor steps. As soon as I released Smoky Joe from his carrier, he dashed from room to room, making sure that nothing had changed since his last visit. I walked into my uncle's open arms.

"I'm so glad to see you, my dear. And what is this you've brought?"

His eyes sparkled as he checked out the contents of the Gourmet Market bag. "Aren't you kind? I'll go put these in the freezer, then it's back to the grill to make sure the chops aren't burning."

I followed him into the kitchen at the rear of the house where Aunt Harriet was preparing the salad. She hugged me, then handed me a tray filled with cutlery, paper plates, and napkins to carry out to the patio where Uncle Bosco was already turning the chops. "Tell your aunt five minutes."

"Uncle Bosco said five minutes," I said when I returned to the kitchen.

"Good, because the corn is just about done. Here's the salad, and please come back for the wine."

Minutes later we were sitting at the patio table, busily passing around platters. I tasted my lamb chop, which was a bit charred, then some of Aunt Harriet's salad, which was perfect. "Everything is delicious," I declared.

"I think I overdid the chops. Next time I'll get it down perfectly," Uncle Bosco said.

"It's because you ran to open the door for Carrie. I told you I could do that."

"Yes, dear." Uncle Bosco winked at me. "How is your friend Angela? I heard one of her guests died while dessert was being served. That young Dr. Harrington. They say he was a damn good surgeon."

"A really nice guy, too. He was married to Angela's cousin Donna."

"I never met him, but I went to his practice when I was suffering from gallstones and was sure I needed an operation. That was about fifteen months ago. Remember, Harriet? I saw Harrington's partner. What was his name—Nick Nolte?"

"No, dear, that's an actor. The doctor's name is Nick Gannon."

"Right. Anyway, turned out I didn't need surgery because the gallstones passed."

"John called me earlier. It turns out Aiden was poisoned," I said.

They fell silent and stared at me. Finally, Uncle Bosco spoke. "I suppose you intend to find out who murdered him."

I shrugged. "I'll be talking to people at the wake."

"Be careful, Carrie," Aunt Harriet said. "Don't provoke anyone. The murderer could very well be there."

Which is what I'm counting on. "I'm going to talk to people, that's all. I won't ruffle any feathers."

Uncle Bosco finished off his wine and poured himself another half glass. "Any thoughts on the town council position?"

I laughed. "I haven't had a moment to think about it. Too busy with Angela's wedding."

"That's what I told Al, but don't be surprised if he calls you next week."

"Thanks for the warning."

We discarded our paper plates, then Aunt Harriet and I carried out a pot of coffee, three mugs, an apple pie, and the gelati I'd brought. I had some pie with the pistachio gelato, but said no to coffee. I helped clear the table and carry in the leftovers to the kitchen. Smoky Joe sat waiting for me with that "feed me" expression, so I gave him some cat food and treats I'd brought along. Afterward he cleaned himself, then curled up in a corner of the living room and went to sleep.

"I'll come by for him no later than eight o'clock. That's when the wake is over," I said as I hugged my aunt and uncle goodbye.

They were somber as they watched me walk to my car, and I wasn't sure if that was because I was going to a wake or because they feared my questions would stir up a hornet's nest.

*   *   *

It was only a few minutes past six when I entered the lobby of the funeral home, but the line of people waiting to sign the guest book stretched almost across the length of the room. I joined the throng and let out a sigh. It must have been louder than I'd intended because the woman in front of me turned around. She was short and round and appeared to be in her early fifties. Her cheery smile lit up her pretty face.

"The line moves faster than you'd think. It was out the door when we arrived."

I smiled back, appreciating her friendliness, but I wondered at her outfit—a screaming orange blouse over a long peasant skirt of blues and greens.

I said, "I should have realized that many people would want to pay their respects to Aiden. He was such a nice person."

"And an excellent surgeon. The staff and our patients all loved him."

The staff and our patients? "Did you work with Aiden?"

She nodded. "I'm the office manager. Vera Ghent. I've known Aiden since he joined up with Nick five years ago." She lowered her voice. "I'm still reeling from his death. And to think someone poisoned him."

So the news was out. No surprise there. John was probably interviewing everyone who worked in the office.

I offered her my hand. "I'm Carrie Singleton. Pleased to meet you."

"Singleton," she repeated as we shook. "That name sounds familiar."

"Bosco Singleton is my great-uncle."

The man standing with Vera finished his conversation with the couple in front of him and turned his attention to us. He appeared to be in his late forties—of medium height, pleasant looking, with the start of a belly.

"I believe he came in for a consultation." He turned to Vera. "When was that? A year or so ago?"

94

"About then," she said.

"I'm Nick Gannon." He extended his hand. "Aiden was my partner. We're so sorry to have lost him—a wonderful physician and a dear friend. I can't imagine why anyone would want to kill the guy."

The line moved forward. I hadn't realized that we'd been inching closer to the viewing room while we'd been chatting.

"How do you know Aiden?" Vera asked.

"A close friend of mine got married on Saturday. Aiden's wife, Donna, is her cousin."

"Oh, the wedding where Aiden died," Nick said. "That must have been awful for the family."

"For all of us," I said. "I was standing right next to Aiden when he collapsed."

Vera and Nick exchanged glances. She said, "How did Roxy react?"

"She was terribly upset. Why do you ask about her in particular?"

Vera shrugged. "No reason, except we'd been seeing a lot of her at the office these past few weeks."

"For medical attention?" I asked, playing innocent.

Vera winked. "You might call it that."

"You mean . . . ?"

She shrugged. "I couldn't *swear* they were having an affair, but my instructions from Aiden were to let Roxy wait for him in his office if he was seeing a patient."

Nick shook his head. "Vera, you're letting your imagination run away with you. They're cousins by marriage, and Aiden was an especially caring person. The poor girl is an emotional wreck, barely coping after her divorce. Aiden was simply being a good friend."

"Good friend, my foot!" Vera protested.

Our conversation came to an end because we'd finally reached the guest book and Vera had started to write her message. I wrote a note of condolence along with my address, then entered the large viewing room. Further down, in front of the rows of chairs, was the casket. Closed, I was glad to see. I remained on line to pay my respects to Donna and Aiden's parents.

Donna wore a black summer suit over a white blouse and seemed to have her emotions under control.

"I'm so sorry for your loss," I said. "I only got to meet Aiden a few times, but I could see what a wonderful person he was."

"Thank you, Carrie." She hugged me. "Aiden was a wonderful husband and father and doctor. A terrible loss to everyone."

She sniffed into her handkerchief and introduced me to Aiden's parents. I expressed my condolences, then stood before the coffin, thinking of the handsome young man who had been cut down in his prime. Aiden's death was a loss to many people. Who had hated him enough to make sure he would never live another day?

A pretty young woman, tears streaming down her cheeks, came to stand beside me. She was crying so hard, I didn't think she noticed I was there. She kissed her fingers and placed them on the side of the coffin. A patient, I figured, and moved on to give her privacy.

Most of the people in the room were strangers to me, which was to be expected. I walked over to Angela's parents, Rosemary and Joe, who were sitting with Donna's parents. We chatted a few minutes. I was about to leave when Tommy came over. He glowered at me, though I couldn't imagine why, then spoke to his parents in low tones before striding off.

Curious, I asked Rosemary, "Is there a problem?"

She sighed. "He's angry because Detective Mathers had him come in to the precinct again and asked the same questions. It seems he considers Tommy a suspect."

"Tommy made no secret of the fact that he was furious at Aiden because he'd decided not to invest in his movie."

Joe turned up his hands. "That's Tommy's way. The kid goes on and on about whatever's bothering him till he flushes it out of his system, once and for all."

"I hope you're right." I proceeded to tell them about Tommy's tirade about Aiden after the wedding ceremony.

To my surprise, Rosemary said, "Joey, it's time Tommy learned to control that temper of his. We should have stopped him from badmouthing Aiden Friday night. No one at the table wanted to hear it, and it upset Angela. Then the poor boy was murdered."

Rosemary blinked back tears. Her sister interrupted her own conversation to lean over and pat Rosemary's shoulder.

I excused myself and headed for the door. But I hadn't gone ten feet when Donna's sister Frankie stopped me.

"Hi, Carrie. I'm glad you came tonight."

"Of course. I'm so sorry this happened."

"Yeah. Aiden was the greatest brother-in-law you could ask for. If it wasn't for him, I never would have gotten through my college math course."

"I only met Aiden because of the wedding, but I could tell what a special, giving person he was."

"Yeah, maybe too giving."

I followed her gaze and saw Roxy in the corner of the room. She was staring at the ground while a good-looking man in his mid-thirties spoke earnestly to her.

"You think there was something between Roxy and Aiden?"

Frankie shrugged. "I don't have any proof, but from the way she acted—always hanging on to him, I'd say something was brewing."

"How did Aiden act toward Roxy?"

Frankie raised her eyebrows. "Hard to say. Aiden was nice to everyone."

"How is Donna getting through all this?"

"That's hard to say as well. My sister's a world-class actress. She took on the role of perfect suburban housewife and mother and plans to stick to it, especially now that she's the mourning widow."

"What do you mean? Weren't she and Aiden happy?"

Frankie glanced around to see if anyone was close enough to overhear us. "Not for some time. She never told me, but she confided in Mom, and Mom was too upset to keep it a secret."

"What was wrong?"

Frankie shrugged. "For one thing, she was annoyed that he worked long hours. He seemed preoccupied but wouldn't say with what. Recently, I saw for myself how Roxy pissed her off, the way she clung to Aiden like ivy."

We both turned toward Roxy in time to see her push aside the man she'd been talking to and dash out of the room.

"There she goes, the drama queen," Frankie said.

"Who was she talking to?"

"Miles, her ex."

"What's he doing here?"

"Didn't you know? Miles was Aiden's best friend."

"Oh, right."

I walked out into the hall and noticed that several people were standing around chatting in small groups. Vera waved to me. I decided to join her when I saw that she was with the young woman who had been weeping in front of Aiden's coffin earlier.

"So you decided to leave before the speeches," Vera said.

"I only stopped by to pay my respects," I said.

Vera laughed. "No criticism here. I'd probably leave, too, except I'm expected to say a few words."

"I'm glad I don't have to," the young woman said. "I'd probably freeze up, speaking in front of a group of strangers."

Vera patted her shoulder. "No worries. Nick and I will represent the office." She turned to me. "Gwen is our RN and my right-hand gal."

"Carrie Singleton," I said, extending my hand.

"Gwen Swithers." She studied me as we shook hands. "You were standing by the casket when I had a meltdown."

At five foot three or four, Gwen had a sturdy, curvaceous figure, with long blonde hair that could use a shaping. She gave me a half smile, and I realized she was young, perhaps no more than twenty-two or three. Working for Aiden and Nick Gannon might very well be her first job out of nursing school.

"I'm glad you're feeling better now."

"I've never known anyone who died. And to think that someone poisoned Aiden . . ." Her eyes welled up with tears. "Who would do such a thing to such a kind and loving man?"

"I have no idea," I said. *But I intend to find out.*

Chapter Twelve

S aturday turned out to be another beautiful June day. Too lovely for a funeral, I thought, and felt a pang of guilt for feeling relieved that Aiden's funeral was only for the immediate family and I wouldn't have to go. Though last evening I'd overheard someone say there would be a memorial service in a week or two, which I planned to attend. I brought my lunch to work, intending to eat it sitting on one of the new benches they'd recently installed on the Green.

I was glad Angela was enjoying her honeymoon, but I sorely missed her and wanted to get her down-to-earth input regarding the latest I'd learned about Donna and Roxy and Aiden's office staff. I also wanted to tell her that her mother was finally seeing her brother as the troublemaker she always knew him to be.

After glancing through my emails, I left my office to see if any of the ongoing programs were in need of attention. The large reading room looked deserted, with only a few patrons thumbing through magazines.

Smoky Joe came bounding over to greet me, and I bent down to pet him. "I'm sorry no one's around to give you attention."

Marion was shaking her head as she walked from the children's section to join us. "I can't remember the last time this place was so deserted. I have a children's book author scheduled this afternoon, but I'm afraid she won't have much of an audience."

"I suppose it's the good weather," I said. "People want to stay outdoors."

Even the knitting and crocheting group that met weekly was much smaller than usual. I had nothing pressing that needed attention. Except those dratted monthly financial reports Sally had us fill out.

The phone was ringing as I reentered my office. "Hi, Carrie. John here. I was wondering if you have any time to answer a few questions today."

"I sure do. We're having a really slow day here at the library. Want me to come down to the station?"

"I'd rather stop by the library, if that's all right with you."

"Of course."

"Be there in ten."

Minutes later, John arrived, a coffee cup in hand. He pulled my assistants' chair from behind the desk and dropped into it, downed what remained of his coffee, tossed the container in the garbage, and stretched out his long legs.

"Did you go to Aiden's funeral?" I asked.

John shot me an amused look. "I thought I was here to ask the questions."

I shrugged. "Just wondering. In the movies, the detective always attends the murdered victim's funeral. To observe if anyone looks guilty."

"I happened to stop by to pay my respects, but no one looked especially guilty."

"Too bad."

John cleared his throat. "So, Miss Carrie Singleton, how well did you know the deceased?"

"Not well at all. I first met him at my friend, Angela Vecchio's, bridal shower, which was held in his home two weeks before her wedding, where he died."

"How did he seem at the shower?"

I thought back. "Fine."

"In good health?"

"As far as I could tell. He came over to congratulate Angela and she introduced him to me and our three library friends. Then Donna's cousin Roxy whisked him off to a seat at her table."

"Roxy did, eh?"

"Yes."

John jotted down a note in his small notepad.

"And the next time you saw Dr. Harrington was?"

"The night of the rehearsal dinner, which was the evening before the wedding."

"Did you get a chance to notice him? Talk to him?"

"I saw him early on with Tommy Vecchio, looking uncomfortable as Tommy rattled on. Though Dylan and I sat at the same table as Aiden, I didn't talk to him. Aiden left the dinner early—while I was in the hall talking to Angela. Dylan said he claimed he didn't feel well."

"Oh? Did he drive himself home?"

"Let me think. I believe he did. Roxy offered to drive him. Donna didn't like that idea. She went home with Roxy later that evening."

"Did Dr. Harrington seem ill to you?"

"He was rather quiet after having an animated conversation with Dylan earlier in the night. Donna said he was probably suffering from his allergies."

"She didn't seem concerned that he wanted to go home early?"

"No. Not at all. She was more bothered that Roxy offered to take him home."

"Roxy again," John commented.

He took me through the wedding, and I said that I'd noticed a few times that Aiden seemed wobbly on his feet and a bit out of it.

"Who was near him when he fell?"

"Dylan and I were the closest. Some guests were nearby. I don't know their names."

"Not his wife or Roxy?"

I thought a bit. "They were ahead of Aiden on the dessert line and had returned to their table. People were pressing forward to see Aiden. Dylan held them back while I pushed through the mob to get my phone to call you. When I looked, Steve and his best man were holding Donna back from throwing herself on top of Aiden."

John took me through the entire series of questions again. He made a few notations in his notebook, then he leaned back and gave me his full attention.

"Anything happen that evening or the preceding days you found odd or suspicious?"

"There's Tommy, for one thing. He was furious that Aiden decided he couldn't or wouldn't back Tommy's movie. Dylan and I heard him telling his girlfriend that Aiden would pay because no one disrespected Tommy Vecchio."

"Anything else come to mind?"

"Roxy was all over Aiden, which annoyed Donna. I don't blame her. Roxy's behavior would annoy any wife, even if her marriage had problems."

John raised his eyebrows. "Was the Harrington marriage in trouble?"

"I'm not saying they were heading to divorce court, but Donna's sister Frankie told me that Donna was unhappy."

"Because of Roxy?"

"I don't know. But when Roxy tried to comfort her right after Aiden died, Donna shoved her away. Those two have a strange relationship—squabbling one minute, best buddies again the next."

"Did you get the sense that Roxy and Aiden were having an affair?"

I shrugged. "I really couldn't say. She acted like she had a right to his attention."

"And how did he respond?"

I thought a moment. "He tolerated her attention."

"Tolerated, eh?"

"Yes. He didn't pursue Roxy or initiate contact when I saw them together. Vera, Aiden's office manager, thought they were having an affair since Roxy was always stopping by the office, but his partner Nick didn't think that was necessarily the case."

John shot me a look of fake surprise. "Vera and Nick? You just *happened* to run into them and they offered you their opinions on Dr. Harrington and Roxy's relationship?"

Oddly enough, that was exactly what had happened, but I had the good sense not to say. "I chatted with them at Aiden's wake. Didn't I mention it?"

"No, you didn't." John grinned. "Carrie Singleton! You can't help investigating a murder, can you?"

I shook my head vehemently. "I'm not *investigating*. Simply keeping my eyes and ears open. Last night I went to Aiden's wake to pay my respects, and Vera and Nick were standing in front of me in line. Vera struck up a conversation. Honest! She's very friendly."

"All right. I believe you." John got to his feet. "Thanks, Carrie."

"Is that all?" I asked.

"Yes, unless you have something more to tell me."

"I don't."

"You sound disappointed," John observed.

"Do you have any more information about the poison given to Aiden?" I asked.

"They're still thinking it was thallium—a colorless, tasteless element that's slow-acting."

"Then the murderer may not have been at the rehearsal dinner or the wedding."

"He or she may have been at those events but administered the poison a day or two earlier. Several possibilities."

John opened the door to let himself out. "If you should happen to learn anything that has a bearing on this case—and I do not want you snooping around—please pass it on."

"Of course. You know I will."

He'd no sooner left than Evelyn made an appearance. Her lips were pursed in disapproval. "I'm surprised at John Mathers—telling you one thing when he means quite the opposite."

I laughed. "He can't help himself. On one hand, he feels obliged to protect me by instructing me to leave the investigation to him. On the other hand, I've been too resourceful in the past for him to ignore my input, especially since I have gotten to know the important people in Aiden's life."

"Who do you think killed him?"

I rubbed my chin as I considered her question. "I don't know. I imagine the police are investigating recent thallium sales and searching homes, but so far there's no evidence pointing to any one person—as far as I know.

"The poison was administered days earlier, and Aiden was in the company of several people—Donna, Roxy, Tommy, the people who work in his office. Patients. Which leads to the question: Who had reason to want Aiden dead? His marriage was in trouble. He might have been having an affair with Roxy. Tommy Vecchio was furious at him. And he planned to talk to Dylan after the weekend."

"Now that's interesting," Evelyn said. "I wonder if he wanted Dylan to investigate a theft or a crime."

"Donna said that recently Aiden had been spending evenings shut inside his home office. Maybe he was worried about his practice."

Evelyn laughed. "Or he could have been sexting with his lover."

"Evelyn!" I said, pretending to be shocked.

"I know. The things I learn from patrons' conversations."

I felt a chill of cold air as she dropped into the chair John had recently vacated. "Have you figured out how you're going to find my brother?"

"I found out where Michelle lives. I went to see her, but she wasn't home. I've been too occupied with Aiden's murder to plan my next step. For all we know, Harold died some time during these past fifteen years."

She shook her head. "I sense he's alive, though I have no idea where he might be. You have to find him! Poor Michelle's about to be turned out of her apartment. I'm worried she'll fall ill or harm herself."

Something about her concern didn't feel right, but I couldn't put my finger on it.

"Michelle's lease is probably up at the end of the month, which is only a week or so away. I'll drive over to her apartment during my lunch hour. Hopefully, she'll be in this time."

Evelyn opened her mouth as if she was about to speak, then closed it without uttering a word. I sensed she wanted to tell me to go see her niece this very minute, then thought better of it. After all, I was employed by the library and couldn't very well leave during working hours in order to investigate on her behalf. But I was happy to do it during my free time. I wanted to help Michelle and that meant tracking her down as soon as possible.

At noon, I exited the library's parking lot and called Dylan on the off chance that he was free to talk. He was playing golf today with a friend who lived a few towns away. I was glad he had found time to do something relaxing. I was in luck. He and his friend and the two men they were playing against were taking a break so we had a minute or two to chat.

"John stopped by the library to ask questions regarding Aiden's murder."

"Yeah. He texted me. I told him I'd stop by the precinct when I was done here."

"I'm on my way to see if Evelyn's niece, Michelle, is home. Evelyn's worried about her, and for good reason, but dropping in like this on the chance that she's home is like shooting fish in a barrel."

"Does she have a car?" Dylan asked.

"I don't know, but I bet her husband took it when he emptied their bank account."

Dylan gave a snort. "A real standup guy. In that case, if she's not home I'd check out stores within walking distance."

I thought a minute. "What a great suggestion. There's a block of shops near her apartment."

I heard voices in the background.

"Gotta go. I'll pick you up a little after seven."

I smiled, thinking of Dylan as I drove to Michelle's apartment. I was getting used to having a man in my life—always in touch to talk about anything good or bad that happened during the day. I liked the sense of continuity we had developed, and that he supported me when I needed support, like when my mother had come to Clover Ridge.

Enough! I told myself. I was beginning to sound like lovey-dovey Angela.

Minutes later I parked half a block from the entrance to Michelle's garden apartment unit. I felt nervous as I climbed the stairs to her apartment since there was no way I could bring up her long-departed Aunt Evelyn as the reason for my visit. I should have worked out my story on the drive over instead of mooning about Dylan.

Still, I rang the doorbell, hoping that a brilliant idea would come to me. I could be a long-lost relative. And then what?

But I needn't have worried because, though I rang and rang, there was no answer. I decided to try her neighbor once again. Before I even stepped in front of her door, it flew open and Bobbie was pushing out a stroller.

"Hi!" she greeted me. "I was wondering if you were ever coming back."

"Well, I'm here, but I see Michelle's out again."

"She's running a few errands. She has to be back by two because I'm driving her to see a room she might rent." Bobbie made a face. "I told her that neighborhood isn't safe, but she said that's all she can afford until she gets another job."

"Has she been looking for a job?"

"She tried once or twice, but getting turned down only made her feel worse. She's hoping the medicine her doctor prescribed will help lift her depression."

I thanked Bobbie and headed for the shops a block away. I peered inside the Dollar Store, the take-out Chinese restaurant next to it, then walked through the small supermarket, but there was no sign of anyone resembling the girl whose photo I'd seen on Facebook. I entered the large drugstore and walked through the shampoo and conditioner aisle when I became aware of loud voices coming from the pharmacy area in the rear.

"I know your prescription is valid, Mrs. Forbes, but if you can't pay for the medicine, I'm afraid I can't give it to you."

Michelle! I walked toward her.

"I know this credit card is okay," Michelle said, her voice shaky. "I keep it for emergencies. Please try it again."

"Sorry. It's been canceled."

"That can't be! How did he get to this card, too?" Michelle burst into tears.

The pharmacist's voice softened. "I am sorry, Mrs. Forbes. Perhaps you can borrow the money from a friend or a neighbor. Right now I have to ask you to step aside and let me help the other customers."

Michelle rubbed her eyes. She left the line and nearly bumped into me. "Sorry," she mumbled.

"I'm sorry you were unable to get your medicine, Michelle."

She stared at me. "How do you know my name?"

Think fast, Carrie. I plastered a wide grin on my face. "My name's Carrie Singleton. I'm a librarian at the Clover Ridge Library. I knew a few of your relatives who used to work there." *True enough.*

"But that still doesn't explain how you know who I am."

I drew a deep breath. "Someone overheard a conversation mentioning you were having difficulties, and I thought I'd stop by to see if I could help."

Michelle's brow wrinkled because she realized there were missing pieces.

"Tell me, how much is the medicine you need?"

"Thirty-five dollars."

"I'll lend you the money for the medicine, if we can stop for coffee nearby so we can talk."

Michelle blinked as she thought. "You went to my apartment! Bobbie said a family friend came by."

"That was me. Let's get your medicine then have a chat."

"All right," Michelle said and led the way.

Chapter Thirteen

M inutes later we were seated in a booth in the coffee shop across the street from the pharmacy. As soon as the busboy brought us water, Michelle gulped down one of the pills she'd wanted so desperately.

"Carrie, thank you so much for getting these for me. They're the only meds that help ease the depression. I promise to pay you back as soon as I can."

"Please don't worry about that now."

Our waitress, a buxom woman in her mid-fifties wearing a nameplate that said "Mary," appeared. "Good afternoon. What can I get you girls?"

Neither of us had glanced at the menus. "Just coffee for me," I said.

"Me too," Michelle said.

"Sure you don't want anything else?" I asked. "My treat."

She shook her head.

"Two coffees coming up," Mary said as she took our menus and left. She returned a minute later with two mugs of steaming coffee.

"So tell me—how did you get into this predicament?" I asked.

Michelle shook her head. "I ask myself that question several times a day. Things started out great. Brad and I moved to Clover Ridge almost a year ago. Despite the awful time when my father left us, I had fond memories of growing up here. Brad was willing. He got a job through a relative who lives in the area—I never met her—and we moved into our apartment." She stopped to put sugar and milk in her coffee, then sipped.

"We hoped to have a baby, but . . . there were complications. I think that's when things began to change. Brad grew distant. Irritable. He started to stay late at the office." She pursed her lips. "Or so he said. I should have realized something was going on."

"Don't blame yourself," I said.

"He encouraged me to find a job. And I did—at an insurance company. But last month they said they weren't doing well and had to downsize, so I was let go a week later. Nothing was going right in my life. I started feeling bad about myself. I found it hard to get up in the morning. Sometimes I slept till noon. I went out less and less."

Michelle sniffed. "One morning Brad was gone. He'd packed up his clothes while I was sleeping. He left me a note saying he couldn't live this way any longer.

"I found out soon enough he'd emptied our savings account, no doubt to spend money on some woman he'd met through work." She began to cry without making a sound. Tears rolled down her cheeks. "And now I'm left with nothing—no money, no home, no family. Nothing."

I reached across the table to hold her hand. "We're going to do something about that."

Michelle looked at me like I was speaking a foreign language.

"Really," I said. "For one thing, you can't be forced to leave your apartment. I'll do some research, talk to my uncle who knows about these things. I may even call the mayor."

"Call the mayor about me?" Michelle asked.

"Why not? I'll find out if there are funds appropriated for people who have suddenly lost their jobs—which is what happened to you."

Michelle nodded. "I never thought of asking for help. Not after I found out I wasn't going to get unemployment insurance because I hadn't worked there long enough."

"And it's time you got yourself a lawyer," I said.

"I can't afford—"

"I know that, but many lawyers take pro bono cases. Your husband had no right to cut off your funds. You're going to need a lawyer to get some of them back. I'm going to give you the name of a lawyer I know well." I jotted down Ken Talbot's name and office number and handed it to her. "I'll be speaking to him too. If Mr. Talbot can't handle your case, he'll find you someone who can."

Michelle gripped my hand. "Thank you, Carrie. I've been so down since Brad left me, but you're giving me hope that maybe I can put my life back together."

I smiled at her. "There's plenty of hope. And now I have to ask for your help."

"Of course, though I can't imagine how I can help you."

I thought of Evelyn and plunged on. "I know this is difficult, but I'd like you to tell me everything you remember about the time your father left you and your family."

I sat back and sipped my coffee, which was now lukewarm. According to the clock on the wall, I should have left for the library ten minutes ago. No matter. I was where I needed to be.

Michelle cocked her head. "Why are you so interested in something that happened fifteen years ago?"

Here goes. "I thought it would be great if you had a relative in your corner." I raised my hand to stop her from uttering the words forming on her lips. "I know your father abandoned you and you haven't heard from him in all these years. He may be dead, for all we know. But there's a chance that he's alive and well, and if he is I'm sure he'd want to help you. I'm a librarian with great research skills. Please tell me it's all right to try to find him and let him know about your situation."

Michelle nodded reluctantly. "How can I say no when you've helped me already."

I waited while she composed herself. "I know it's painful, but please tell me everything you remember about that period in your life."

"My father was an accountant," Michelle began. "He worked for a large company in New Haven. We were a happy family—my parents, my brother Harvey, and me. Sometimes my parents argued because my father liked to gamble. I never thought much about it, never thought it was anything serious. Just that Mom thought gambling was like throwing away money, money that we could use for home improvements or family trips.

"I was sixteen when my world, as I knew it, came to an end. I felt the tension and fear in the house. My parents speaking in worried whispers. Then suddenly Dad was gone and Mom had no idea where he was."

"I can only imagine how frightening that was," I said.

"I turned numb. I had trouble breathing. Moving. I didn't go to school for two weeks."

"Brad's behavior must have brought it all back."

Michelle nodded. "Another man leaving me. The story of my life."

"Did you eventually find out why your father took off?"

"Oh, yes. This time Mom didn't hide it from Harvey and me. Dad had run up a large debt at the tables. He had to pay it back or something really bad would happen to him, so he took money from one of the company accounts. He heard that the feds were coming to headquarters and figured they were after him." She made a scoffing sound. "The irony was the feds came, all right, but they were after the CEO and top officers for corporate fraud."

"And you never heard from your father again?"

Michelle shook her head. "Mom was sure he'd come back when word got out about the arrests, but after a week of not hearing from Dad, she tried to track him down. She contacted everyone he knew—friends, relatives, people at the firm—but no one knew anything. His disappearance crushed her spirit. My aunt urged her to move to Ohio, so she sold the house and the three of us went there."

"I was sorry to hear that your mother died. Are you in contact with your brother?"

"We lost touch a few years ago. Poor Harvey's in and out of rehab. I wish there was something I could do for him, but . . ."

"Was there anyone your father was especially close to? Someone with whom he might have stayed in touch?"

"Instead of his own family? I don't think so."

"Michelle, I didn't see much of my father when I was growing up. He was in jail some of the time. Other times, he simply stayed away from the family. Eventually my parents got divorced."

Michelle grimaced. "Another wonderful father."

"Except Jim made big changes in his life. Now he has a good job and he's in my life again."

Michelle shot me a look of disbelief. "I hope you're not expecting that to happen in my case."

"I just thought it might be worth the effort to find your father. He might be in a position to help you."

"I doubt that. For all we know, he's dead."

"That's possible." I waved to Mary. When she hurried over, I asked for the check. "I have to run," I said to Michelle. "Please stay and have a sandwich or something to eat."

She smiled for the first time. "Thanks, Carrie. Maybe I'll have a tuna salad sandwich, after all."

Mary jotted down Michelle's order and gave me the bill. I left her a nice tip and handed Michelle my card. "Please call if you can think of anyone who was especially close to your father. And call the lawyer on Monday. Meanwhile, I'll talk to my uncle. He knows a lot of people in Clover Ridge. I'm hoping he might be helpful finding you a job."

"A job," Michelle echoed wistfully. "I think I'd welcome that most of all."

* * *

The library was even quieter—if that was possible—when I returned thirty minutes past my lunch hour. Smoky Joe was waiting for me outside my office door.

"Poor baby," I said, sweeping him into my arms. "You must be starving. And since it's the weekend, neither Trish nor Susan was here to let you inside."

He gobbled down the food I set out for him, then ran to the door. "Off you go," I said as I watched him race into the reading room. I checked my email, then texted Ken Talbot to expect a call from Michelle. I called Uncle Bosco, who said he would ask around about a job for Michelle. I decided to call Al Tripp on Monday to see what funds might be available to someone in

Michelle's situation. Besides, he knew everyone in Clover Ridge. If Uncle Bosco couldn't find her a job, Al certainly could.

When Evelyn showed up, I filled her in on my conversation with her niece. "She seemed calmer when I left her," I said, "but she has no idea where her father is now. I gave her my phone number, in case she remembers someone who might know something about him."

"Thank you, Carrie." Evelyn shot me an enigmatic smile. "I have a feeling you'll be hearing from Michelle before a week is past." Then she disappeared.

I went downstairs to look in on the one program in progress, a crafts class, then I headed to the hospitality desk to relieve Marion's assistant, Gayle, till closing time. A few patrons stopped by to chat. I appreciated having a spell of quiet time after the turbulent emotions I'd experienced listening to Michelle's sad story.

At ten to five I stood and was about to return to my office when Tommy Vecchio came striding toward me. He set both palms on the hospitality desk and leaned forward. I stumbled back into the chair. "Tommy. What are you doing here?"

His eyes were popping with rage. "I've come to tell you to keep you nose out of my business."

"I don't know what you're talking about."

"You don't, eh?"

I felt a pang of real fear as he jutted his face forward until it was inches from mine.

"No. Please move back."

He ignored my request. "You didn't tell that police captain I had it in for Aiden and planned to give him what he deserved?"

My face grew warm. Sure I had told John what I'd seen and heard, but he'd never share that with a suspect. "Chief Mathers never told you that."

116

Tommy's face took on the crafty look of a fox. "Maybe *he* didn't tell me, but you're the reason I have to stick around here instead of flying home."

"Don't put that on me. I heard you tell your father you were staying in town to see some people about backing your movie."

Tommy made a scoffing sound as he straightened up. "Like I'd really poison my cousin's husband!"

Rosemary must have told Tommy what I'd overheard him say about Aiden to his girlfriend after the ceremony. "Plenty of people heard you say hateful things about Aiden because he decided not to back your movie."

"I was just letting off steam."

"Really?" I was getting annoyed. "Is that what you're doing now—letting off steam?"

He reached out and gripped my upper arm. "I'm warning you, don't mess with me, Carrie."

Before I could think what to do, a meaty hand settled on Tommy's shoulder. "You don't want to do that, son."

Tommy swung around to face Max, our senior custodian. "Keep out of this!"

"I will not," Max said. From his height of six two, he peered down at Tommy. Then he glanced over at me. "Carrie, want me to call the police?"

I shook my head, too flustered to speak.

Max took hold of Tommy's upper arm as Tommy had seized mine seconds earlier. "In that case, I'll escort this *gentleman* out of the library."

Chapter Fourteen

The incident with Tommy had shaken me more than I was willing to admit. He really was a thug and capable of doing physical harm. I felt a flash of pity for Angela, who'd had to put up with his mistreatment throughout her childhood. Dylan and I had dinner in a quiet restaurant, then came back to the cottage and turned in early. It was comforting to fall asleep in his arms with Smoky Joe snoring gently at my feet.

We woke up early the next morning and spent over an hour at the gym. Back at my cottage, I made blueberry pancakes for breakfast. Then we stretched out on the living room sofa to read the Sunday papers. A quiet day, the kind I welcomed after the tumult of the day before.

At one point I reached for the Sunday crossword puzzle and caught sight of Dylan going through the sports section. I must have been beaming because he looked at me quizzically.

"What's up?"

"Nothing," I said. "I just love being with you."

He reached over to pat my leg. "Same here, babe." Then he went back to reading the paper.

How would it be, I wondered, to spend all our days and nights together? Raise a family? Would our relationship remain magical and loving, or would we grow apart like my parents had? Like so many marriages?

Why am I thinking about marriage when Dylan and I have only been dating for seven months? I probably had marriage on the brain because of Angela's wedding. I forced myself to focus on the crossword puzzle and writing in the first clue.

The landline phone rang and I stood to answer it. It was Rosemary Vecchio, panting as if she'd been running.

"Carrie! I'm so glad I caught you at home. I don't have your cell number and I really didn't want to bother Angela on her honeymoon."

I felt my anxiety rising. "What is it? What's wrong?"

"I need your help. Your friend Lieutenant Mathers just left. He came to talk to Joe and me about Aiden and the terrible way he died. Not that he thought either of us was responsible for that sinful act, but he asked lots of questions about Donna and Tommy. And even Roxy, my brother's daughter." Rosemary exhaled a gush of air in my ear. "I'm afraid they're all suspects."

"I'm sorry you're upset, Rosemary, but what do you want me to do?"

"Prove that none of them killed Aiden. Why would they? Aiden was family." Rosemary sounded like she was on the verge of tears.

I rephrased her impossible request. "You want me to investigate Aiden's murder?"

"Please, Carrie. You've solved other murder cases. Angela's told me you have a knack for finding out things that people try to hide."

"Rosemary, I liked Aiden and want desperately to see his murderer caught, but I can't interfere in a murder investigation."

"Why not? You've done it before. This is your friend Angela's family we're talking about. Can't you find it in your heart to help us?"

I closed my eyes. "Of course I want to help, but I'm not an investigator like Dylan. Once I start looking into Aiden's murder,

I have no idea what I'll discover. I'd feel awful if I found out that Tommy or one of your nieces poisoned Aiden."

"I'm certain that you won't, Carrie, but I'll face whatever really happened. All those years I didn't listen to what Angie was telling me. I need to know the truth."

Rosemary's logic was screwy, but I understood what she was after—proof that no one she loved had ended Aiden's life. "In that case I'm going to start by telling you a few home truths."

"All right."

"We'll start with Tommy. He stormed into the library yesterday and, in an ugly and menacing manner, claimed he was a suspect because I told John Mathers I had heard him make incriminating remarks. And now he has to stick around here instead of going home. Now why would he say that?"

After a pause, she said, "I'm so sorry, Carrie. I was trying to reason with Tommy. Get him to see how his behavior made him look like a suspect. I should never have brought you into the conversation."

"No, you shouldn't have. Our custodian escorted him out of the building. If he confronts me again, I will tell John. And I will press charges."

"I understand. I promise not to tell Tommy that I've asked you to investigate."

"Then there's Donna and Roxy." This was more difficult for me. I hated to have to tell Rosemary things about her nieces she probably didn't know, but if she wanted me to look into Aiden's murder I couldn't sugarcoat the facts. "Anyone close to a murder victim is considered a possible suspect. Donna was married to Aiden. What's more, they were having problems."

"I had no idea," Rosemary said. "My sister Marie never said a word."

"Well, Frankie told me. Again, I have to ask you not to mention this to Marie and Vinnie."

"Of course not. But why is Lieutenant Mathers interested in Roxy? The poor girl's high strung at the best of times, and now she's having a terrible time adjusting to her divorce."

"It seems she turned to Aiden for support and he was happy to provide it. There was talk that they were having an affair."

"I don't believe it!"

"I have no idea if it's true or not, but she often stopped at his office. And I saw for myself how possessive she was of Aiden."

"All this is making my head spin."

"Rosemary, I'm sorry you had to hear things about Tommy, Donna, and Roxy you would rather not have known, but I want you to understand why the police are interested in them. It doesn't mean any of them killed Aiden."

"Please find out what you can."

"I will," I said.

"They're holding a memorial service for Aiden on Friday afternoon. I hope you will attend."

"Of course I will."

I hung up the phone and returned to the living room. "That was Rosemary, asking me to look into Aiden's murder."

"It figures since he's a family member."

"She's upset because John is looking at Tommy, Donna, and Roxy as suspects."

Dylan laughed. "Of course he is."

"I explained in detail why John is interested in them. I think it left her kind of dazed."

"So, you're on the case, babe."

"Looks like it." I kissed his cheek, glad he now trusted me to be cautious when investigating mysteries on behalf of family and friends.

He bumped his shoulder into mine. "That gives you a homicide and a missing person to solve. You have almost as many active cases as I do."

* * *

The rest of the day belonged to Dylan and me. I banned all thoughts of Aiden's murder and Michelle's problems from my mind as we drove east along Route 1 to Old Lyme. We wandered through the town and visited the Florence Griswold Museum. We had a light bite in Old Saybrook and, on impulse, stopped to listen to a band concert in a park by the Sound. Dinner was in a rustic restaurant that served lobster, my favorite summer fare.

Dylan and I held hands as we rode back to Clover Ridge. The traffic on 95 was bumper-to-bumper at times, but neither of us cared. It was close to ten when he dropped me off at the cottage.

"I had a wonderful weekend," he said as he kissed me good night.

"Me too."

"Talk to you in the morning."

* * *

"So you're going to look into who murdered the good doctor," Evelyn said. She'd turned up in my office Monday afternoon, a minute after Trish had left for the day.

"I am."

"I hope it doesn't sound callous when I say I hope you'll still have time to help my niece, Michelle."

"Of course I will. Uncle Bosco called me earlier to say he's asking around to find out who can use office help."

Evelyn beamed at me. "Thank you, Carrie. I never should have thought that you'd let something this important slide."

The jingle of my cell phone sounded.

"Hello, Carrie. This is Michelle. Michelle Forbes," she added. She sounded cheerful.

"Hi, Michelle." I glanced at Evelyn. "Have you gotten in touch with Mr. Talbot?"

"A few times. When I told him what Brad did, he was furious and said he wanted to handle this case himself."

"You're in luck. Ken is a very capable lawyer, but be prepared. It may take some time before he can get any money back for you."

"I know. He explained how the system works. But the important thing is he said I couldn't be thrown out of my apartment, and he might be able to get me some funds in the meantime."

"I'm so glad."

"That's not all. A Mr. Rockland just called. He's a friend of your uncle."

"Sorry, I don't know him."

"He has an advertising and marketing firm in Branford and needs someone to do general office work—at least for the present. It might turn into something more."

"That sounds promising," I said.

"Doesn't it? Bobbie's driving me to my interview tomorrow morning."

"Branford's not that far away, but you'll need transportation."

"There's a bus that goes there, but not very often. I'll figure it out."

"I know you will," I said. "I'm very happy for you."

"Thanks, Carrie. You've turned my life around."

We disconnected and I grinned at Evelyn. "Things are improving for Michelle. Looks like she'll be keeping her apartment and she may very well have a job."

"Did she mention her father?"

"No. Why would she?"

"You did ask her to let you know if she remembered anyone he was especially friendly with at the time he left Clover Ridge."

"I did, and she probably couldn't think of anyone who might have stayed in contact with your brother." I pursed my lips. "Besides, now that she's getting help, she'll manage without him."

Evelyn's gaze was piercing. "Carrie, think how much you appreciate having your father back in your life."

I shrugged. "Jim came to me, remember?"

"Asking you to act as go-between for him and his partner-in-crime. But all that's water under the bridge," she quickly added.

I burst out laughing. "Evelyn, you want me to find your brother Harold because you miss him."

She hung her head. "I admit there's some truth to that."

"And if by some unforeseen method or magic, I managed to whisk him back to Clover Ridge, you would no doubt ask me to find a way of getting him to come to the library so you could see him for yourself."

Her silence told me I was right.

"Okay, I'll call Michelle and ask her again to try to recall the names of anyone her father was close to before he disappeared."

"Will you call her now?"

"In a while."

My cell phone sounded again.

"It's me again. Michelle."

"Hi, Michelle."

Evelyn, who had been on the verge of disappearing, returned to hear the latest news bulletin.

"I'm such a ditz. I was so excited to share my good news, I forgot to tell you I got to thinking about my father. There was someone he was friendly with—a neighbor who lived a few houses down from us. Salvatore DiSanto. He and his wife were older than my parents. They had three kids a few years older than Harvey and me. Dad and Sal used to watch wrestling together—of all things."

I felt my pulse quicken. "Do the DiSantos still live there?"

"No idea. I never looked them up when I moved back to Clover Ridge, though I suppose I should have."

"Not to worry. Tell me the street they lived on, and the number, if you remember it. I'll check it out."

"Thanks, Carrie. But I doubt if Sal would know anything about my father. Not after all this time."

Evelyn was beaming at me as I said goodbye to her niece. "I have a good feeling about this, Carrie. I eagerly await your report." And with that, she took off to parts unknown.

I looked up Salvatore DiSanto's address online. Sure enough, there was an address in Clover Ridge: 37 Marcellus Lane. I jotted it down along with the phone number. I planned to stop by the house when I left the library, figuring I had a better chance of finding him at home later on in the day.

The landline rang.

"Hello, Carrie. This is Al Tripp, your mayor calling. How are you today?"

I swallowed my annoyance. I knew this call was coming, but I still had no definitive answer. "Good afternoon, Al. I'm fine. And how are you?"

"Wonderful. Just wonderful. My wife has me on a diet and the food's not half bad. I've lost fifteen pounds already."

"I'm glad to hear that," I said, meaning it. I remembered how concerned I'd been last month when Al had huffed and puffed as I followed him up the library stairs.

"And I'm waking up an hour earlier every day to get in an exercise session with a personal trainer."

"Good for you. Soon you'll be in shape to run a marathon."

Al chuckled. He had a good sense of humor. "Anyway, enough about me. I suppose your uncle told you about the upcoming vacancy on the town council."

"Uncle Bosco mentioned it, but—"

"Before you give me a but, I wish you'd hear me out."

"But—"

"Carrie, if you let me lay it all out for you, explain why I think you're the perfect person to replace Jeannette Rivers on the board and why you'll thank me in the end, I promise not to pursue this further. Will you hear me out?"

"Okay."

"In that case, if you're free Wednesday evening I'd like to take you to dinner to discuss it—at the Inn on the Green, if you like their food."

"Do I!" I said, forgetting to follow my rule to pause five seconds when asked to do something I had doubts about. "That is, if you realize you'll be wooing a reluctant candidate."

Al sounded jubilant when he said, "I'm well aware of your feelings. Shall we meet at the Inn at seven?"

"Sure," I said, wondering what I was getting myself into.

Chapter Fifteen

Two midsized cars stood in the DiSantos' driveway, so I parked on the street in front of their modest home. The lawn had been mowed recently, and the flowers and shrubs bordering the house looked well cared for. I rang the bell. A woman who appeared to be in her early seventies answered the door. The fragrant aroma of food greeted me. That and the fact that she was wearing an apron told me the DiSantos were about to sit down to an early dinner.

"Hello, can I help you?" Though she was smiling, she appeared bewildered to have found me at her doorstep.

"I'm so sorry to interrupt your dinner preparations. I'm Carrie Singleton. I work at the library—"

"Of course! Two of my friends belong to the knitting and crocheting group that meets on Saturday. I've often thought of joining but somehow never managed to get there."

"Who's at the door?" a male voice called from another room. As the man approached, I recognized Sal DiSanto, a thin balding man in his mid-seventies. He sometimes read the newspaper in the reading room and occasionally came to the current events group well-known for its heated discussions.

"Oh, hello, Carrie! What brings you to our humble abode?"

Before I could respond, he was waving his hand, inviting me into the house. "Come inside and tell us what's on your mind."

"Well, I have Smoky Joe in the car and—"

"Bring the little guy in. We still have some of Muffins' toys around somewhere, don't we, Daisy?"

"I suppose we do. In a carton in the back of the coat closet. I'll go get them."

"Please don't bother," I protested, but Daisy had gone off to look for cat toys and Sal was urging me to get Smoky Joe. "Be right back," I said and walked quickly to my car.

Minutes later, I found myself accepting the DiSantos' invitation to dinner. I sat sipping a glass of sangria at the DiSantos' kitchen table while both Daisy and Sal prepared the finishing touches to our meal. Smoky Joe had scampered off to the living room with a toy mouse that had belonged to the deceased Muffins after gobbling down several cat treats that Daisy said she kept on hand—just in case they had a feline visitor. They were the warmest, most hospitable couple. I could well understand why Evelyn's brother had been drawn to Sal. He was that unusual person who attended to every word you said, and his comments were always thoughtful and wise.

They wouldn't let me explain why I'd come to talk to them until we'd finished our antipasto and had started on our eggplant rollatini, one of my favorite dishes.

"So, what brings you here this evening?" Sal finally asked.

I finished chewing what was in my mouth and grinned. "I'll tell you, but first let me say how much I'm enjoying my dinner. Daisy, you are a fabulous cook!"

Daisy beamed as she patted my hand. "Thank you, Carrie. I love feeding people."

I looked at Sal. "Do you remember Harold Davis?"

"Of course I do. We were pretty good friends—until he took off and left his family."

Daisy was nodding. "The two of them used to sit in our den or out on the patio when the weather was good, talking about everything under the sun."

"Frankly, he was one of the few people who could discuss issues in an intelligent way." Sal shot me an apologetic smile. "Sorry, but some of those regulars in the library current events group are too pigheaded to be believed. Even after the nonsense they spout is proven wrong, they refuse to see reason."

I laughed. "Sometimes I can hear you guys going at it from behind my closed office door."

Sal shook his head. "Then you know what I mean. But why are you asking me about Harold?"

"I know he disappeared fifteen years ago."

"He did." Sal set down his knife and fork and eyed me speculatively. A shiver shot up my spine. *He knows something!*

"The thing is, his daughter Michelle moved back to Clover Ridge about a year ago. She's not doing very well."

"Oh, no!" Daisy placed her hand on her heart. "Is she ill?"

"No. Her husband left her, which I imagine brought up the trauma caused when her father abandoned the family. She lost her job and was told she'd have to leave her apartment. The poor girl was despondent when we talked." Because of the guarded way Sal was now watching me, I decided to omit the fact that Michelle was already doing considerably better.

Daisy opened her mouth to speak but a sharp glance from her husband silenced her.

"Why have you come to tell us this?" Sal asked.

"Because, except for a kind neighbor, Michelle has no one in the world to help her. She remembered that you were her father's closest friend at the time he disappeared. I was hoping you might know how we could contact him."

"I see," Sal said. My loquacious host had suddenly become a man of few words.

"Can you tell me where he is? Or what name he's using now?"

My second question had startled him. Whatever Salvatore DiSanto was privy to, he was reluctant to share it with me.

I leaned closer to him. "Is there a reason why, after all these years, you won't tell me what you know about Harold? Is he still alive?"

Sal released a deep sigh. "That I can't say. We lost touch a few years ago."

Daisy tsk-tsked. "Sal did his best to convince Harold to give himself up, but the poor man was afraid for his life. He didn't want his family to know where he was going. He figured this way the people he owed money to wouldn't hurt them."

"Where did he go?" I asked.

"To Mexico. He had just enough money for the flight. He had a college friend who'd moved down there. Of course, he didn't fly anywhere near the town where his pal lived. He ended up taking a long bus trip to the place and changed his name."

"To?" I said.

Sal chuckled. "Lee Kirby. Lee because he always liked the name and hated Harold. Kirby because, like George Kerby, the ghost in the Topper books and movies, he was becoming a ghost, only he changed the spelling. And so Lee Kirby was born."

"That's where he is now? In Mexico?"

"He left a year or so later and moved to Texas, then settled down in New Mexico. Eventually found himself a wife and started a new family. Started attending Gamblers Anonymous religiously and got involved in his new wife's family business. They own a few car dealerships. Was running one of 'em when I last heard from him."

"Nice guy," I said.

"I don't condone what he did," Sal said, "but Harold never lost the fear that the client he'd stolen from would come after him, even after he'd paid all the money back some years later. I helped him do that." Sal nodded. "The man's old now. Still, he was a rough customer so the fear lives on."

"Then there's no real reason why Michelle couldn't contact her father. I bet he'd love to hear from her. And she could really use a parent's support."

Sal shrugged. "You can try. Last I heard from him, they were living in Albuquerque."

"Thanks, Sal. I know Harold must have sworn you to secrecy, but that was fifteen years ago."

"I never told a soul but Daisy till just now."

"Tell me one thing. Why did the two of you lose touch?"

Sal's smile was bittersweet. "Harold didn't need me any longer."

* * *

Dylan called me as I was driving home from the DiSantos', mulling over what I'd learned about Michelle's father.

"Hi, babe. Did you go to the gym after work? I tried the landline, and when you didn't pick up I figured that's where you were."

"I'm on my way home. I ended up having dinner at Daisy and Sal DiSantos'."

"And they are?"

I laughed. "Sal knew Michelle's father and kept in touch with him for years after he left Clover Ridge. He told me that Harold changed his name and was living in New Mexico last time he heard from him."

"That's terrific! Rosalind can probably find the guy now, unless he changed his name again or croaked. Listen, do we have any plans this weekend?"

"I don't think so. Aunt Harriet is having a barbecue July Fourth, but that's next Thursday. Why?"

"I thought it would be nice to take Gary out to dinner Saturday evening. Maybe start out midafternoon, if you're free, and show him the area."

"Sure, I'm off Saturday. Though my weeknights are fast filling up, and not with work," I groused.

"What did you let someone talk you into?" Dylan asked.

"Al Tripp's out to put me on the town council."

"Your uncle warned you he'd be calling. Just say no if you want."

"I will, after our dinner at the Inn on the Green."

Dylan whistled. "Dinner at the Inn! He's dead serious about wanting you on the board. Talk to you later. I'm on my way to the gym."

I was in high spirits when I turned onto the road that led to the Avery estate. Complaining to Dylan about Al wanting me on the town council made me realize something. As Dylan had pointed out, I could have said no. But I hadn't. Which meant I was interested in finding out more about the position and what was involved. Dylan hadn't told me what he thought I should do, but respected whatever decision I made.

It meant a lot to me that Dylan wanted me to get to know Gary Winton, the young investigator he'd just hired. Further proof—as if I needed any—that our lives were entwined. Yet we still had our work and our personal space. Our situation suited me just fine.

* * *

The first thing I did when I got to my office Tuesday morning was call Rosalind to tell her that Harold Davis now called himself Lee Kirby, and was quite possibly living in Albuquerque, New Mexico.

"And he's about—how old would you say?" she asked.

"Anywhere between mid-fifties and mid-sixties. I could call Michelle to find out."

"Please do that," Rosalind said. "And find out the color of his hair and eyes. I can do some photo research, though given his history, he might shy away from photos."

I called Michelle's cell phone. She was out of breath when she answered.

"Hi, Michelle. It's Carrie. I've got some news for you."

"Oh, Carrie! I'm on my way to the interview for that job I told you about."

"Sorry. I won't keep you, but I wanted to tell you I saw the DiSantos. Sal told me your father changed his name and might be living in New Mexico."

"Really? So he kept up with Sal but not with his own family except to send Mom money twice." She sounded hurt and angry. I couldn't blame her.

"Michelle, a description of your father would help. What color eyes does he have?"

"Brown."

"And his hair?"

She laughed. "Brown—what there was of it. Could be gray by now."

"Balding and brown or gray hair. Did he wear glasses?"

"Yes. Tried contacts once but hated putting them in his eyes."

"Thanks. I'll let you know when I get results. Good luck with the job."

"Thank you, Carrie."

Evelyn must have been lurking around my office because she appeared the moment I ended my call to her niece.

"Sounds like you're hot on Harold's trail."

"So it would seem." I speed-dialed Dylan's office. "I'm calling Rosalind to give her your brother's description now."

Rosalind said she'd get back to me ASAP, but that might not be till the afternoon because there was some office work that she had to take care of first.

"Of course. I understand," I said and relayed what she'd told me to Evelyn.

"In that case, I'll be back later," Evelyn said as she disappeared.

I looked in on the programs in progress, then answered a few emails and phone calls. Trish arrived, bubbling over with news about her children, who had started day camp the day before.

"Let's work on the August–September newsletter. I'd like to have it ready to go to the printers on Friday," I said. "Most of the layout is done, and we have more than enough of Susan's sketches to choose from."

Trish grimaced. "We're still waiting for articles from the usual procrastinators."

"Don't I know it. I'll walk over and give Marion a gentle prod and text Harvey a reminder."

Trish smiled. "I'll tackle Harvey for you."

"Thanks. Much appreciated."

"In fact, I'll go right now."

I watched Trish close the office door behind her, thanking my lucky stars that I had her and Susan as my part-time assistants. Trish was ultra-efficient and Susan was artistic, and I made great use of both their talents. Harvey Kirk, the head of the library's computer department, was acerbic and not very sociable. What's more, he was the only one of my colleagues who had a gripe against me because I'd once suspected him of having murdered a fellow librarian. What's more, he probably also resented the fact that I knew about his gambling problem and that he sometimes used library time to check out gambling sites and place bets online.

I walked over to the children's section, where Marion was involved in an activity with a group of preschoolers. I found Gayle, her assistant, in their office and told her I needed their report ASAP. That accomplished, I returned to my office.

The library phone was ringing. "Hello, this is Carrie Singleton, head of programs and events."

"Hi, Carrie. This is Angela's cousin, Donna. I know it's short notice, but I'd like to talk to you. Is there any chance I can treat you to lunch today?"

Why does everyone want to feed me? "Sure, that should work. I usually have lunch with Angela at noon but she's still away on her honeymoon."

"Would it be possible to make it one o'clock instead? I'm running errands and don't think I can get to Clover Ridge until then."

"All right. Where shall we meet?"

"Have you eaten at Tea and Crumpets?"

"Not yet," I said. The new bakery-restaurant was located on the west side of the Green, the side that had been neglected by developers until recently.

"The food is scrumptious. They have excellent sandwiches, quiches, and salads."

"So I've heard. But you don't have to—"

"Don't be silly. It's my pleasure. See you at one."

I stared at the phone, the click of her hang-up echoing in my ear. Donna Harrington didn't sound like a woman who had just lost her husband.

Chapter Sixteen

Three hours later, I was ushered past a line of diners—mostly women—waiting for a table and led to a small booth for two where Donna was just ending a phone call. I glanced around, admiring the décor. Blonde wooden booths with salmon-colored backs and seat padding filled the room. Plants spilling over their wicker baskets hung from the pitched-beam ceiling. Sunlight poured through the long, narrow skylight. The owners must have paid a pretty penny for the acoustics because, though the restaurant buzzed with conversation, diners had no need to raise their voices to hear themselves speak.

"Thanks so much for meeting me on such short notice," Donna said as she slipped her cell phone into her large leather pocketbook. She wore a bright yellow summer dress with cap sleeves and a diamond pendant at her throat. Today her hair was arranged in a loose knot on top of her head. She wore mascara, blue eye shadow, and coral lipstick and looked as elegant as a New York model ready for a photo shoot.

"Of course," I said, feeling dowdy in my white shirt and black capris. "It sure is a busy restaurant. I'm glad you managed to get us a table."

She smiled. "The owner was Aiden's patient." She reached for one of the menus lying on the table. "Why don't we order first?"

"Okay." I picked up the other menu, feeling like a child being treated to an outing. I was glad I'd been spared from having to deal with a take-charge cousin growing up. Even Roxy must have felt ill at ease at times.

When our smiling fortyish waitress whose name tag said "Sandra" arrived, I asked for a turkey and pesto on an artisan ciabatta roll and iced coffee. Donna ordered blueberry scones and clotted cream. The *American* version of clotted cream, she explained when Sandra left to fill our orders, as real clotted cream was made with unpasteurized milk, a no-no in this country.

"What did you want to talk to me about?" I only had an hour for lunch and was tired of Donna calling the shots.

"What do you think? My husband's murder."

I nodded. "Go on."

That surprised her, but not for long. "I want to know who murdered Aiden. Aunt Rosemary said you agreed to help find out who did it. Have you learned anything the police have overlooked?"

"Sorry. Nothing yet."

Donna rolled her eyes. "Lieutenant Mathers seems to consider me a likely suspect, which is ridiculous. I didn't poison my husband."

"The spouse is always a suspect where murder is concerned."

She nodded. "I know that, but I swear—"

"Especially when a couple wasn't getting along."

"Who told you that?"

"It doesn't matter." I met her gaze. "If you're innocent as you claim and want me to help find the person who murdered Aiden, I need two things from you."

"Yes?"

"Everything you can tell me about Aiden's behavior, his conversations, who he saw and talked to the last two weeks before he died."

She nodded. "Of course."

"And the truth, no matter how ugly it sounds. I'm here to help, not to judge."

"Okay. This may take longer than I thought," Donna said.

"Then let's get started. Did Aiden seem upset the last week or two before he died?"

"He did. It might have had something to do with the office or a patient or finances. I don't know because he wouldn't tell me. He'd hole up in his home office for hours and come out looking as worried as he had when he'd gone in and closed the door behind him."

"Would you mind if I looked at his computer?"

Donna shrugged. "Sure. Be my guest. The police have returned most everything they took. I read Aiden's will and so did our lawyer. He left everything to me. I've spoken to our financial adviser twice. He assured me the kids and I are in pretty good shape."

"I'm glad. One less thing to worry about."

We brought our conversation to a halt because Sandra had arrived with our food. Donna ordered a mango lassi and offered me a taste of her scone and fake clotted cream. "Yummy, isn't it?"

"It sure is." I offered her a taste of my sandwich, but she shook her head.

We ate in silence. My sandwich was delicious. I made a mental note to return to Tea and Crumpets with Angela in the very near future, but right now I had to make the most of my time with Donna.

"How did Aiden get along with the people in his practice?" I asked.

"Okay, I suppose, though he and Nick butted heads at times. Nick's older, and it was his practice to start with, so he thought he had the right to make decisions regarding the practice. Aiden set him straight." Donna laughed. "They still argued, but not as much. Nick's divorced and not dating anyone, so we didn't socialize with him."

"What about Vera, the office manager?"

Donna snorted. "Vera's a busybody. Talks on and on with every patient. Loves to gossip. Aiden said she clearly favored Nick since she'd worked with him before Aiden came on board."

"Did that bother him?"

"A bit, but Aiden decided to ignore it unless it affected scheduling patients and scheduling surgery, which it never did."

"And Gwen Swithers?"

"Oh, the new nurse. She was competent, Aiden said. Quiet."

"She seemed really broken up when I saw her at the wake."

"I noticed," Donna said, though her thoughts were clearly elsewhere. I glanced at my watch. I had to leave soon, but I needed to hear what was on Donna's mind. Finally she sat erect and looked me in the eye.

"Aunt Rosemary asked you to find out what you could because she wants to protect Roxy, Tommy, and me. I know I didn't poison Aiden, but I can't say the same about Roxy or Tommy."

I feigned innocence. "Aren't you and Roxy best pals?"

"We were, until recently. I know she's high strung and having an awful time since her divorce, but she had no business making my husband her psychiatrist. She got in the habit of running over to his office for sympathy. And Aiden, softie that he was, let her." Her mouth tightened in a grimace. "Just because he—"

"He what?"

"Was the one to let the cat out of the bag about Miles's latest affair. Aiden felt responsible for Roxy going nuts and divorcing Miles." Donna rolled her eyes. "Which was such a mistake. Miles loves Roxy. He just can't seem to keep it in his pants."

Too Much Information about one relationship I didn't need to know about. "But I can't understand why you think Roxy might have poisoned Aiden."

"Roxy's not in her right mind these days. She attached herself to Aiden, and believe me, there's no one as supportive as Aiden when you need a shoulder to cry on." Donna hesitated. "But the other day she went too far. She tried to talk him into going to bed with her."

"Aiden told you this?" I asked.

Donna nodded. "Roxy pretended she wasn't upset when he told her it wasn't a good idea and continued to act like Aiden was her good buddy, but inside she was steaming big time. She dropped a few comments about all men being liars and cheats and how some deserved a slow death. At first I thought she was talking about Miles, but lately I've been wondering if she meant Aiden as well."

"Wow!" I thought a moment. "And your cousin Tommy?"

"He's a brute, and not just a jerk with a big mouth. Aunt Rosemary and Uncle Joe tried to keep it from the family, but we found out that Tommy was sued for getting into a fight and breaking some guy's jaw. Which was why Aiden decided not to back his movie."

"It wasn't because he was short on cash?" I asked.

"No." Donna sighed. "But maybe he should have gone along and backed Tommy's movie. Maybe then he'd still be alive today."

* * *

Donna dropped me off in front of the library. I thanked her again for lunch and said I'd let her know when I was free to stop by to check out Aiden's computer and papers.

"Thanks, Carrie. I hope you find the person who did this, no matter who it turns out to be," she said as I climbed out of her Mercedes.

Smoky Joe came running toward me as soon as I entered through the front door. I bent down to pet his gray flank. "Are you hungry, boy?"

Bushy tail held high, he accompanied me to my office. Though I'd posted signs around the library, instructing patrons not to feed him, I knew that a few people still did. But he must have been really hungry, judging by the way he gulped down his food.

After Trish gave me the lowdown on who had called and I ran through my emails, we spent the next hour finishing the layout of the newsletter. Both Harvey and Gayle had sent over a short paragraph of news, which left more space for Susan's wonderful sketches.

I stretched my arms overhead. "And we're done for the next two months."

"I'll take it over to the printer's tomorrow," Trish said as she got ready to leave.

Minutes later, Rosalind called sounding excited. "I found him!"

"You did?"

"It was easy, once I had his new name and the city where you thought he was living. The good news is he has no outstanding criminal charges that I could determine—not for Lee Kirby or Harold Lester Davis. And from the looks of it, he's semiretired. I'm giving you his home and business phone numbers."

"Thanks, Rosalind." I jotted down the information she'd uncovered. "Now comes the hard part—deciding what to say when I contact him."

"That won't be easy, Carrie."

"I know," I said. "I imagine he'll be skittish and wary."

"I have faith you'll come up with something that won't scare the man into an early grave."

Evelyn made her appearance a few minutes later. She looked happier than I'd seen her in some time when I told her that her brother Harold had been found. "Thank you, Carrie! I knew if anyone could find him, it would be you."

"I had no idea you were so attached to your brother Harold." *Who I never knew existed until a week ago.*

"The three of us—Frieda, Harold, and I—were close when we were growing up. Then Harold went off to college, which is where he met Glenda. After they married, we never saw much of him, even though they were living right here in Clover Ridge. Glenda was very possessive of my brother and her children and didn't want to have anything to do with my sister and me. So after being rebuffed a few times, Frieda and I decided not to force the issue. And then—he left."

"I'll hold off telling Michelle the news until I find out if he's willing to contact her."

"Good idea. But I'm hoping Harold will want to see his daughter. He was always a loving person."

A loving person who left his family, I thought, but felt it was better left unsaid.

* * *

Driving home that evening, I thought about the new developments in the two cases I was involved in.

Finding Aiden's killer was the more crucial problem. Any one of several people could have murdered him—someone in his practice, a member of his family, or a friend I'd yet to meet. Donna suspected both Roxy and Tommy, and had done her best to persuade me that she was innocent. I appreciated the effort but wasn't totally convinced. Not if their marriage was on the rocks, as her sister had said. Then there was Miles, Roxy's ex-husband and Aiden's best friend. Miles had cheated on Roxy several times, but that didn't mean he didn't love her. In which case, he might have resented Roxy's sudden attachment to Aiden. I intended to talk to as many people as I could at the memorial on Friday.

In the meantime, contacting Michelle's father and convincing him to offer her emotional and financial support wasn't going to be easy. I needed advice from someone with psychological savvy because I had only one shot to get this right.

After dinner I called my father on his cell phone. I hadn't spoken to Jim in close to two weeks, which was quite a long spell in our new relationship. Though I'd been busy, I could have found the time to call him sooner, but I figured he could have called me as well. I couldn't help wondering if my father was falling back into his old ways of dropping out of contact with the family—in this case, me. It was one of the reasons my mother had divorced him.

Then I'd tell myself that Jim and I had been through too much together these past few months to doubt that he had changed. For one thing, he'd given up his life as a thief and now held a respectable position in Dylan and Mac's investigative company. And hadn't he flown to Clover Ridge from Atlanta, where he was based, to give my mother, his ex-wife, emotional support when her husband was a suspect in a murder case? No, I had to give him the benefit of the doubt and assume his new lady friend and work were keeping him totally occupied.

"Hello there, Caro!" he boomed across states the moment he heard my voice. "I was just talking about you."

"Really? Who to?"

"Meredith. Here, say hello."

"Dad, what—?"

I heard the sound of feminine laughter, then a woman said, "Hello, Carrie. How nice to finally speak to Jim's daughter. He talks about you incessantly."

"Does he? He hasn't told me one thing about you."

"I advised him to—several times—but I think he wanted to wait until we could come and visit you."

I found myself grinning. "You're planning a trip to Clover Ridge?"

"We're thinking of the second weekend in July—if that's a good time for you and your significant other to spend a few days with us."

"Sure. Dylan and I have no plans to leave town."

"I'll put your father on. I know he wants to talk to you."

"Dad! You're too much." I managed to convey my happiness that his relationship was serious enough for him to put Meredith on the line, yet exasperated that he'd held her back for such a long time.

"I know. I know. I didn't want to say anything until—I don't know—Merry and I were on the same page regarding a few issues."

"Whatever that means," I said.

"Exactly. She's a good one, Caro. I'm one lucky bastard."

"I'm glad for you, Dad."

"So am I."

I drew a deep breath as I thought about Jim Singleton, past and present.

"So how goes it in Clover Ridge?"

"Things are good. I'm busy."

"Dylan told me about the poor doctor who dropped dead right in front of you both at Angela and Steve's wedding."

"Really? I didn't tell you because I didn't want to worry you."

"Caro, it was in all the papers." Jim chuckled. "I know it's not a laughing matter, but 'Death by Chocolate' was how one headline put it. I would have been worried if Dylan hadn't been keeping me informed."

"He never mentioned he's been giving you updates."

"That's because I asked him not to."

"Oh." *This was getting complicated.*

"Are you planning to do any sleuthing?" Jim said.

"Angela's mom asked me to prove that her dear son—a thug who produces movies—is innocent of poisoning Aiden, along with her niece Donna, Aiden's widow, and Roxy, another niece who may or may not have been Aiden's lover."

"Sounds intriguing. I know better than to ask you not to get involved. Just promise me you'll be careful."

I swallowed, touched by his concern. "I will. I'm glad that you and Meredith are planning to visit this summer."

"If you and Dylan will have us. Or the four of us could plan a short motor trip somewhere."

"Either sounds fine. I'll talk it over with Dylan."

"Of course, honey. Whichever you prefer."

"Has Dylan met Meredith?"

"He's known her for years. Merry does freelance work for the company."

"I see," I said.

Now I really felt left out of the loop. But before I could comment, my father asked, "Have you heard from your mother?"

"She called a few weeks ago to tell me Tom's got a small but important part in a TV series."

"That must have made her happy. Linda and her actor hubby aren't your usual couple, but somehow they make it work. I suppose you won't be seeing them for some time."

"I don't know. Mom invited me to visit them in Hollywood. I may take her up on it."

I heard someone speak. My father muffled the phone as he answered, then returned to me, "Sorry I have to cut this short. We've got dinner plans and we're late."

"Call me when you have some free time. I miss you."

"We'll talk soon and firm up our plans. You're always in my thoughts."

When Dylan called later that evening, I told him that I'd sort of met Meredith.

Dylan let out a loud exhalation. "I'm glad that's finally out of the bag."

"What do you mean? Why didn't you tell me that you knew my father's girlfriend?"

"How could I? Jim swore me to secrecy. He was so worried you'd be upset because he was seeing someone."

"But I knew he was—or suspected as much."

"That's not the same thing as meeting the woman who has an important place in your father's life. Jim was afraid if you knew how much he cares for Merry you'd feel abandoned all over again."

I burst out laughing. "I'm happy that he has someone special."

"That's what I told him. I'm glad he called you."

"No, I called him."

"Figures. But now it's over and done with."

"Yes, he wants to bring Merry to Clover Ridge for a visit. Or have the four of us go on a road trip."

"Okay."

"He also said you filled him in on Aiden's murder and the fact that he died in front of us."

"I did," Dylan said. "I figured he'd heard about the incident and I didn't want him to worry, so I've been keeping him up to date."

When I didn't answer, he said, "What's wrong with that?"

"I don't like having my boyfriend and my father keeping secrets behind my back."

"You could have told Jim about Aiden," Dylan said.

"And you could have mentioned that you knew Meredith."

"I suppose I could have, but I was respecting Jim's request. Carrie, you're going to have to accept that your father and I have a close relationship. And it's based on the fact that we both love you."

"I know," I said, ashamed for being so hypersensitive. "It's just—I don't like feeling left out."

"I get it. Being close to a parent when you're an adult is something new. For both of us."

"You mean you were never close to your parents—"

"Let's not bring them into the conversation," Dylan said.

"All right."

As I got ready for bed, various thoughts ran through my head. I was happy that my father had met someone he cared about, and I looked forward to meeting Meredith. And I was glad that he and Dylan had grown close. I wondered if my reaction earlier was due to jealousy—that Jim and Dylan shared certain things like work that didn't include me—and realized I had to get past it. And truly accept I had an important place in both their hearts.

For the first time, I found myself wondering about Dylan's parents, who were both deceased. Dylan rarely spoke of them, and when he did it was in a casual, offhand way. I yawned as sleep came over me. I'd find out more about Cal and Estelle Avery, but that was for another day.

Chapter Seventeen

Wednesday turned out to be a busy day at the library. Most of our morning was devoted to a meeting of library department heads, the library board, and a committee made up of Friends of the Library and other local groups. Our subject: the library expansion.

Like most of the buildings around the Green, the one abutting the library had once been a private home, though nowhere near as large as the one that had become the library. Centuries old and unoccupied for some time, it was in need of a good many repairs. But a lengthy inspection proved that the basic structure was sound, and the library board and town council members agreed that the interior walls and floors would have to be rebuilt anyway to accommodate the library's requirements. The stadium-seating auditorium that I wanted so badly would be located in the new addition.

Construction, or I should say the reconstruction, was expected to begin sometime in September. The library would continue to function as usual until it came time to break down part of the wall that the two buildings shared in order to erect an archway linking the old and new sections.

A good part of the meeting was devoted to how we intended to utilize the new addition. I wanted more rooms for more programs,

Marion wanted an outdoor area for the children, and Harvey wanted a large area for more computers and other electronics. The discussion grew loud and a bit contentious. Sally brought us to order, reminding us that though the referendum that had taken place months ago was paying for most of the expenses, more money still needed to be raised via fundraising. We agreed to discuss it at a later meeting.

Back in my office, I filled Trish in on the meeting, then went through my emails and phone messages. She left early to take care of some personal business while I contacted two people to discuss programs they wanted to present to our patrons.

After a quick trip to the library coffee shop and a pleasant chat with Marion, Smoky Joe followed me back to my office. As usual, my furry friend hissed because Evelyn was there, waiting to speak to me. I doubted that Smoky Joe could see her, but he sensed her presence and didn't much like it. Then, as usual, he decided to ignore her and sat by his dish while I filled it with kibble.

"Have you contacted my brother yet?" she asked by way of a greeting.

"You know I haven't."

"What's wrong with right now?"

"One thirty in the afternoon? He could be having lunch somewhere." I looked down to avoid her scowl. "But it's earlier in New Mexico and worth a try, I suppose. I'll call the business number first."

I dialed one of the phone numbers Rosalind had given me, and felt a surge of excitement as we waited for someone to answer.

"Carville Motors," a young woman's voice rang out.

"Hello, is Lee Kirby there?"

"Who is this, please?"

"It's a personal matter."

"I'm afraid Mr. Kirby isn't in today."

"Thank you. I'll try him at home."

I disconnected and called the second number. The phone rang four times. I was about to set it down when a man's voice said, "Kitty, where the hell are you? You were supposed to be home an hour ago. The Vandervilles will be here soon for bridge, and I haven't even had my lunch."

"Sorry, this isn't Kitty, Mr. Kirby."

"Who the hell are you?"

"Carrie Singleton. I'm calling from Clover Ridge, Connecticut."

Silence. I sensed he was debating whether or not to hang up and was leaning toward ending the call. "Please don't hang up! I'm calling about your daughter."

"Michelle." The word sounded like a sigh. "How is she?"

"She's all right for now, but things aren't good in her life, and she could use your help."

"Is that so?"

I wasn't sure if he was being sarcastic or trying to absorb what had to be a shocking experience. "It's very much the case."

More silence. Then, "How did you find me?"

I didn't mean to, but I chuckled. "With great difficulty." Evelyn glared at me. "But don't worry. No one is after you or—"

"I can't talk now," he said quickly. "Give me your number and I'll call you tonight."

I gave him my cell number. "Please call me."

"I will," he said and hung up.

I stared at Evelyn, who had a broad grin on her face. "There!" she said triumphantly, as if she'd been the one to track down her brother. "Was that so difficult?"

I called Dylan to tell him the good news.

"Don't be surprised if he doesn't call," Dylan said.

"I think he will, but I hope it's not when I'm having dinner with Al Tripp."

* * *

At five o'clock, I found Smoky Joe in the reading room, lounging on the lap of one of his favorite patrons. I carried him back to my office, coaxed him into his carrier, and we set off for home. Despite my protestations, part of me was looking forward to my dinner with our esteemed mayor this evening. Al Tripp loved his role as mayor of Clover Ridge and never missed an opportunity to give a speech. But underneath it, he was a good guy with a big heart, and I knew from my aunt and uncle that in the four years he'd been mayor, he had constantly striven to do what was best for Clover Ridge.

I fed Smoky Joe his dinner, then showered and slipped into a pretty floral dress I'd bought on sale a few weeks ago and patent leather high-heeled sandals. I put on lipstick and added eye shadow and mascara for the occasion. That accomplished, I grabbed my pocketbook and a light cardigan and drove back to the center of town.

Al spotted me the moment I entered the Inn's large dining room half-filled with diners. He beckoned me over to a table in the rear. An older man I recognized but whose name I couldn't place hovered over Al as he spoke fervently. When he paused to draw breath, Al whispered something. The man sent me an apologetic glance and moved to another table. I sat down next to Al.

"So nice to see you, Carrie." He welcomed me with a wide grin.

"I'm happy to be here."

We chatted about the lovely weather until the waitress, a pleasant blonde woman in her mid-fifties, came to take our drink order.

I said I'd like a glass of white wine and left the specifics to Al. He surprised me by asking for a bottle of fine white Burgundy that I knew was rather expensive.

"I've been cutting back on hard liquor and making a study of wine," he told me when our waitress left to fill our order.

I lifted my large menu and scanned the entrees. They were many and varied.

"You might want to hear the specials before you choose," Al said with a wink. "I'm pretty sure they have prime rib tonight."

I laughed. "You sure know the ins and outs of the place."

"I should," he said drily. "I eat here often enough."

Our waitress returned and opened our bottle of wine with a flourish. She had Al taste it and declare it up to his standards, then poured. I sipped, taking delight in the wonderful flavor.

"This is delicious," I said.

Al beamed. "So glad you like it," he said and sipped his wine.

We ordered the Inn's special salad and the prime rib—both medium rare. Al asked for more veggies to make up for the Inn's signature stuffed baked potato. When the waitress left, he said, "I promised Dolores I wouldn't cheat on my diet tonight."

"Good for you," I praised him. "You've lost weight recently."

He smiled. "I have, as a matter of fact. And I feel good. I'm also working out with a personal trainer at Parson's Gym."

I grinned. "Billy Harper?"

"Yep! He's the best!"

"He sure is."

Al winked. "And I know you helped reunite Billy with his mother."

Just in time, our waitress arrived with our salads and asked if we'd like some ground pepper, saving me from having to talk about Billy or his mother. I wasn't sworn to secrecy regarding the people I'd helped, but neither did I consider them a subject of idle conversation.

I finished off one of the Inn's delicious rolls with my salad, and noticed that Al refrained from doing the same. He was serious about his diet.

Al turned to me as a busboy removed our salad dishes. "Have you given any thought to joining the council since last we spoke?"

I shook my head. "I must admit that I haven't. I've been busy with other matters."

"You know what they say—if you want to get something done, ask a busy person to do it," Al said.

"So they say."

"I heard you had a pretty vocal meeting this morning regarding the library addition."

I laughed. "We sure did." I looked at him sideways. "How did you know?"

Al shrugged.

"Uncle Bosco."

"I make it my business to know what's going on all over town. The referendum and large private donations cover a good part of the building expenses, but the addition means the library will be offering more activities and programs and those will require more funds."

I nodded enthusiastically. "I'd like to invite theater groups in to put on plays. If we do, we'll need decent lighting, a good sound system, and I don't know what else."

"If you were on the council, you could bring attention to the library's growing role in our community and encourage support for the library's budget."

"I suppose."

Al put his hand over mine. "Carrie, I've seen how you've developed these past few months into a responsible, proactive member of our community. You're young and vital. Full of new ideas. Our town council needs someone like you."

"I don't think I'm the type to sit on any council," I protested. "Listening to homeowners ask for a variance so they can add an extension because it's close to their property line."

"We don't get many of those. And believe me, they're settled quickly, unless a neighbor has a reason to object. Being on the town council will give you a chance to learn about all the various aspects of life in Clover Ridge. For example, where and to what extent do we allow new housing and industry to be developed so that it doesn't overload the infrastructure and our school system."

I looked at Al. "What makes you think I'm interested in all that?"

"Because you're a Singleton," he said, surprising me.

"So?"

"The Singletons are one of the families that settled in Clover Ridge generations ago. There aren't many of you left. Most up and left the area."

"You have my Uncle Bosco. Seems to me he's active enough—being on the library board and running Haven House."

Al sighed. "Of course. But Bosco can't go on indefinitely."

I shot him a look of distress. "Are you telling me Uncle Bosco isn't well?"

"I'm simply saying we need fresh blood on the town council. Someone who's young and who cares about this town. And that's you, Carrie."

Our main course arrived and we focused on enjoying our prime rib and veggies that were done to perfection. Lucky for me, Al didn't utter another word regarding the purpose of our dinner. Not even when we were having coffee and sharing a serving of tiramisu.

Finally, we'd eaten as much as we could. We leaned back in our chairs and regarded each other.

"I've enjoyed our dinner together immensely," Al said.

"You know what? I did too. Oh!" I glanced at my watch, surprised that two hours had passed.

"Feel free to leave," he told me. "You must be tired, after putting in a day's work."

I walked around the table to kiss his cheek. "Thanks for a great evening, Al."

"Please think about what I've said and let me know what you decide."

"I will."

I drove home slowly in the afterglow of the wonderful dining experience I'd shared with Al Tripp. I had to admit that everything he said made sense. I *was* invested in Clover Ridge, and not just because of my position in the library. I felt an allegiance to the community, not, I hoped, just because I was a Singleton. That sounded so—elitist and snobby. I wanted the town to remain picturesque and respectful of the centuries-old buildings around the Green and elsewhere, while keeping pace with the times. And I knew from my experience with Haven House how easy it was for ruthless people to turn a town project into a personal moneymaker.

But did I want to be on the town council? My cell phone jingled, interrupting my thoughts. "Hello?"

"Miss Singleton, Carrie. This is Michelle's father."

I grinned. I'd forgotten that he'd said he'd call tonight. "Hello, Mr. Kirby."

"Lee is fine. Please tell me more about my daughter. You said she was having problems."

"She's doing a little better than when I first met her. She and her husband moved to Clover Ridge a year or so ago."

"Michelle's married! Does she have any children?"

"No children. And her husband left her and cleaned out their bank account, which sent her into a depression."

"Oh."

"She lost her job and was under the impression she'd have to leave her apartment. But I explained that she wouldn't have to. And

I—" I stopped, afraid that if I made it sound that everything was now under control, he'd have an excuse not to contact his daughter.

"Yes?" he urged.

"I know that hearing from you would mean the world to Michelle. Her only friend is her young next-door neighbor, and she's busy taking care of her baby."

"How did you get involved in all this?"

Good question. "I work in the library and learned about Michelle's problems, so I did what I could to help."

"That was nice of you."

In the pause that followed, I wondered if I should mention that it would be safe for him to come visit her. I breathed a sigh of relief when Lee said, "I had a spot of trouble when I left Clover Ridge, but that's been settled. I made some calls this afternoon, just to make sure."

Phew! "That's good." *Now for the big question.* "Does that mean you'll come see Michelle? I know she'd love to see you."

"Of course I want to see her! For years I've wanted to see my family. But I kept putting it off, planning to do it when I was settled. Then I heard my wife had died and I figured the kids would blame me for her early death, so I kept away."

"Let me give you Michelle's phone number. She'll be thrilled to hear your voice."

Chapter Eighteen

Midmorning Thursday, I received a call from Fran telling me to come down to the circulation desk because Angela had stopped by! She wasn't scheduled to return to work until the weekend, but it turned out she couldn't stay away from her besties at the library. In fact, Angela had been so eager to get home, they'd changed their flight to an earlier one and took a redeye home.

I hurried to join the throng around the circulation desk where Angela was holding court talking about her honeymoon and gave her a hug. She looked well-rested, deliriously happy, and had a glorious tan.

"Free for lunch at noon?" she whispered.

"Of course."

"Good. Need to talk."

At twelve sharp we met at our usual spot—the door leading to the library parking lot.

"Any place in particular?" I asked as we walked to my car.

"The Indian restaurant would be nice."

We climbed inside and I drove out of the lot. "So, how does it feel to be an old married woman?"

"I love it. Waking up next to Steve every morning, knowing I'll see him later in the day."

I glanced over, saw her solemn expression. "But?"

"But we have to find out who murdered Aiden. I'm worried about my parents. I've never seen them so upset, praying that no one in our family is responsible. My brother's staying with them and driving them nuts. Every time he's questioned at the police station, he comes back to the house raging like a maniac." Angela shuddered. "I'm so glad I'm not living there any longer."

I drove slowly toward Mercer Street, where the Indian restaurant was located. "Your mother asked me to investigate, but so far I haven't been able to find out much. Donna invited me to lunch. She swears up and down that she didn't kill her husband, but she can't say the same about Roxy. Or your brother."

Angela snickered. "That's Donna for you. I'm not saying she poisoned Aiden, but she's been known to lie and blame others when it serves her purpose. Her interpretation of 'a woman's prerogative.'

"As for my brother—my mother paid John Mathers a visit at the precinct to tell him what an upstanding citizen her son is. You know what John told her? That Tommy was hauled in *twice* in the past eighteen months for assaulting crew members working on his movie *and* that a director he'd fired had accused Tommy of putting a laxative in his drink, though it was never proven that my dear brother was responsible."

I was pulling into the restaurant's parking lot when Angela added, "We're all worried about Roxy. Aiden's death seems to have unraveled her. She sobbed continuously at his funeral. My uncle has tried to get her to see a shrink, but she refuses."

"Tomorrow is Aiden's memorial," I said as I clicked off the motor. "Let's both speak to as many people as we can and compare notes afterwards."

"Good idea." Angela squeezed my arm. "I'm glad to finally be taking an active role in one of your investigations. I only wish most of the suspects weren't my relatives."

We walked to the restaurant's back entrance. "There are plenty of other possibilities—Aiden's coworkers. A disgruntled patient." I pulled open the door and was greeted by tantalizing aromas. "Now let's enjoy our lunch while you tell me more about your new life as Angela Prisco."

* * *

That evening, I decided to do some computer research in preparation for Aiden's memorial the following afternoon. I started with the website for Clover Ridge General Surgeons, Aiden's medical practice. There was a definition of what general surgery consisted of—surgery of the abdominal cavity including the esophagus, stomach, small and large intestines, liver, pancreas. The list went on to include colonoscopies and other procedures. Next appeared photos of Aiden and Nick Gannon's smiling faces and, beneath them, the photos of two nurse practitioners, neither of whom I'd met, and one of Nurse Gwen Swithers. Finally, there was a photo of Vera Ghent, looking considerably younger and thinner.

I clicked on Aiden's photo and was taken to his medical background: he had attended an Ivy League medical school and did his residency at an excellent Manhattan hospital. Aiden had his ABS board certification and a fellowship in the American College of Surgeons. His specialties were esophageal and stomach surgeries and those in the small and large intestines as well as robotic surgery.

Next, I checked out Aiden's ratings by his patients. He had four stars out of five. Seven patients gave him a five-star rating. An eighth patient gave him one star, complaining that he had to wait hours before his scheduled surgery, something I knew was out of a doctor's control. I jotted down the man's name: Marcus Zilliag.

Nick's background was less impressive. He had attended medical school in Mexico and done his residency in a hospital out west. His specialties were hernia repair, appendectomies, and gallstones. His twelve reviews were mostly threes and fours, with three ones, none of which gave any explanation for the low rating. Interesting. From what I could see, Nick's status had improved when he'd taken Aiden on as his partner. Now I was curious to check out Aiden's home computer and find out what had kept him so busy the evenings before he died.

Aiden's Facebook page was filled with photos of him, Donna, and the kids. I went back six months. There were several of him and Donna, Roxy, and Miles—skiing and some on a cruise ship. Interesting to learn that the two couples had often vacationed together.

The only information Marcus Zilliag's Facebook page had to offer was that he was a machinist, divorced, and lived outside of Clover Ridge. Judging from the one photo he'd posted of himself with his dog, he was slight, balding, and in his early fifties. There were several photos of his German shepherd named Duke.

My cell phone jingled at nine thirty as I was about to jump into the shower. It was Michelle, bubbling over with joy.

"Carrie, I just got off the phone with my father!"

"I'm so glad he called you."

"We had a long talk. Dad said he'd been wanting to contact Harvey and me for years but was afraid we wouldn't want to hear from him after he'd abandoned us."

"Really?" I didn't mean to sound as sarcastic as it came out, but Michelle was too excited to notice.

"Yes, and he wants to make up for it. He's going to come visit soon, but meanwhile he's sending me a check to cover two months' rent and enough so I can buy a secondhand car to get to work."

"I am so glad, Michelle. You deserve a break."

"I told him about my brother's condition, and he's going to see to it that Harvey gets into a rehab facility."

"That's good."

"It's all thanks to you, Carrie. I was feeling so down, I don't know what I would have done if you hadn't helped me."

"I'm glad it worked out, Michelle. Please let me know when your father comes to Clover Ridge. I'd like to meet him."

"I certainly will! Thanks again. You've made a tremendous difference in my life."

* * *

I spent most of Friday morning interviewing the two people who had called me about presenting a program at the library. Annette Phillips was a woman in her forties who had a service animal—a golden retriever she brought to hospitals and senior residents—that she wanted to include in her presentation along with a blind friend and her seeing-eye dog. She spoke enthusiastically about her subject—how animals help us lead better lives—including facts and figures to back up her premise. I told her I was definitely interested and gave her the forms to fill out to return to me ASAP.

The next potential presenter was an older gentleman who was eager to discuss and show slides of his gastronomical trip through France. He was well spoken and enthusiastic about his subject. He showed me photos of two restaurants and meals he wanted to talk about and regaled me with an amusing anecdote about each dinner. As with Annette, I said yes on the spot, adding that we were starting work on the library extension in a few months and I wasn't sure how that would be affecting fall and winter programs.

That accomplished, I ventured to call a local theatrical company that had an excellent reputation for putting on plays in libraries. I explained to the young woman who took my call that our library would have a stage in the near future and I was eager to find out what if any suggestions or requirements we should include if we planned to put on theatrical productions. We got into a discussion of lighting and sound systems, and she promised to send me a packet of information that included their current repertoire.

At one fifteen, I fed Smoky Joe and reminded Trish that she'd agreed to keep an eye on him while I had a quick lunch, then attended the memorial service for Aiden. Not that Trish needed reminding. Her mind was like a computer and she was efficient at multitasking. I'd already asked Susan to check on him occasionally when she came to work earlier than usual. I needed to talk to as many people as I could at the memorial service and wasn't sure when I'd be returning to the library.

The Cozy Corner Café was busy, so I ordered a sandwich and iced tea to go and ate it sitting at one of the outdoor tables in the rear. Then I set out for Aiden's memorial service in Town Hall, only a few blocks away.

As I stopped in the ladies' room to freshen up, my thoughts flashed back to another memorial service which had been held here in October for a retired police lieutenant who had been murdered while investigating a cold case. I'd helped flush out the murderer and came close to becoming a victim myself.

I nodded to a group of elegantly dressed women chatting in quiet tones in the hall. Friends of Donna's, I thought. Or possibly Aiden's patients. I pulled open one of the doors leading to the large meeting room. About a dozen people sat scattered around the room but no one looked familiar. Perhaps family members had gathered in another room to wait until the service began.

I walked down the aisle and took a seat about seven rows from the front. Farther along the row, a woman sat hunched over her knees, her face in her hands. She gave a start when she realized she was no longer alone. I recognized Gwen Swithers, the nurse who worked in Aiden's office.

"Hello, Gwen."

Gwen blinked, not remembering who I was.

"Carrie Singleton. I met you at the wake last week. I'm a friend of Donna's cousin, Angela."

"Oh, yes." She blinked, this time in an attempt to hold back the tears that were spilling down her cheeks.

I reached in my pocketbook for a tissue and handed it to her. Gwen moved closer to me and dabbed at her eyes. "Thank you. I'm sorry for being so emotional."

"I'm sure it's very difficult for you—losing someone you worked with every day."

"Very difficult. Aiden meant the world to me."

"Oh," I said.

"I mean," she quickly explained, "I'm from Ohio and I don't have any real friends here in Clover Ridge. Aiden was always helpful and supportive." She blew her nose. "I miss him so much."

"I know what it's like to move to a new place where you hardly know anyone," I said.

"To think that someone hated him enough to poison him."

I reached over to take her hand. "Gwen, I'm sorry for your pain. Would you like to meet for coffee and talk?"

She nodded. I fished in my pocketbook for one of my new business cards I'd had made up. "Feel free to call me on my cell phone."

We both looked up as a large group of people entered the room through a side door at the front of the room. I spotted Angela and Steve, Angela's parents, Donna and her parents, and Donna's sister Frankie.

I stood. "I'm going to pay my respects to the family. I'll be back."

As I headed down the aisle, I turned around. Gwen was gone.

Chapter Nineteen

I hugged Angela and Steve, Rosemary and Joe, and told Donna how sorry I was. She looked regal in a long navy dress. Her eyes were red from crying, but she seemed calm and appreciative that I was there.

"Thank you for coming, Carrie. Aiden's purpose in life was to help people. The world has lost one of its angels."

"I didn't know Aiden well, but I can see he was well loved," I said, thinking of Gwen's emotional outburst and Roxy's frequent visits to Aiden's office. In fact, where was Roxy?

I caught sight of her a few rows away, sitting with, of all people, her cousin Tommy.

"We'll talk later," Angela said.

And compare notes, I thought as I returned to my seat where I'd left my sweater, and moved closer to the aisle. As the room filled up, I recognized a few library patrons. I nodded to Nick Gannon and Vera Ghent, who had slipped into the row behind me. And there was John Mathers standing at the back of the room. I caught his eye and smiled. John glanced upward, as though asking God to give him strength. Somehow he knew that I was sleuthing again and there wasn't anything he could do to stop me.

To my surprise, Miles Forlano stepped up to the lectern at the front of the room, a handsome, fit figure of manhood in his prime. He wore a blue summer blazer, gray slacks, and an open-necked white shirt, appearing both casual yet respectfully dressed for the occasion. He held out his arms and asked for silence.

"It is with great sadness that I stand here before you as we remember my dear friend Aiden Harrington, cut down in the prime of his life by a miserable coward. Aiden was a warm and generous human being and a gifted surgeon. He loved his family, cared for his patients, and was a loyal friend. I miss him terribly, as I imagine all of you do."

Miles went on for another five minutes, then invited Donna to say a few words. She thanked everyone for coming and went on to say what a wonderful father Aiden was, and how much his patients meant to him. Then a tall, stooped man who appeared to be close to seventy got up to speak. Aiden's father. He talked about Aiden as a boy, introducing an element of humor when he spoke about Aiden's fascination with science experiments and how once he almost blew up the garage with an experiment gone awry.

Frankie, Donna's sister, shared how Aiden had helped her pass a college math course. Then Vera walked up to the lectern. She looked pretty in a deep purple dress with tiny white and yellow flowers, though her curly hair was disheveled.

"Aiden Harrington was my boss for the past five years, some of the happiest working years of my life. He was kind to everyone in the office and never lost his cool, even when I accidentally over-booked his schedule." She stopped for the small ripples of laughter that ran through the audience. "His patients loved him, and with good reason. Aiden was a wonderful doctor. We all miss him."

An elderly woman rose and spoke, praising Aiden's medical skills. As she returned to her seat, I heard a commotion on the other side of the room. Roxy came stumbling down the aisle. Was she drunk? High? She stood before the lectern and clutched the mic as if she were afraid someone would grab it from her.

"Yeah, Aiden was a great guy, but he had one fatal flaw. He gave generously to the people he loved, never expecting anything in return." Roxy's gaze darted around the room in search of a target. It settled on Donna. "Too bad his wife, my *dear* cousin, never appreciated him."

I stared, transfixed, hardly believing what I was hearing.

"Oh, Donna loved being a doctor's wife, and all the perks that went with it—the beautiful house, money for vacations—but did she care about the man himself? Poor Aiden. He deserved someone who truly loved him."

Miles, who had leaped out of his seat and raced up to Roxy, now put an arm around his ex-wife's shoulders. We all watched as Roxy struggled to free herself from his grasp, but Miles held firm and led her swiftly out of the room.

People looked at one another, at a loss regarding what to do next. Miles had been the person directing the memorial, and no one else was volunteering to take his place.

"Well, that puts an end to this little show and we can go back to work."

I glanced around to see who had spoken. As I'd suspected, it was Nick Gannon.

Vera nudged him and whispered. "Show some compassion. The girl was in love with him."

Nick laughed. "Like half the people here. They should have known the real Aiden."

A minute later, a man I didn't know walked to the front of the room and thanked everyone for coming. As we stood to leave the room, I tapped Nick on the shoulder. "What did you mean—people should have known the real Aiden? What was he really like?"

Nick stared at me.

"Sorry. I'm Carrie Singleton. I didn't know Aiden well, but he died in front of me at my friends' wedding. I'm just wondering what he was really like."

"Right. We met at the wake."

"Yes, we did."

Nick shrugged. "Don't get me wrong. Aiden was a good guy. He had a big heart, like everyone said, but he couldn't see the big picture."

"What do you mean?" We both, along with Vera, had joined the crowd in the aisle slowly exiting the building.

"I had visions of opening another office in Merrivale, but Aiden refused to consider it."

"I think he was too busy with other affairs to have his mind on business matters," Vera said with a meaningful smile.

I stared at her. "You mean—Roxy?"

"I said *affairs*, didn't I?" Vera fluttered her eyes. "Silly man, when he had a gorgeous wife like Donna at home."

* * *

Affairs? Plural? Surely not Aiden! I wasn't being naïve about how some men played around, but Aiden didn't seem the type. I walked slowly back to the library, as I tried to process what I'd learned about the people surrounding Aiden and the possible motivation any one of them might have had to poison him. Nurse Gwen's insistence that he had been an especially caring employer didn't explain her extremely emotional reaction to his death. And how weird was it that she took off when I had left to talk to Angela and her family. I wondered if Gwen was one of the affairs that Vera had alluded to. How I'd love to ask Gwen and watch her reaction.

Poor Roxy was in a bad way—coming to the memorial drunk or high and blasting Donna in front of everyone for not being a good wife. Seeing Roxy with Tommy made me wonder if they might have planned Aiden's death together. After all, they each had a grievance against him. Though Aiden had been supportive of Roxy, she hadn't managed to win his affection and convince him to leave Donna. Sometimes murderers were beset with grief even though they themselves had killed the person they still loved.

I walked across the library's parking lot as I considered Nick's comments. He had hinted there was a side to Aiden that most people either didn't know about or were ignoring. Was he referring to the supposed affair with Roxy and/or Gwen, or was he just being spiteful because Aiden had refused to go along with his plan to open another office? Maybe Gwen could fill me in on what was really was going on in the office. I'd contact her after the weekend. And if she was reluctant to meet, I'd simply explain that I'd been asked to find out who had murdered Aiden. Surely she would want to help me find his killer.

* * *

Dylan arrived at the cottage a little before seven, a bottle of wine in hand, looking handsome and sexy in shorts and a T-shirt. I served our dinner—a large salad I'd made to which I'd added grilled sirloin tips that I'd picked up at the Gourmet Delight, along with focaccia bread that was warming in the toaster oven. Dylan filled our wine glasses. We smiled and toasted each other, then sipped.

Dylan was full of talk about Gary Winton, his new protégé, pleased by how quickly Gary picked up whatever he was explaining and by his eagerness to start working on cases.

"Sounds like you made the right choice," I said.

"You'll see for yourself when we take him out tomorrow," Dylan said as I cleared our dishes and set out plates for dessert. "I know you want to run a few errands in the morning, so I signed us up for a three o'clock boat ride around the Sound."

"What a great idea! I went on one of those boat rides when I was six years old."

"Then I thought we'd have dinner at the Sea Maiden. I managed to snag a reservation for seven thirty. That gives us an hour and a half between the boat ride and dinner. We can drive around town, show Gary some of our favorite spots. Or have drinks at my place."

"I'm sure he'll go for either one," I said.

We drank our coffee and munched on one of Aunt Harriet's cakes that I'd defrosted earlier.

"Tell me more about Aiden's memorial service," Dylan said.

I had told him about Gwen's disappearing act and Roxy's outburst earlier. "His partner Nick Gannon made a comment, implying that Aiden wasn't the Golden Boy everyone was praising. That could have been a reference to his supposed affairs with Roxy and/or Nurse Gwen, as Vera the office manager implied."

"Were Nick and Vera sitting together?" Dylan asked.

"Well, sure. They work together, don't they?"

"Did they go to the memorial service together?"

"I wouldn't know. Why do you ask?" I laughed. "You don't think they're having an affair, do you? Vera's about fifteen years older than Nick."

Dylan shrugged his shoulders. "Just wondering."

"Anyway, Nick was annoyed that Aiden didn't want to go along with his plans to set up another office—in Merrivale."

"Not exactly a reason to kill your business partner," Dylan said.

"No." I exhaled loudly. "And there's no clue anywhere leading to the poisoner. Anyone could have bought the stuff."

"I'm sure John's checking that out," Dylan said.

"Speaking of John, he was at the memorial service, but I didn't get a chance to talk to him. I'm hoping that Angela's learned something from her relatives."

We settled down in the living room to watch a movie. Like an old married couple, I thought, and quickly brushed the thought aside. Then Angela called. Since Dylan was engrossed in the movie, I spoke to her in my guest bedroom/office.

"We've just finished dinner at my parents' and soon we're off to Aunt Marie's for dessert." Angela released a deep sigh. "I can't wait to go home for some peace and quiet."

"What's been happening? Have you learned anything?"

"My brother's gone completely berserk. Suddenly he insists he *has* to get back to California ASAP to start filming his movie, which is bogus. I mean, how can he do anything with that movie if he doesn't have enough funds? He's furious that John Mathers wants to interview him again about Aiden's murder." Angela giggled. "I won't bother repeating the rest of what he said. Though they don't say it, I'm pretty sure my parents wish he'd go home. On the other hand, they're worried about him. I think they're finally seeing the kind of person Tommy really is."

"What about Donna? How did she take Roxy's little performance?"

"I have no idea, but we're going over to Donna's parents' house in a little while, so I'm sure I'll get an earful."

I filled Angela in on Aiden's colleagues' comments. "We have nothing concrete to go on. The only thing left to do is find out what kept Aiden holed up in his home office all those evenings before his death. Though I'm sure John went through everything there already."

"I'll go with you. You never know what will turn up."

"Good idea. I wish we knew what Aiden wanted to talk to Dylan about."

"Oh, that's right," Angela said. "Aiden did want to talk to Dylan. Which meant something was troubling him. Something he wanted investigated."

"Something illegal, I imagine."

Angela laughed. "Let's not get ahead of ourselves. By the way, would you like to come over for a barbecue early Sunday evening? Steve can't wait to try out our new grill."

"I'd love to. Give me a minute to run it by Dylan."

"Sure," was Dylan's quick response. "Shall we bring wine or beer?"

"Beer," Angela answered.

We chatted a minute more, then I went to join Dylan in the living room. He gave me a quick kiss and I nestled against him. A quiet evening at home was just what I needed.

A few hours later I must have dozed off because Dylan was nudging me. "Your cell phone's ringing."

I hurried into my bedroom where I'd left my phone and wondered who was calling. My mother? With the three-hour difference between Connecticut and California, she sometimes misjudged the time. Not that it was late. Only a quarter to ten. And not that she called very often.

"Hello, Carrie?" The voice was so muffled, I couldn't identify who was speaking.

"Yes?"

"This is Gwen. Gwen Swithers. You said I could call. I know it's late, but . . ." Her voice faded away, and I was worried she was about to hang up.

"I said to call and I meant it. Are you all right?"

"Not really. I can't get past this terrible sadness. And I keep wondering if I should have told the police—" Gwen stopped suddenly. "I—I don't know what to do."

"Would you like to meet for breakfast tomorrow and talk about whatever's bothering you?"

"I'd like that, Carrie—as long as you keep what I tell you in confidence."

"Of course," I said. *Unless you poisoned Aiden.*

We made plans to meet at a diner a few miles east of Clover Ridge at nine fifteen. I told Gwen to get a good night's sleep.

"I think just knowing we're meeting in the morning, I'll be able to sleep for the first time in weeks," she said.

And maybe tomorrow morning some of the mystery surrounding Aiden Harrington will be revealed.

Chapter Twenty

G wen was waiting for me outside the entrance to the diner. Dressed in a T-shirt and jeans, her long hair pulled back into a ponytail, she looked no older than eighteen.

Her anxious expression turned into a smile as I approached. "I was worried you wouldn't come," she said.

I pulled open the door and we entered the diner. A pleasant young woman greeted us and ushered us into the mostly empty dining room. "Sit wherever you like."

"Over there's fine," I said, pointing to the corner window booth for four at the far end of the room.

"Enjoy," she said, dropping off two large menus.

A handsome young server stopped at our table. "Would you like coffee while you decide on your breakfast?"

"Thanks," I said.

"Please," Gwen said.

A few minutes later we were sipping coffee and placing our order—a Belgian waffle with blueberries and strawberries for me, something I never made at home, and an omelet with mushrooms and Swiss cheese for Gwen. That taken care of, I gave her my undivided attention.

"So how are you feeling this morning?" I asked.

Gwen smiled. "Much better. I slept through the night for the first time in weeks."

"I'm glad."

"It's a relief to have someone to talk to."

"What about the people at work?" I asked.

Gwen grimaced. "It's been very hectic since Shari and Colette left. And now that Aiden's gone, there's never time to sit around and chat."

"Who are Shari and Colette?"

"They're nurse practitioners who used to work in the office. I'm still not sure why they left. I only know that Nick and Aiden argued about it. And then they were gone. Aiden never explained."

I raised my eyebrows. "Why would he have explained it to you?"

"Aiden and I were . . . involved."

"Ah."

"You're not surprised," Gwen said.

"Not when I saw how much his death affected you."

"His murder, you mean."

"That's right. His murder."

Gwen paused, then her words came in a torrent. "It's not what you think—I didn't go after him. I'm not a home wrecker."

"So how did it happen?"

"As I told you, I have no friends in the area and I often felt lonely. Aiden was always kind—recommending places to go to on my days off, things to do—stuff like that."

"I see."

"We got into the habit of talking after everyone left the office for the day. A few times we went for coffee. Once we went for a drink."

"You knew he was married."

"Of course I did!" Gwen glared at me. "I told Aiden I didn't want to get involved in a seamy affair where I was bound to get hurt as well as hurt his family."

"But?"

"But it just happened." Gwen looked down at her hands. "One warm Friday afternoon in early May, Aiden asked me if I'd like to go for a drive. I said sure. We stopped to pick up some wine and cheese and ended up in a cabin that he and Nick own. It's near a small lake not far from the office. And, well, things got out of hand."

An affair between a doctor and his nurse. How cliché is that? But I refused to come off as judgy, so I simply nodded.

"You're thinking how trite, aren't you? But we suddenly realized how much we cared for each other. Aiden told me he and Donna hadn't been getting along for some time. He'd tried to talk to her about it, but each time she blew him off."

"What about Roxy?"

Gwen laughed. "Cousin Roxy who stopped by the office most days?"

I nodded as our waitress arrived with our breakfast. We thanked her and asked for coffee refills. When she left, I said, "Yes, that Roxy. What was going on between her and Aiden?"

Gwen exhaled her exasperation. "Aiden was supportive—like a big brother—because he knew she was unstable. At the same time, he did his best to convince Roxy that Miles still loved her. Only Roxy had set her sights on him—Aiden. When she spelled out her intentions, Aiden reminded her in no uncertain terms that she was his wife's first cousin and he had no intention of leaving Donna."

Gwen sighed. "She took it very badly."

And how did you take the part that he didn't plan to leave Donna? "Do you think Roxy killed Aiden?" I asked.

"I don't know. The last time she came in, she left the office shouting at him. I can only imagine what the patients in the waiting room were thinking. That was a week before he died."

"And Donna?" I asked. "Do you think she might have killed Aiden?"

Gwen's gaze met mine. "Aiden once told me something Donna said that sent a chill down my spine. It's been troubling me since I found out he was poisoned."

"Do you want to talk about it?"

She sighed. "I keep thinking I should tell the police. Except then they'll ask me how I know this and I'll have to explain about Aiden and me. Then maybe they'll think that I killed Aiden . . ."

"And so you keep going around in circles."

"Exactly. And it's taking its toll on me."

"I won't repeat what you share with me, but I will tell you what I think."

Gwen nodded. "In that case," she exhaled loudly, "Donna told him she would kill anyone who tried to ruin her lifestyle. He laughed it off, claiming it was her way of saying 'don't try to divorce me even if you no longer love me.'"

"Was Aiden planning to divorce Donna?"

"We talked about it. He thought it might be best to make the break soon, while the kids were still quite young."

He tells you one thing, tells Roxy another. "And marry you?" I asked.

"Eventually. I loved Aiden but I made it very clear that I wasn't going to rush into marriage. He had issues to work out before marrying again."

"That's very mature of you," I said.

Gwen must have thought I was being sarcastic, because she made a scoffing sound. "Mature? Not rushing into marriage was something I've learned the hard way. I was married for a short time. The ending was awful. It was the reason I took a job so far from home."

We made casual conversation as we ate, and I called over our waitress to refill our coffee cups. When she was gone, I said, "Gwen, do you think Donna knew that Aiden was planning to ask for a divorce?"

"I do. He said that's why she kept avoiding the subject when he tried to talk about their relationship."

"Do you think she knew he was in love with you?"

"I doubt it. If anything, she thought Aiden was having an affair with Roxy. Vera, the office manager, was the only person who caught us in a less than professional situation." Gwen grinned. "All she did was say 'go for it.'"

"So Vera knew you and Aiden were involved. Do you think she told anyone—like Nick?"

Gwen shrugged. "Maybe. They're close friends, but I doubt either of them would say anything to Donna. They're not big Donna fans."

"Why?" I asked, suddenly curious.

Another shrug. "They think she's a beautiful bubblehead."

"What about Aiden's relationship with Nick? They were partners, but Nick said he wanted to open another office and Aiden refused to consider it."

"I really don't know. We didn't talk much about the business end of things." Gwen thought for a moment. "Aiden did seem worried about money, but I think that was because he knew that a divorce would mean giving up a large part of his income to Donna and the kids."

"From what you've told me, I think you should tell Lieutenant Mathers everything we've discussed. He can't arrest Donna Harrington based on what she said to Aiden since it's considered hearsay, but it gives him a broader picture of the people involved."

"But what if it gets back to Donna that Aiden and I were in love? Or Lieutenant Mathers starts to think that I killed Aiden?"

"Why would he think that? You wanted Aiden alive."

"Of course I did!"

"And he certainly wouldn't tell Donna about your involvement with her husband."

Our waitress cleared our dishes and brought over the check. Gwen reached for it. "This is on me, Carrie."

"Don't be silly," I protested.

"No, I asked you to meet me and you helped me decide to talk to the police."

I smiled at Gwen, pleased that she was looking more relaxed. "In that case, many thanks for a delicious breakfast."

She clasped both my hands in hers. "Thank *you* for listening and helping me decide what to do."

As I ran a few errands in town, I thought about my conversation with Gwen and what had been weighing on her mind. She was in love with Aiden and wanted his murderer apprehended. Gwen considered Donna's comment about killing anyone who tried to change her lifestyle a threat aimed at Aiden. But whether or not Donna had meant it literally was another matter. Still, Gwen considered it her responsibility to repeat it to John Mathers.

On the other hand, telling John meant Gwen would have to come clean about her relationship with Aiden. What she hadn't mentioned and might not even be aware of was that she probably felt guilty about pointing a finger at Donna. Guilty because she'd become involved with Donna's husband and was part of the reason why Aiden had pulled away from his marriage.

So, if Donna killed Aiden because he was planning to leave her, wasn't she, Gwen, partly responsible for her actions?

"Guilt makes people do strange things," I murmured as I turned onto the private Avery road. The good thing was, Gwen was going to tell John what she knew. Circumstantial evidence, a lawyer would say in court, but helpful in giving John the total picture of who might have a motive for killing Aiden Harrington.

* * *

When Dylan came over for lunch, I told him about my meeting with Gwen.

"So you've crossed her off your list of possible suspects," he said when I was through.

"I never thought she poisoned him. After talking to her at length, now I'm certain of it."

Dylan chuckled then leaned over to kiss my cheek. "I love your objective investigative methods."

I brushed him away. "I'm entitled to my take on people. Besides, why would Gwen go to all the trouble to tell me about her and Aiden when as far as she knew I had no idea that they'd been involved?"

"Because this way she can offer the same information to John, thinking it makes *her* look innocent. Then add the incriminating line that Donna is supposed to have said. If Donna actually said it." Dylan winked. "After all, who else can verify it, right?"

"Right," I mumbled. "The important thing is Gwen's now intending to tell all this to John."

"So we hope."

"So I'll find out," I said. "Case closed."

Dylan tried to hold my hand as we drove to pick up Gary Winton, but I wouldn't let him. After a few miles, my pique was over and I took his hand in mine. Dylan was a trained investigator and it went against his instincts to swallow whole what a person told him without checking it out thoroughly. All well and good, of course, but I had my own methods which included a respect for my gut feeling concerning the people surrounding a homicide. So far I'd never been wrong.

We found Gary leaning against his apartment building texting. He was tall and gangly—at least six four—with a cowlick that spilled over his forehead and a ready smile. Dylan got out of the car and made the introductions. I got out, too, as I figured that Gary would be more comfortable sitting in the front seat. He demurred at first but finally agreed, and I climbed into the back.

Exuberance and enthusiasm accompanied every comment Gary shared with us—from how excited he was to work with Dylan to anecdotes about his Granny who lived in Maine. He settled down as soon as we stepped aboard the boat for our ride around the Long Island Sound and our guide began her spiel about the history and geography of the area. But as soon as we were on solid land again, driving around the outskirts of Clover Ridge, Gary responded to every comment Dylan or I made with one of his own that had little connection to what had just been said. I found it irritating until I realized the poor guy was trying his best to impress us. When Dylan caught my glance in the rearview mirror, I rolled my eyes.

He rested his hand on Gary's arm. "Relax, kiddo."

"Sorry. I've been running off at the mouth." A blush rose on Gary's neck and ears.

"No problem. We're just out to enjoy the day."

"Yeah. Sure."

"You already aced the interview. And Carrie likes you. I can tell."

"I do," I said, clamping my hand on Gary's shoulder.

He was quiet for a while as Dylan continued to drive through the countryside, pointing out some of our favorite spots. I joined in occasionally, and eventually Gary did, too. He was smart, curious, and perceptive, I decided, after hearing his comments regarding the case notes of his first assignment that Dylan had given him to study. Dylan had chosen well when he'd hired Gary to work in his company.

Gary was twenty-three, the same age as Gwen Swithers. Though they were as different as could be in their personalities and life experiences, their lives had yet to take shape. Gary was starting a new career in a new town, and Gwen had just lost the man she loved and her life was in flux. They were young. And though I was only seven years older, I felt as though I were in a different age group entirely. Not ancient, perhaps, but my life had settled into a pattern. I was in a relationship with the man I loved and had a satisfying career. What's more, I was beginning to find a place in my community.

"Earth to Carrie," Dylan said.

I looked up, surprised to see that we'd arrived. I exited the car and walked arm-in-arm with Dylan to the entrance of the Sea Maiden, one of the larger seafood restaurants on the Sound.

The maître d' led us around to the back and seated us at a lovely table close to the water. After glancing at the extensive menu, all three of us decided to share the restaurant's mammoth signature salad and to order a two-pound lobster each. Dylan looked over the beer list and read off some suggestions. When we'd made our selections, he put his arm around me. "Happy, babe?"

I smiled at him. "Very."

Dylan turned to Gary. "Carrie's a librarian by training, but she also investigates the occasional crime."

"Really? You mean, if people don't return books on time she goes after them?"

I laughed. "Usually homicides."

His brown eyes grew large. "Awesome! Any cases you're working on right now?"

I shrugged. "Nothing I can talk about. But I did help track down someone who left town fifteen years ago. Actually, Rosalind helped me with that one."

"I'm impressed," Gary said.

"So am I," Dylan said.

Hearing that, I totally forgave him for his earlier comments regarding my methods of detecting a suspect's guilt.

The baby greens and beet salad had a marvelous ginger dressing, and the lobster was tender and tasty. We shared a piece of chocolate fudge cake three ways, along with the largest dollop of whipped cream I think I'd ever seen.

Gary told us about the birthday cake he'd made for his girlfriend in college that sank in the middle. He ate a spoonful of cake and managed to get a smudge of whipped cream on his nose. Without thinking, I reached over and wiped it away with my napkin.

"Thanks," he said and continued talking.

But I'd managed to shock myself. I wasn't in the habit of cleaning the face of a young man I'd met a few hours ago. As if I were his mother. Like Dylan and I were his parents and he was—

I shook my head, refusing to pursue this ridiculous train of thought. When I glanced at Dylan and Gary, I was relieved that they were in the middle of discussing a case. I leaned back and sipped my coffee, noting that I was deliriously happy.

Chapter
Twenty-One

The next morning, Dylan drove to our favorite deli for fresh bagels, cream cheese, and lox. We had a leisurely breakfast, read the Sunday papers, then went to the gym. Later, back at the cottage, I made us a light lunch. Then Dylan went home to his manor house, as I thought of it, to do some work, and I baked a blueberry cobbler for that evening's barbecue, then watched an old movie on TV with Smoky Joe asleep on my lap. Suddenly it was five o'clock and Dylan and I were on our way to Angela and Steve's.

Angela showed me their new décor purchases while the guys, beers in hand, were out on the patio, supposedly to start up the grill.

In the kitchen we sipped our beers as Angela removed a platter of cold appetizers from the fridge and placed it on a tray.

"Looks like married life agrees with you," I said.

"It does, though I'm having trouble wrapping my head around the idea that someone in my own family may have poisoned Aiden. Good thing I have Steve." She shot me a lopsided grin. "Sometimes I get this happy feeling in the middle of the day just knowing I'll be with him after work. He listens to me when I'm happy, when I'm sad. We're there for each other." Angela exhaled loudly.

"Now I can step back from all the craziness in my family and not react—at least not the way I used to."

"Has something new developed?"

Angela removed a tray of pigs in a blanket from the oven and began placing them on a platter. "After the service, Steve and I were having dinner at my parents' when Aunt Marie called, begging us to come over to her and Uncle Vinnie's house for dessert. She insisted that Donna needed our support. Steve and I didn't want to go, but Mom pleaded so off we went like good soldiers."

She made a scoffing sound. "There we were—my parents, Steve, and I—sitting around my aunt and uncle's living room. Tommy was smart. He didn't bother to show up. You know what? Neither did Donna. So much for supporting her. Aunt Marie disappeared, probably to call and convince her to come over, because Donna arrived with the kids a few minutes later.

"Then Uncle Dominic and Roxy came by. I can't imagine what my aunt was thinking, inviting them over after the drama queen's performance at the memorial. Or why Roxy agreed to go."

"That must have been something."

Angela rolled her eyes. "Like straight out of a movie. Donna went right for the jugular. She punched Roxy in the stomach, then before Roxy could react, butted her head into Roxy's chin. Roxy recovered and grabbed Donna's hair and let loose with her fist."

I stared at her. "No!"

"Yes. At which point, Steve and my father came to life and separated the two contenders. Good thing the kids were in the kitchen with their *nonna* at the time."

I shook my head in disbelief. "Then what happened?"

"They were forced to sit on opposite sides of the room, but that didn't stop them from hurling insults at each other. They each accused the other of murdering Aiden. At one point, Roxy said she'd only come there to tell her side of the story, but now it was too late for that. Finally, Uncle Dominic apologized and he and Roxy left."

"Wow."

"Steve and I took off after that." Angela pointed to two platters of appetizers. "Grab one and let's go outside and join the guys."

The heavenly aroma of barbecue greeted us as soon as we stepped onto the small patio off the kitchen. Dylan and Steve were deep in conversation about baseball as Steve deftly turned spareribs and kebabs with a long fork, then lowered the gas and closed the lid. Their eyes lit up when they saw the appetizers. They scarfed down several, then Angela and I placed the half-empty platters on the card table nearby.

"I borrowed the table and folding chairs from my parents," Angela explained. "We're buying outdoor furniture next weekend."

Angela and I sat down at the table, which was already set with paper plates, napkins, and plastic cutlery. Dylan and Steve joined us a minute later.

"I was filling Carrie in on my family saga," Angela said as we continued to munch on the appetizers. She gave Dylan a quick summary of what had taken place at Donna's parents' house Friday evening.

"And Tommy's making our lives miserable, complaining about being a suspect just because he got annoyed at Aiden for reneging on his promise."

"At least he's gone most of the day, trying to talk everyone he knows into backing his movie," Steve said.

"I wish Tommy would go home," Angela said. "I can't relax when he's around."

Steve leaned over to kiss her cheek, then speared a shrimp with a toothpick.

"Roxy sounds like a loose cannon," Dylan said. "And I don't understand her relationship with her ex-husband. Carrie said Miles drove her home from the memorial service on Friday."

"We get the definite feeling he wants to get back together with Roxy," Angela said.

"Speak for yourself, my angel," Steve said. "Miles is a player. He'll always be a player. But he feels responsible for Roxy going off the rails, so he pretends to be a good guy."

Angela glared at her husband. "For your information, Donna said Aiden told her that Miles loves Roxy and wants to marry her again. He never wanted the divorce in the first place."

Steve made a scoffing sound. "Roxy's drinking again and acting crazy. She's not capable of being in a relationship."

Dylan and I exchanged glances. I made a big show of sniffing the air. "I think our dinner is ready. Angela, should we bring out the side dishes?"

"I think that's a great idea."

"Hon, I'll need a platter for the meat," Steve said.

Angela and I each picked up the now empty appetizer platters and headed for the kitchen.

"Men. They're so cynical," Angela said as she scooped rice pilaf onto a dish from the pot warming on the stove.

I removed the salad from the fridge, along with the potato salad, coleslaw and a few cold bottles of beer, and placed them on a platter. "I can't see how Roxy could trust Miles after his bad behavior."

"He's really a good guy," Angela said as she got a large platter down from the cabinet above the oven. "I think she'd get out of her funk if she could see her way to forgive him."

"Still, what assurance can he give her that he won't go wandering again?" I asked.

Angela didn't answer. I think she was too bedazzled by the wonders of marriage to consider how despondent Roxy was feeling. She had given her heart, her husband had deceived her, and her world fell apart. Being in love made you vulnerable.

Minutes later we were too busy to speak as we devoured the wonderful meal that Angela and Steve had prepared. But not too busy, I noticed, to keep Angela and Steve from exchanging glances. I finally sat back and let out a deep sigh. "I believe this was one of the very best meals I've ever eaten," I said.

"Me too," Dylan said.

Our hosts beamed at each other and clinked their now empty beer glasses. "Success," they said in unison.

"I hope you left room for dessert," Angela said.

I rolled my eyes. "I don't think so."

"We'll see about that," Angela said.

I helped her clear the table, which was easy enough as we threw our paper plates into a big black plastic bag. We carried the leftovers into the kitchen while Steve took care of the gas grill.

Angela started the coffee, then took a large white cake box from the fridge, which I promptly opened. "Miniature Italian pastries!"

She winked. "If you don't mind, I'll save your cobbler for later."

The doorbell rang. Angela went to answer the door and returned to the kitchen followed by Frankie, Donna's sister. Frankie plunked down a bakery box full of cookies.

"What a pleasant surprise," I said as we hugged.

"Ange said you guys were coming for dinner so I thought I'd stop by."

Angela got out another platter—she seemed to have an unending supply of them—on which she set out several kinds of cookie. Frankie reached for one of the mini-pastries and devoured it in two bites. "Yummy."

We placed the desserts on trays, and when the coffee was ready, carried everything outside. Steve and Dylan greeted Frankie with hugs, then we settled down to eat.

"Anything new regarding Aiden's case?" Angela asked her cousin when we'd all had our sugar fix.

"Lieutenant Mathers questioned Donna again this afternoon." Frankie glanced at her watch. "I better get going. Donna asked me to be back at her house at seven. I'm babysitting the kids."

"Why?" Angela asked. "Where's she going?"

For a minute it looked like Frankie wasn't going to answer. Then she said, "She's meeting Miles somewhere."

"Miles!" I exclaimed.

"It isn't a date!" Frankie sounded flustered. "Miles loves Roxy."

"How do you know that?" Dylan asked.

"He told Donna. It's one of the reasons he wants to talk to my sister—to discuss what she thinks he should do to win Roxy back."

Steve scoffed. "That's a good ploy if I ever heard one. It's Miles's way of making Donna think he's caring and what a great guy he is. Then he'll make his move—on Donna!"

"That's not the case at all!" Frankie said, her dark eyes flashing. "Miles was an idiot for running around on Roxy. He never expected her to throw him out. And now he sees what a mess she is. And it's all his fault."

Partly, anyway. "Does Miles have another reason to talk to Donna?" I asked

"Yes." Frankie reached for another mini-pastry. After she'd bitten into it, chewed, and swallowed, she said, "According to Miles, Aiden was concerned about the office finances."

"Did he go into specifics?" Dylan asked. He was probably remembering that Aiden had wanted to talk to him after the wedding.

"No," Frankie said. "Miles told Donna he was planning to mention it to Lieutenant Mathers. But then *he* was questioned as if he were a suspect. After that, Miles figured that telling the police there were problems at the office would only be viewed as his way of pointing the investigation away from him."

"Miles was Aiden's best friend," Angela said. "Why would John Mathers think Miles had a motive to poison him?"

"Because suddenly Roxy was in love with Aiden, and many people thought they had something going," Steve said.

Angela threw up her hands. "What a mess!"

Frankie nodded. "I wonder if they'll ever find out who murdered my brother-in-law."

* * *

Frankie left a few minutes later and Dylan and I followed shortly after. Angela and Steve walked us to our car.

"We had a terrific time," I told Angela as I hugged her good night. Then I couldn't help whispering, "Marriage agrees with you. I'm so happy for you."

My BFF glanced at our two guys deep in conversation. "Try it, you'll like it," she whispered with a wink.

I drew back as if from a roaring fire. "Don't forget—tomorrow evening we're going to Donna's to look at Aiden's computer and papers."

"She said eight o'clock was good. I'll call to remind her we're coming," Angela said.

A minute later Dylan and I were starting for home.

"Well, that was fun," he said as we exited the condo complex.

I yawned. "It was. And now I'm ready for bed."

Dylan turned to me. "Want me to stay over?"

"Of course."

"Then I will."

I reached over and squeezed his hand. *That makes three nights in a row.*

"I like spending the whole weekend with you," Dylan said.

"Me too."

"Then let's do that from now on."

"Okay."

We didn't say much the rest of the trip. We didn't need to.

Chapter
Twenty-Two

"Talk to you later. Go back to sleep." Dylan kissed me and left for an early Monday breakfast meeting with a client.

"Mmm." I looked at the clock, saw it wasn't even six, and caught sight of Smoky Joe following Dylan out of the bedroom.

"I'll feed him," Dylan said.

"Thanks." I drifted back to sleep feeling nurtured and cared for. It was almost like being—no, I would *not* say the M word, not even in my mind.

When the alarm sounded an hour later, I leaped out of bed, eager to start the day. I hummed as I showered, dressed, and ate my breakfast. I babbled to Smoky Joe as we rode to the library—about the lovely summer weather and Aunt Harriet and Uncle Bosco's upcoming Fourth of July barbecue later on in the week.

I hadn't been in my office more than five minutes when Evelyn showed up. She perched on the corner of my assistants' desk and crossed her arms. "Someone's in a chipper mood," she observed.

I shot her a sidelong glance then turned on my computer. "And someone's making an early appearance. What gives?"

Evelyn shrugged. "I was in the neighborhood and thought I'd stop by to find out if you've heard anything further regarding my brother's upcoming visit."

"Nothing since I spoke to Michelle on Wednesday."

"Oh."

She sounded so disappointed, I offered to call Michelle later to find out when he was planning to come.

"Thanks, Carrie. Much appreciated. Any new developments in finding Aiden's killer?"

I pursed my lips. "Nothing concrete, but I'm sure learning plenty about the people in his life. Nurse Gwen claims she and Aiden were in love and he was planning to divorce Donna. She insists Aiden was not having an affair with Roxy but trying to get her back together with Miles, only that backfired and Roxy seems to have fallen in love with Aiden instead." I finished with Roxy's outburst at Aiden's memorial service on Friday.

"So any one of them—Roxy, Miles, Donna, even Gwen—might be the murderer." She shot me a sidelong glance. "Or Tommy."

"That wouldn't surprise me at all. But let's not forget Aiden's partner, Dr. Nick Gannon. Nick wanted to expand their practice to another location, but Aiden wasn't keen on the idea."

Evelyn made a scoffing sound. "That's a reason to kill someone?"

I laughed. "By now you should know that people kill for all kinds of crazy reasons."

"Unfortunately, you're right."

"Tonight Angela and I are going over to her cousin Donna's house to check out Aiden's computer, files, and papers. According to Donna, before he died Aiden spent several evenings holed up in his office going over . . . well, she's not sure what, except that she's pretty sure it had to do with his practice. It's probably what he wanted to talk to Dylan about."

"That sounds promising," Evelyn said.

"Of course John Mathers searched Aiden's office and might have discovered what was troubling Aiden. If only I could figure out a way to ask John what he found."

Evelyn chuckled. "Though our police chief is a good friend of yours, you can't very well ask him to share whatever clues he's unearthed."

"Sometimes he shares, but not always." I grimaced. "Our exchange of information often goes in one direction."

"How is Angela? She looked very pleased with herself when I saw her this morning."

I grinned. "She and Steve are very happy. They had Dylan and me over for a barbecue yesterday."

"And how are you and Dylan getting along?"

"Great."

Evelyn's ghostly blue eyes twinkled. "Yes. That's the impression I'm receiving this morning."

My cell phone's jingle played, saving me from responding to her comment. It was Michelle. She sounded excited.

"Oh, hi, Michelle. I was hoping to hear from you."

"My father's coming today! I'm picking him up at the airport in an hour! He can only stay till Wednesday, but isn't that wonderful?"

"It sure is!" I thought quickly. "Michelle, I was wondering—I'd love to meet your dad. I know you both have a lot of catching up to do, but do you think you could stop by the library sometime tomorrow afternoon? I would so much like to meet him."

"Of course, Carrie. I don't see why not. Especially since I've got you to thank for getting us together in the first place."

Those can't be tears in Evelyn's eyes since ghosts don't cry. Must be the reflection of the overhead light.

"That's great! I'm looking forward to meeting him," I said, ending the call.

"Oh, Carrie! I'm so happy, I wish I could hug you!" Evelyn said.

"But you won't," I said, shivering at the thought.

"Of course not. And now I must let you get on with your library duties. After all, that's what you're being paid to do," she said as she faded away.

And leave me more curious than ever as to why you just have to see your brother Harold after all these years.

* * *

The rest of the day was quiet and uneventful. The pulse of the library had slowed down—probably because people took vacations in July and August or simply because it was summertime and they preferred being outdoors enjoying the warm weather. At any rate, fewer patrons attended daytime activities. Which could be why the library was closed on Sundays from Father's Day through Labor Day. Whatever the reason, I was happy to have Sundays off for the next two months. Since the newsletter was taken care of, I looked in on the few ongoing programs, then concentrated on the dreaded monthly financial report that was due next week.

Angela had offered to feed me barbecue leftovers for dinner that evening, but I thanked her and drove Smoky Joe home. After having a light dinner, I started out for Angela's place so we could go to Donna's house together.

Steve welcomed me with a hug. I followed him into the kitchen, where Angela was ending a phone conversation.

"That was my mom," she said. "She told me to thank you for investigating Aiden's murder and to please let her know if you've found out anything new."

"I only wish I had something worthwhile to report."

Angela grimaced. "John called the house earlier today wanting to know where Tommy was since he wasn't answering his cell. Mom got upset when John asked her to tell Tommy to call him ASAP but wouldn't say why. Now she's worried Tommy's in trouble with the law."

"You're John's good buddy," Steve said. "Has he told you anything about the case?"

"Nothing."

"Maybe we'll learn something important tonight." Angela kissed her husband and grabbed her bag. A minute later we were on our way to uncover what Aiden's home office might reveal.

Donna greeted us at the front door, her finger to her lips. "Ssh! I just got the kids into bed. If they see you they're going to want to come down and visit. I'll take you to Aiden's office, then go upstairs to read them a story."

Angela and I nodded and followed Donna. As we crossed the hall, a young voice called out, "Mommy, hurry up."

"Be right there, Liam!" Donna called back. "Pick out the book you want me to read."

"Two books!"

"Okay, then let your sister choose one too."

When Liam was out of sight, Donna let out a sigh. "How I miss my au pair Chloe. She flew home to France yesterday for a two-week vacation that was planned months ago. I'm counting the days till she returns."

She opened the door to Aiden's office and switched on the overhead lights. "I keep the door closed so the kids won't come in here."

And the shades are drawn as well, I noticed, glancing to my left at the two long windows facing the back lawn and, beyond that, the Sound. The wall opposite the doorway had built-in shelves filled with medical books and stacks of medical journals. Before it stood a large leather chair and a sleek modern desk, bare but for a laptop and a lamp. In the corner farthest from the windows stood two large metal cabinets.

A lounge chair and a magazine rack occupied the corner of the room to the right of the doorway. The wall facing the windows was covered with family photos and copies of Aiden's diplomas.

"I imagine Lieutenant Mathers has already looked through everything," I said.

"He had his IT guy go through Aiden's computer along with every paper and file in hopes of finding clues pointing to Aiden's killer. Everything's back the way it was."

I pointed to the file cabinets. "What did Aiden keep in them?"

Donna shrugged. "Records pertaining to the house and the cars. Old tax returns. There are files related to the practice—the rental lease, the partnership agreement. I glanced at them briefly. I'll have to go through every one of them when my accountant comes next week."

"You said Aiden was probably upset about something related to his practice," I said. "Did he bring home paperwork related to the office?"

"I don't think so. Why would he? Vera handled billing, payroll, appointments, and patients' records on the computer."

"Do you know if Lieutenant Mathers found anything helpful?" Angela asked.

"If he did, he didn't tell me."

"Mommy."

We all turned as little Emma, barefoot and in her nightgown, opened the door.

"Feel free to look around—not at my tax returns, of course, but anything else."

Donna carried Emma out of the office, and Angela and I got to work. "I'll check the computer and desk drawers. Why don't you go through the file cabinets?"

"Will do," Angela said.

The desk had two drawers—a narrow center drawer and a right side drawer about a foot wide and two feet deep. The top drawer was crammed with pens, staples, paper clips, rubber bands, and a row of stamps—the usual supplies expected to occupy a desk drawer. I collected a few pieces of paper and Post-its, which I placed on the desk top. Two had a name and telephone number on them. The others were old receipts.

The side drawer was used to hold larger items. There was an address book, a current appointment book, which I pulled out to study, a personal checkbook, several empty file folders, and a few envelopes. I opened the appointment book, which Aiden had used for personal engagements. I smiled to see he usually drew icons instead of writing down words: A drawing of a molar on a page in early June—no doubt a dental appointment. Another had the outline of a car. Inside the car was written "oil, lube, tires rotated."

I turned to the week in June when the poison had been administered. Three of the days before Angela and Steve's wedding had dollar signs next to large question marks. Okay. That meant he was concerned about expenses. Home expenses? Expenses Donna was maxing out? Or expenses related to the practice? It didn't say.

I turned to the week after the wedding. Monday's icon was a stick figure in a deerstalker bent over a magnifying glass. Next to it was a phone number. I felt a jolt in my solar plexus when I recognized Dylan's office number.

"Find anything?" I called out to Angela.

"I have the folder with a copy of Aiden and Nick Gannon's partner agreement, along with a copy of their lease."

"Anything else?"

"There's a folder filled with printouts of services the office billed for the past four months."

I walked over to take a look. "That sounds interesting."

"Okay, but what does it mean?" Angela asked as she handed me the folder.

"Maybe Vera overcharged some patients and pocketed the difference," I said as I rifled through the papers. "But Aiden hasn't made notations. Without seeing his charts or whatever records he and Nick keep, we can't possibly know if some expenses are bogus."

"My thoughts exactly," Angela said. "But why this folder?"

"I haven't checked out his computer yet," I said. "Maybe he created a document where he goes through these charges. But before I start, I'm going to need to find a bathroom."

"There must be one close by," Angela said.

I left the office and walked down the short hall and stopped at the first door. Sure enough, it was a small powder room—just large enough for a toilet, a small sink and a tiny stand that held a sprig of dried flowers. I was about to step inside when I heard Donna's voice coming from the kitchen at the end of the hall. She was speaking to someone on the telephone. There was a secretive tone to her voice that made me curious.

"Really? That's so sweet." She laughed, a seductive, intimate laugh.

I edged closer to the kitchen, not wanting to miss one word of the conversation.

"Of course I've been thinking about you, but I haven't—" Then sharper, "if you'll remember, I recently lost my husband."

Pause. "No, the police aren't any closer to finding his killer. If you ask me, I think it's my ape of a cousin. He was furious when Aiden decided not to put money in his movie. I told Aiden that Tommy was a loose cannon and he listened to me. My husband was brilliant but gullible. If I didn't put a stop to some of the things people wanted him to invest in we'd be living in a hovel."

So she knows more about the family's finances than she claims.

Silence as Donna listened to her caller.

"Impossible. My au pair's away, and I can't leave the kids alone . . . No, you can't come here!"

I peered around to catch a glimpse of Donna. She paced as she listened, her lips pursed. Finally, she said, "I can meet you tomorrow when the kids are in day camp."

A smile bloomed. "I'm afraid that will have to wait."

Pause.

"Until I let you know. Jeez, I just buried my husband."

Donna cocked her head from side to side as her caller ranted. Finally, she said, "I'm sorry, but meeting at the museum is the best I can do right now. Unless you'd rather not."

Pause.

"Of course I miss you."

Pause.

"Me, too." A little laugh. "Then shall we say eleven thirty, a half hour before the museum opens? We can walk through the grounds as usual. And I'm hoping they have a new exhibit of paintings."

The conversation was winding down. I hurried to the bathroom and splashed cold water on my face.

So Donna has a lover! Why was I so surprised? She was a beautiful, vibrant woman in her prime stuck in a marriage that had gone stale. Her husband had found someone else, why shouldn't she?

The list of suspects had suddenly grown longer. If Donna had thought so little of her marriage vows, maybe she was the person who had murdered Aiden, after all. Or maybe her lover, whoever he was, had killed Aiden. From the little I'd just heard, he'd been the more eager of the two to get together.

They'd made arrangements to meet at a museum tomorrow. I had no idea which museum, but I intended to find out.

*   *   *

Angela's mouth fell open when I reported what I'd overheard. I put my finger to my lips and quickly added, "I know. It's a lot to take in, but we'll talk about it later." I was whispering, even though I'd closed the door to Aiden's office. I didn't want Donna to find out we knew about her affair.

Angela nodded. "You're right, but my head is spinning. My mother used to call Donna and Aiden the perfect couple."

The computer wasn't password-protected so I was able to glance through the list of Aiden's recent documents and downloads. He even kept a document labeled "passwords" so there was no difficulty getting into his personal files, his Facebook page, even his emails.

After a half hour of going through document after document, I gave up. "There's nothing here that relates to the practice."

"What about his emails?" Angela asked.

"There are a few to and from Nick in which Aiden tells Nick in no uncertain terms that he won't even consider expanding the practice until certain issues are resolved—I have no idea what he's referring to. Aiden writes in one of the last emails that he wants them to meet. Nick says sure."

"Anything else?"

"There are email exchanges with Roxy. The ones from Aiden are short and supportive. Roxy's fall into three categories: depression, anger at Miles, and excessive gratitude toward Aiden for being so caring."

I turned off the computer, and we went to look for Donna. We found her in the kitchen, talking on her cell phone again. She gestured to us to sit down while she continued speaking. Finally, she ended the call a few minutes later.

"Sorry. That was my lawyer. I needed his input regarding a few matters and he filled me in on some others that require my attention." She shook her head. "I had no idea things could be so complicated."

What an accomplished liar you are, I thought as I spun out my own fib. "I'm sorry. I suppose Aiden took care of everything financial."

"He did," Donna said. "My accountant sat me down last week and started explaining things to me. At first it seemed like a jumble of numbers with all sorts of rules and regulations, but I'm catching on.

"Would you like some coffee? I'm eager to find out if you learned anything helpful."

Angela and I exchanged glances. "Sure," I said. "That would be lovely."

Donna started a pot of coffee—regular, we all agreed—and placed a platter of cake on the table. "People have been so kind—bringing over casseroles and desserts. I have enough to feed the kids and me for months."

When we were seated at the table, she asked, "So, what did you learn?"

"Nothing very new or revealing," I said.

"Aiden printed out pages of office charges, but we have no idea why or what they mean," Angela said

"I could ask Vera or Nick," Donna said.

"I wouldn't do that," I said quickly.

"No, I suppose that wouldn't be wise," Donna said.

"Where's Aiden's cell phone?" Angela asked. "Then we'd know who he called and texted."

"Unfortunately, the police still have it. I'll be getting it back soon."

I drank the last of my coffee and shook my head when Donna asked if I'd like more. "Aiden wanted to see Dylan, which means he was possibly concerned about something illegal. Is there any place where he might have hidden papers or a flash drive?"

Donna made a scoffing sound. "Why would he? Aiden knew I didn't take an interest in the business end of his practice. Though I must admit, I once checked his email and read all those pathetic messages that Roxy sent him."

Roxy. "Frankie mentioned that Miles asked you to intercede for him to try to convince Roxy to give him another chance," I said.

Donna raised her eyebrows. "She did, did she? My little sister should learn not to talk about things that don't concern her."

"Come on, Donna, the family's worried about Roxy," Angela said. "From what I've heard, she was very happy when she was married to Miles."

"Miles is a great guy," Donna said, frowning. "Aiden considered him his best friend. He's generous and supportive, but though he claimed to love Roxy, he ran around."

"I didn't know that at the time," Angela said, "but then I wasn't close to Roxy." She thought a minute. "Did you know?"

Donna shrugged. "I guess. Aiden knew and one day it slipped out."

"How did Roxy find out?" I asked.

Donna gnawed at her lower lip. "I thought she should know what her husband was up to."

So Donna told Roxy and Roxy divorced Miles and turned to Aiden. "Did Roxy resent you?" I asked.

"Of course not! Why should she? I only told her what she had a right to know."

Time to change the subject. "Donna, please think. Aiden was worried about something, and it might very well be connected to the practice, but we didn't find any evidence of it in his office. Where would Aiden put something he didn't want anyone to see?"

Donna threw up her hands. "I have no idea."

"Let's try to figure this out. Aiden was planning to call Dylan a day or two after Angela's wedding and probably set up an appointment. Could he have put a folder or papers in a brief case and left it in his car?"

"We can check, though I think Lieutenant Mathers examined both cars."

We went into the garage and looked through Aiden's Lexus. There was no sign of a large envelope or briefcase that could hold a folder.

"What about a flash drive?" Angela asked.

"He used them occasionally," Donna said. "He said this way he didn't have to clog up his computer."

Now she tells us! "Let's check the pockets and crannies in the car," I said.

The three of us looked for a small flash drive in every possible compartment. We even checked the ashtray. No flash drive.

"Sometimes he kept one on his key chain," Donna said.

"Where are his keys?"

Back in the house, Donna led us to the front hall. She stuck her hand in the small bowl on the narrow table and pulled out a bunch of keys. On the ring was the very thing we'd hoped to find.

"Finally!" I said, holding up the flash drive. "Now we're getting somewhere."

Chapter
Twenty-Three

Angela drove like a madwoman to her condo. We ran inside and she slipped the flash drive into her laptop. Of course we'd offered to view it on the computer in Aiden's office, but Donna said she was exhausted and would never be able to fall asleep after learning what was on it. Most likely she was planning to call her boyfriend back as soon as we left. We said one of us would call her in the morning to tell her what was on the flash drive and hand it over to John Mathers.

Angela and I peered at the screen as we ran through the contents of the flash drive. There was only one document, and that seemed to run on for pages.

"What is this?" I asked.

The Excel spreadsheet was filled with a listing of names, dates, diagnoses, and numbers. Then two columns of numbers running side by side. Below it was a list of eight or ten treatments or diagnoses and a figure after it.

"Patients' names," Angela muttered, "and their diagnoses."

"I think the columns reflect what each patient was billed!" I said.

"Why two columns then?" Angela said.

I studied the two rows of numbers. In each case, the number in the second column was higher than the first. I thought a bit. Could it be? I scrolled down to the last part of the document, jotted down the various numbers after each diagnosis, then scrolled back up.

"What are you doing?" Angela asked.

"Figuring out if the difference between the numbers in column A and column B add up to the numbers at the bottom of the document."

"I'll do it, too," Angela said.

A minute later we grinned at each other and slapped a high five.

"That's what was troubling Aiden!" Angela said. "Someone in that office was padding the bills."

"It sure looks that way," I said. "It must have been going on for a few months, at least."

Angela smiled. "Could be Aiden mentioned it to Nick or Vera, and whichever of the two was behind the scam killed him to shut him up." Her smile faded. "At least, that's what I'm hoping. This new development doesn't let my relatives off the hook, especially Donna."

We went over the telephone conversation I'd overheard, carefully and in great detail.

"So, she's had this lover—whose identity we don't know—for some time," Donna summed up. "And she's the one responsible for changing Aiden's mind about backing my brother's movie."

"Seems she had a good handle on Aiden's blind spot and knew more than she let on about their finances," I said.

"Then why did she bother to have us come over and look at Aiden's records?" Angela asked.

The answer came to her before I could speak. "To make herself look innocent."

I nodded. "Donna figured we'd only find what the police had already seen."

"But she didn't know about the flash drive—or did she?"

"I don't know. But she didn't seem concerned. Right now I'm more interested in finding the museum where she's planning to meet her lover."

"That should be easy," Angela said. "A museum that's in the vicinity, has woods on its property, is open on Tuesdays, and opens at noon."

I patted her shoulder. "Gee, Mrs. Prisco. You've turned into one shrewd detective."

Steve wandered into the room. "You're still at it?" he asked.

"Almost done," Angela said. She returned to what she was tapping out on her laptop. A minute later she let out a shriek. "I have it!"

She turned the screen to face me. "Horlick House. A seventeenth-century stone house converted into an art museum. Wonderful walking paths on the property."

"Yes, I believe this is it." I sent the website to my phone. "It's not far from Clover Ridge. I can make their rendezvous and get to work in plenty of time. It's a late day for me."

"I could change my schedule and come with you," Angela offered.

I shook my head. "No, one of us will be less conspicuous. Even if I get there fifteen minutes early, it's going to be tricky keeping out of sight."

I removed the flash drive and slipped it into my bag. "Meanwhile, I'll drop this off at the precinct tomorrow."

"And I'll call Donna and tell her what we found," Angela said.

"See you tomorrow," she said, stifling a yawn as we hugged good night.

It was after eleven o'clock when I started for home, my head spinning with everything we'd learned this evening. I decided to wait until the following morning to tell Dylan about our discoveries. Though I couldn't swear that the names belonged to patients and that one column listed actual charges and the other the inflated charges that were sent to Medicare and insurance companies, it was the only thing that made sense. I chuckled. It was John's job to check it out as well as to find the guilty party.

Since there wasn't much traffic that late in the evening, I drove on autopilot as I mused over a new set of questions. Had Aiden been poisoned because he'd confronted the person responsible for the fraud? Why wasn't Donna more curious to learn what was on the flash drive? I wondered about Roxy and whether she'd consider taking Miles back. The age-old questions: Could he really change? Was she better off without him?

When I glanced in the rearview mirror, I recognized a dark sedan that had been behind me earlier. I'd noticed it a few times now. *No big deal*, I told myself, especially since it had turned onto the parkway right after I did. We were driving at the same rate of speed, so it wasn't surprising that it continued to remain close to me.

I changed lanes. The other driver changed lanes. A frisson of fear snaked down my back. Was Aiden's murderer following me? *Don't be ridiculous!* I told myself. *No one knows where I've been.*

No one but Angela's relatives, who knew I was looking into Aiden's murder and was spending the evening poring through Aiden's papers and computer.

And some of them were suspects.

I floored the gas pedal. The car sped up. I slowed down. The car slowed down too. The exit before mine was fifty feet ahead. I veered off the parkway, hoping this was the end of it. The car stayed on my tail.

I drove back onto the highway and sighed with relief when I saw no sign of the other car. But as I approached my exit, it loomed behind me. I glanced in my rearview mirror as the car passed beneath the street lamp, but the light was too dim for me to make out if a man or a woman was at the wheel.

Frantic, I called Dylan. He picked up immediately.

"There's a car tailing me home from Angela's!"

"Where are you?"

"Turning off at our exit."

"Is he getting off, too?"

I looked. "Yes. What should I do?"

"Keep on driving. I'll call John and wait for you outside my house."

"Okay. It's a dark sedan. I can't tell you anything about the driver."

"Don't worry. Just get here safely."

The Avery property was two miles from the parkway exit. I was breathing heavily as I drove onto the private road. Surely, my pursuer wouldn't dare follow me here! The manor house was several hundred feet down the road. I glanced in the rearview mirror. No headlights shone behind me. There was no sign of the car that had been following me.

I pulled into the semicircular driveway in front of the house where Dylan was waiting. Judging by the dazzling brightness, he must have switched on every light, inside and out. I threw open my car door and ran into his arms.

* * *

Minutes later I was sitting in my kitchen with Dylan and John. Smoky Joe must have sensed I was upset because he'd leaped onto my lap, where he remained purring and occasionally licking my hand. Dylan handed me a shot of Scotch, which I only kept in the house for guests. "Sip it slowly."

The strong, pleasant liquor slid down my throat.

"There's no sign of the car that followed you," John said. "Unfortunately, there aren't any security cameras on the parkway between here and Angela's condo."

"Who knew you and Angela were going to Donna's house?" Dylan asked.

"You and Steve, of course. Rosemary, Angela's mother. I have no idea which family members she and Donna might have told—they're all very close."

Dylan and John exchanged glances. "So Roxy might have known," Dylan said. "And Miles, if she's in touch with him. And Tommy."

John fixed his attention on me. "Bad as it is, I'm thinking this unknown person was out to frighten you, not harm you. Maybe he or she figured you were onto something, though I can't imagine what it might be. Danny and I combed Aiden's home office. We're still going through his cell phone."

I squirmed, not knowing why *I* was feeling guilty. "We didn't find anything there either, so I asked Donna where else Aiden might have hidden information. She said Aiden occasionally used flash drives. We found one on his key chain. We took it to Angela's house and viewed it on her laptop. From what we could tell, it might be a record of medical fraud."

John's mouth fell open. Before he started to lecture me, I added, "I was going to bring you the flash drive tomorrow." I stood. "I'll get it for you now."

When I returned a minute later, both John and Dylan were laughing.

"What's so funny?" I asked. "It's not my fault you didn't bother to ask Donna a few pertinent questions."

John reached over to slip his arm around my waist. "Carrie, sometimes I get the urge to lock you in one of my two cells. Other times I'd like to hire you."

"Really?" Flattered, I handed him the flash drive.

"For your information, Mrs. Harrington wasn't available when we searched her husband's home office, so we never got the chance to ask for her input."

"I don't suppose you'll fill me in about what you'll be doing with this evidence."

"You suppose right," John said, getting to his feet. "I'll be talking to you and Angela if I have any questions."

"You know where we'll be," I said, walking him to the door. "Thanks for coming out tonight. Made me feel safer."

I returned to the kitchen where Dylan was surveying the inside of my fridge. He opened the fruit bin and removed a handful of cherries.

"I thought I'd stay tonight, in case you were feeling nervous," he said over the running water as he rinsed the cherries in a strainer.

"Thanks, I'd like that."

"Me too."

Later, as I was drifting off to sleep, I realized that amid the turmoil of last night's events, I'd forgotten to tell John and Dylan about Donna's conversation with her lover. Oh well, I could always tell them tomorrow—after I stopped by Horlick House.

*　*　*

When I woke up Tuesday morning, Dylan had already left. The cottage felt empty and I was aware that, except for Smoky Joe, I was alone. I shuddered as the memory of someone tailing me home filled my head. Maybe going to spy on Donna and her lover wasn't such a great idea after all.

I fed Smoky Joe, had my breakfast, and decided to make my double-fudge brownies for Aunt Harriet and Uncle Bosco's barbecue on Thursday. The act of doing something domestic calmed me considerably and I decided to go ahead with my plan.

After I slid the brownie batter into the oven, I called Angela at the library.

"I called Donna to tell her what was on the flash drive," Angela said. "But she didn't answer her phone. I left her a message to call me."

"She doesn't sound very eager to find out what we learned," I said. "Meanwhile, someone followed me home from your house last night."

"Oh, no! How scary. Did you see who it was?"

"No. John and Dylan came by. John's going to see if there were any security cameras on my route home. I gave him the flash drive."

"Who could have known you were at my house last night?" Angela said.

"I hate to say it, but the only people who knew we were going to Donna's house together—"

"Were members of my family," Angela finished for me. "I'm so sorry, Carrie."

"Not your fault."

"Are you still planning to go to Horlick House?" Angela asked, her voice lowered. "I mean, after someone tailed you home."

"I am."

"Stay safe and let me know what you find out ASAP."

"Of course."

A few minutes later, I was leaving the house when Michelle called on my cell phone. In the tumult of the latest events, I'd forgotten that I'd asked her to stop by the library today.

"How did yesterday go?" I asked her.

"Not quite as I expected," she said. "I was so looking forward to seeing my father, I didn't realize how angry I was at him—for abandoning us the way he did. I really let him have it."

"Oh." So much for happy endings. "Did he leave?"

"No, he sat there and took it. And when I was finished he apologized. After that we talked—about his gambling problem, my life, his life—until three in the morning."

"You must be exhausted. I understand if you won't have time to stop by the library."

"On the contrary. Dad wants to thank you for helping me. He'd like to take you to lunch."

"That's sweet of him, Michelle, but today's my late day and I'll be getting to the library at one thirty. Why don't the two of you have lunch, then stop by for half an hour or so? Does that work for you?"

"Sure. We don't have anything solid planned this afternoon. How does two, two thirty sound?"

"Fine. If I'm not in my office, my assistant Trish will know how to find me."

"Then we'll see you later." Michelle lowered her voice. "In addition to what he's already given me, Dad's going to pay whatever other expenses I have until I'm back on my feet."

"I'm glad—for both of you."

Now it was up to Evelyn to show up so she could witness her brother's visit.

Chapter
Twenty-Four

Horlick House was a fifteen-minute drive from my cottage. I arrived a little after eleven o'clock—plenty of time to check out the area and find a place to hide when Donna and her lover arrived. I parked at the far end of the parking lot and walked over to the house. It was made of stone and appeared to be well preserved. It would be a lovely place to visit with Dylan one day.

I noticed a small wooden structure, covered but open to the elements, and figured that had information regarding the acres of land behind the house. Sure enough, along with the listing of rules and regulations for how to behave in the park there was a large map showing the various trails.

A car pulled up, startling me, but I relaxed when I saw a man and a boy of about ten get out of the car and start down one of the trails. The father waved to me as they passed.

"Beautiful day, isn't it?" he said.

"Sure is," I agreed.

I decided to wait for Donna and Mr. X behind a group of trees. I hadn't gotten there a moment too soon, when a man Dylan's age pulled into the lot in a Camry. He got out of his car, looked around, then reached for his cell phone. He looked familiar, though I couldn't remember his name or where I'd seen him—most likely in the library. He paced nervously as he spoke on his phone.

A few minutes later, Donna drove up in her Mercedes. Her lover ran over to her. I watched them hug, look around to see if anyone was in the vicinity, then embrace and kiss passionately.

"I've missed you so much," he said.

"I missed you too," Donna said, not as fervently. "Shall we walk?"

I noticed she was wearing sneakers and a loose T-shirt over bicycle shorts while Mr. X was dressed for the office. He nodded and fell into step beside her

I had no choice but to follow them. The path they had chosen had woods on both sides. I couldn't trail behind them. They'd spot me immediately. I glanced to my left and noticed the start of a very narrow path. If I remained silent, I could walk on this parallel path and hopefully hear what they had to say to each other.

I grinned as Donna picked up the pace and Mr. X began to trail behind. Was she here for a romantic rendezvous or out for some exercise? Or was she intent on making a point?

"Hey, slow down," he complained. "I want to be with you, not race you."

"You need to get into shape. I told you to join a gym."

After they continued in this manner for what seemed to be two blocks, Donna took pity on him and pointed to a bench. "Let's sit down."

I was as happy as Mr. X to hear this. I crept closer in order to make out their words.

Donna let him draw her into his arms for another passionate kiss. When she pulled away, he appeared puzzled. "Hey, what gives? Are you mad at me?"

"Of course not. Why would I be mad at you?"

"You seem so different from before. So—distant. When you need me now more than ever."

"I need you?" Donna laughed. "What makes you think I need you now . . . more than ever?"

"Because now you're alone. Your husband died."

"Yes, Aiden is dead. Someone murdered him." Donna narrowed her eyes. "Did you do it?"

"Me?" The guy looked shocked. "Why would I murder Aiden?"

"So you could have me to yourself."

I stared at Donna. Did she think this man had poisoned Aiden? Had she told John about this person in her life? Somehow I didn't think so, since John had never so much as hinted that they were looking at another suspect. Donna had managed to keep her affair under wraps. I felt a pang of guilt for not telling John about Donna's lover last night.

Or was Donna simply a wonderful actress and actually the person who had poisoned her husband? Once again, I remembered there was good reason why the spouse was always the first suspect in a homicide case. She had motive and opportunity, and thallium wasn't difficult to get hold of.

Donna's lover rallied, proving he wasn't the pushover I'd originally taken him for. "Don't be ridiculous. I'm not the murdering kind," he scoffed.

"No? I seem to remember you swearing you would do anything to have me."

The sidelong glance he threw Donna was close to a sneer. "Please. That was in the heat of the moment."

I wanted to cheer him on. Until I heard Donna's next words.

"Come on, Brad. You left your wife for me, remember?"

Shocked, I bit my lip to keep from yelling at the lowlife. No wonder he looked familiar. I'd seen his photo on Michelle Forbes's Facebook page. This was Bradley Forbes, her errant husband!

Brad nodded. "I admit it. I left her because I was crazy about you. Have been since the day we met."

"That was so odd, running into you at Aiden's office, since I hardly ever went there. But there you were, Vera's nephew. New to the neighborhood."

Vera's nephew? All these revelations were making my head spin.

Donna suddenly turned nervous. "Vera doesn't know about us, does she?"

"Are you kidding? I love my aunt, but she's the biggest blabbermouth. I like to keep my life private."

"Good," Donna said. "It's better that way," she murmured.

"I fell for you on the spot." Brad looked at her beseechingly. "From the way you acted, I thought you felt the same way."

"I enjoyed our time together, but things are different now that Aiden's gone."

Brad stroked her arm. "We can have a great life together, Donna. We'll get married. I'll even adopt your children."

Donna leaned back and shook her beautiful mane of hair. "I don't want to get married again, at least not for a long time. I'll have enough money from Aiden's life insurance policy and the practice. I'll be fine on my own." She gave a little laugh. "And if I need more to keep up the house, I'll get a job."

"If it's money you're worried about, I'm doing fine." Brad smirked. "Especially with that little sideline I have going at the insurance company where Aunt Vera got me the job."

Donna's head jerked up. "What sideline?"

Brad studied her face for a minute then smiled. "Just business. Nothing for you to bother your pretty head about."

Donna shrugged, losing interest. "Whatever."

They were silent for a minute while I pondered what I'd just learned. Vera must have gotten Brad a job at one of the insurance companies she dealt with, where he was in a position to approve the medical office's bloated expenses.

Donna seemed not to know or care to know what Brad was talking about. How fortuitous it was that she hadn't answered her phone when Angela called to tell her what was on Aiden's flash drive. I was pretty sure she knew nothing about the medical fraud.

She reached out to take Brad's hand. "I wanted us to meet today because I owe it to you to say what I have to say in person. You've been so sweet." Donna stroked his face. "I couldn't have gotten through the last few months if I didn't have our meetings to look forward to."

"Are you saying what I think you're saying?" Brad's voice rose with every word. "You're dumping me, just like that?"

The smile she gave him was bittersweet. "It was fun while it lasted, but my life has changed drastically. I have other priorities now."

"Priorities? What other priorities?" he demanded.

But Donna didn't hear him. She'd already set off jogging down the path.

* * *

I drove slowly back to my cottage, trying to wrap my head around everything I'd just learned. Donna. Brad. Vera. Michelle. All these connections. Not that it pointed a finger at any one suspect.

And it's not my job. For once, I was glad it was John's job to take it from here. John. I drew a deep breath and exhaled loudly as I called him on my cell phone. It went to voice mail. I said it was important, and he called back just as I'd turned onto the Avery private road.

"I have something to tell you," I said, "but I need your word that you won't lecture me when I'm done."

"All right. Spill it."

I slowed down as I approached my cottage. "It seems Donna Harrington has a lover. I mean *had* a lover. She broke it off a short while ago."

John was good as his word, literally, if not in spirit. I ignored his snorts as I told him about the call I'd overheard last night and today's meeting I'd witnessed.

"The guy's name is Bradley Forbes. He's Vera Ghent's nephew. She got him a job at an insurance company, and it sounds like he's involved in the medical fraud scheme."

"Anything else you care to share?" John barked.

"Hey, easy there," I said. "You said you wouldn't lecture me."

"I am *not* lecturing you. You'll know when I lecture you about doing stupid things that can land you in the morgue!"

"That's all I have for you," I said quickly and disconnected.

John was pissed, but he'd get over it.

Chapter Twenty-Five

I fed Smoky Joe, ate a quick lunch, and headed for work. So much had happened this morning, I'd almost forgotten that Michelle and her father were stopping by. Evelyn made an appearance the moment I entered the library. Poor Smoky Joe let out a howl as I released him from his carrier. Being in Evelyn's presence always spooked him. Cool cat that he was, he immediately regained his composure and, tail in the air, trotted off to visit with patrons.

"We have to find a place where we can talk," Evelyn instructed. She knew that Trish worked till midafternoon and was probably in my office.

"Sure, soon as I drop off the cat carrier."

I greeted Trish, told her I'd be back in a few minutes, and joined Evelyn, who was hovering outside my door.

"Let's go downstairs to the supply closet," I said. "Nobody hangs out there."

As we headed for the staircase, Mabel Obsprey, a talkative patron, stopped to ask me when they were planning to start work on the new library addition.

"In September. I'm not sure of the date."

"I hope the library won't have to close," she said.

"Almost all the construction work will be outside this building. I don't know if they plan to close the library when they link the two buildings. But I'm afraid there will be a good deal of noise at times."

"That's too bad. Speaking of noise, they've already started shooting off fireworks to celebrate the Fourth. Last night I couldn't fall asleep until well past midnight."

Evelyn exhaled her annoyance, a sound only I could hear.

"Excuse me, Mabel, but I really must take care of something."

"Don't let me keep you, Carrie." She smiled and went on her way.

When we reached the supply closet, I switched on the light and glanced around before closing the door behind me. It was a good-sized space with shelves that were well stocked with various stationery items, paper goods, even a few old printers and computers. I leaned against the shelves facing the door and nodded to Evelyn. "Okay. Talk."

"When are Harold and Michelle coming?" she asked.

"Very soon. Within the hour."

Evelyn beamed. "I can't wait to see him."

"Why?"

She blinked several times, as if I'd offended her. "Why? Because he's my brother."

"There's more to this story." I pursed my lips. "After finding Harold and arranging to have him come here so you can see him, I think I'm entitled to know."

"Yes, you are." Instead of looking annoyed, there was a glint of admiration in her eyes. "You're entitled to know why I must see for myself that Harold is well and happy."

I waited.

Evelyn cleared her throat. "The last time I saw my brother, I'm afraid I wasn't very kind or charitable. He was desperate and wanted me to lend him a large sum of money to pay back the money he'd taken.

"I talked it over with my husband that evening, and Bob was adamant that I not give him a cent. He said gamblers threw away their own money along with whatever they could beg, borrow, or steal. Bob said we couldn't afford to make Harold a gift of that much money because we'd never see it again. I must have felt the same deep down because I didn't argue. I called Harold to tell him we couldn't help him. The next day he was gone."

Evelyn looked so sad, I wished I could comfort her with a hug. "And you feel responsible. For him taking off and leaving his family."

She shrugged. "I didn't make him gamble away the money and I never would have told him to take it from a client, but he's my brother and I didn't help him."

"Bob was right. You never would have seen that money again. You weren't in a position to cover his debt."

"My sister told me the same thing. He'd asked Frieda for money too, but she had no problem saying she couldn't afford to pay his gambling debts. Still, he's my baby brother. I can't help feeling I should have done something to help him."

I smiled. "I think it's time you stopped feeling guilty and gave yourself credit for helping your niece *and* your brother. Michelle is starting over with many options in front of her, and Harold has his daughter back in his life."

"I suppose I could look at it that way."

"Please do." I grinned. "And now I have another surprise for you. One you're going to really appreciate."

"Really? Do tell."

When I finished telling Evelyn how upset Bradley Forbes had looked after Donna broke up with him, she was laughing uproariously. "How fitting," she commented when she could speak.

"And it looks like he'll be up on criminal charges as well."

"Getting what he deserves."

"Now let's go upstairs so we'll be in my office when your brother and his daughter pay us a visit."

* * *

Donald, or Lee as he preferred I call him, turned out to be a pleasant man in his sixties. He kept telling me how grateful he was that I'd managed to track him down and reunite him with Michelle. His love for his daughter was obvious.

"I want Michelle to come to Albuquerque to meet my new family. I know they'll love her."

"I will, Dad. I promise. But first I have to get settled in my new job."

"Of course. I understand," Lee said, then he turned to me. "I know I'm no one to talk, but I'm furious at that miserable excuse of a husband—deserting Michelle the way he did."

"I don't blame you," I said.

Michelle touched her father's arm. "Dad, don't get worked up over Brad. I'm better off without him. Besides, Mr. Talbot will deal with him. Then I want to divorce him as quickly as I can."

Lee patted her hand. "Honey, I don't mean to cause you any more grief, but that creep deserves a kick in the butt. Not a free pass to take up with some other woman."

While Michelle calmed her father down, Evelyn and I exchanged knowing glances. *Yes, Mr. Bradley Forbes. You'll be getting what's coming to you!*

Michelle and Lee left shortly after, and Evelyn and I rehashed my conversation with them. I'd never seen her so happy. She didn't stop beaming, even as she began to fade.

"Thank you, Carrie. I'll always remember this afternoon." She blew me a kiss as she disappeared from sight, and I finally settled down to do some work.

Chapter
Twenty-Six

John called me on my cell later that afternoon. *Here comes the lecture*, I thought. But he'd called to tell me they'd found the person who had been tailing me the previous night.

"Sorry, Carrie. It was Tommy Vecchio."

I got a sinking sensation in my stomach.

"Turns out there was a camera, after all, and it caught the license plate. Belonged to a rented car, which was easy enough to trace."

"He must have followed me from Angela's house. But why?"

"He claims he was out for a drive and happened to be near his sister's place when you left. He just happened to be going in the same direction that you were."

"Yeah! Practically right to my door."

"Do you want to press charges?" John asked.

I sighed. "Well, he scared me, all right, though he didn't actually harm me. But I don't want to have to worry if he's going to bother me again while he's in Clover Ridge. What do you think I should do, John?"

He sighed. "You'll save yourself a lot of time and grief by not pressing charges. Let me deal with Tommy Boy. I don't think he'll be bothering you after that."

"Thanks, John." I paused for a minute, then asked, "Have you gotten a chance to follow up on the information that's on the flash drive?"

"If it is what you and Angela figured it to be—and I think you're right—then regarding the homicide, this goes to possible motive. Still, it's not proof that anyone in that office poisoned Dr. Harrington. As for the fraudulent charges, I've notified the Health Care Fraud Unit. They'll investigate their own way in their own time frame."

"And they'll check out Bradley Forbes's role in all this?"

"I've added his name to the report. And of course I'll be interviewing him myself. As the homicide victim's wife's lover, he's now a person of interest. Mrs. Harrington was very remiss not to mention him."

I smiled, thinking, *And you'll tell her so in no uncertain terms.*

"Thanks for that piece of information. You did good, Carrie."

And with that, I knew that John had forgiven me for taking a risk.

* * *

The rest of my work day was uneventful. I had the Cozy Country Café deliver one of their wonderful salads for my dinner and treated myself to a cappuccino in the library's coffee shop. As I drove home, I kept on the lookout for a car that might be following me. Thank goodness there weren't any. However John dealt with Tommy must have taken effect. When I arrived at my cottage I discovered I was thoroughly exhausted. And so, after feeding Smoky Joe some treats, I called Dylan one last time—having brought him up to date earlier—and crept into bed for an early night.

*   *   *

The jingle of my cell phone woke me from a deep sleep. It went on for a minute or two until I had the coordination and presence of mind to reach for it on my night stand and croak a sleepy "Hello."

"Carrie, Roxy was in an accident. She's dead." Angela sounded as upset as I'd ever heard her. And no wonder. Another member of her family was gone.

"I'm so sorry, Ange. What happened?"

"She was driving last night and crashed into the ravine near her apartment."

I shuddered as I remembered the car tailing me home the night before. I hadn't yet told Angela that it was Tommy who had followed me home, and now wasn't the time. Though it made me wonder if he was responsible for this latest death.

"Was it really an accident or does John think someone ran her off the road?"

"Two witnesses saw her weaving all over the road. John said they'll do a tox screen to check to see if she was drunk or high."

Roxy had definitely been under the influence at Aiden's memorial service. "How sad."

"John is considering it a suspicious death," Angela said, "given Aiden's murder and Roxy's close connection to him."

"I get his reasoning, but who would want to murder Roxy?"

"Carrie, don't be naïve."

"You're not thinking Donna would—"

I held the phone away as Angela exhaled loudly into my ear. "I don't know what to think. I'll be in late to work today. Soon as I get dressed, I'm driving over to Uncle Dominic's. Mom asked me to pick him up and bring him to the house. She doesn't want him being alone at a time like this."

I disconnected. Since it was six o'clock and Smoky Joe was nudging me to get out of bed, I decided to do just that and get an early start on the day.

Poor Roxy, I thought as I brushed my teeth, then stepped into the shower. She seemed so desperately unhappy. First her husband betrayed her, then she'd had the bad judgment to fall for her cousin's husband, whose kindness she'd misinterpreted as romantic interest. She'd been drinking a lot these past several months and might have finally resorted to taking drugs to cope with her overpowering emotions. Drink or drugs, one of them had killed her in the end. Death by misadventure.

Or was someone else responsible? I mused as I got dressed. Had the person who had poisoned Aiden also driven Roxy to her death? Two deaths in one family was . . . downright suspicious.

I fed Smoky Joe, then put on a pot of coffee and slid a slice of bread into the toaster oven for my breakfast. Now that my mind was in better working order, I realized that Roxy's sudden death didn't necessarily mean that she hadn't murdered Aiden. If Gwen, Aiden's lover, was to be believed, Aiden had rebuffed Roxy's advances. In Roxy's disturbed mind that might very well count as another betrayal by a man she trusted.

I was about to call Dylan when he called to tell me that the local TV channel was airing a segment about Roxy's car crash. I ran to the TV but only caught the tail end of it. I'd watch it later as they were sure to run it several times throughout the day.

I called Dylan back and asked if he thought someone had caused Roxy's so-called accident.

"Difficult to say. From the looks of it, she was high on something and driving erratically, finally crashing into the ravine. On the other hand, she was close to Aiden, who was poisoned. John will look very closely into Roxy's death. Don't be surprised if he stops by for a chat."

"Why would he?" I asked. "Roxy never confided in me."

"No, but you've been in her orbit these past few weeks and you're in touch with her family members. Besides, John admires your powers of observation and deduction."

I felt myself swell with pride. "Did he say that?"

"Let's just say, he wouldn't bother talking to you about his cases if he didn't value your input."

* * *

John didn't call or stop by, which meant he was chasing down more important leads. Nor did I hear from Angela again. She finally stopped by my office around three o'clock, looking frazzled.

"I went with my dad and Uncle Dominic to ID the body at the morgue. I didn't go in, of course. Still, it was awful. Uncle Dominic was in a bad way when we brought him back to the house. Aunt Marie came over and she and my mother comforted him as best they could."

"I'm so sorry," I said. "Did John question anyone in your family?"

"My cousin Donna. She stopped by my parents' house just as I was leaving. It turns out she and Roxy had a heart-to-heart yesterday afternoon and got everything out of their systems. She forgave Roxy for what she'd said at Aiden's memorial service and Roxy apologized for turning Aiden into her private therapist."

"So, according to Donna, she and Roxy patched things up."

"Right. She was really broken up about losing Roxy. She told John that Roxy never did drugs, though she drank too much when she was upset. And Roxy wasn't at all upset when she left. In fact, she'd suddenly turned into a woman with a mission. Donna said Roxy told her that something made sense now—like pieces of a puzzle fitting—and she was going to find out if she was right."

"Whatever she realized must have come out of their discussion," I said.

"You'd think, but Donna had no idea what triggered it. She said Roxy's mind often jumped from subject to subject without rhyme or reason. But she loved her dearly and now she has to cope with two losses."

"Very sad for everyone in your family." I hesitated, then said what was on my mind. "Angela, it was Tommy who followed me home from your house the other night. They caught him on a security camera."

"Oh, no! I'm so sorry, Carrie." Her apologetic expression quickly changed to anger and she uttered a word I'd never heard her say before. "I hope they throw him in jail!"

"John's going to talk to him, if he hasn't already."

"He deserves more than a lecture and a slap on the wrist." Angela glanced at her watch. "I'd better get moving. I told Fran I'd relieve her at three o'clock and it's a quarter past."

She flew out of the office and was immediately replaced by Evelyn, who took up her favorite spot, the corner of my assistants' desk.

"So, there's been another murder in Angela's family."

I nodded. "Looks that way."

"Interesting—if you consider that in both deaths, poison or a drug was administered to the victim."

"Do you think someone gave Roxy something?" I asked.

"Even a sedative could have impaired her driving," Evelyn said. "And from what I gathered, this accident took place at night when she might have been tired. Or had been drinking earlier in the day."

I nodded. "The question is who did she see after she left Donna, and how did this person manage to get Roxy to take something?"

"And why did this person want both Roxy and Aiden out of the picture?"

I frowned. "Donna could easily have put the poison in Aiden's food. And it's possible her conversation with Roxy didn't go the way she's been telling it. Donna had been furious with Roxy for coming on to her husband. Given their volatile relationship, I could see Donna becoming furious if Roxy so much as mentioned Aiden, then under the guise of friendship, added something to whatever food or drink she offered Roxy yesterday afternoon."

Evelyn sighed. "I'm sure the possibility hasn't escaped John Mathers's attention."

"Which is why he questioned Donna so closely."

"And will no doubt question her again."

Chapter
Twenty-Seven

Other than hearing about the car crash that had ended Roseanne Forlano's life on the local TV station, I received no
further updates about the investigation. Dylan came over for a
light dinner of omelets and salad. Then we settled down in the
living room and watched a rom-com against the sound of fireworks being shot off in the distance. Tomorrow was Independence
Day and my aunt and uncle's barbecue.

I called Aunt Harriet to ask if she'd like me to bring over
something in addition to the brownies. At first she said no, but
then realized she could use a few bottles of seltzer.

"On second thought, don't bother, Carrie. I'll send Bosco out
in the morning."

"Don't be silly," I said. "I have several bottles here. How many
shall I bring?"

"Two will do nicely, thank you. See you both tomorrow at two."

I smiled as I disconnected. Great-Uncle Bosco and Great-Aunt
Harriet were two of my favorite people and I was looking forward
to spending time with them.

* * *

Thursday turned out to be a perfect day for a barbecue—sunny, in the low eighties, with a balmy breeze that would keep us comfortable. I was happy to see my cousins Julia and Randy and their delightful children. I got to meet a second cousin, Judy Reiner—a tall, statuesque woman in her early forties—her husband Carl, and their twelve-year-old son Todd as well as Willis Singleton, a potbellied, white-haired first cousin of Uncle Bosco's. Willie, as everyone called him, regaled us with old Singleton stories while our hosts plied us with chicken and steak kebabs and various side dishes.

Some time later I was wondering if I had room for another sliver of Aunt Harriet's strawberry-blueberry pie, when Judy cast a glance at Randy and Carl playing tag with the children on the lawn and then said to me, "Harriet told me you were at the wedding where Dr. Harrington died. Poisoned, they say."

I nodded, not liking where this was going. I hadn't thought about the murders all afternoon, and hated to have the subject brought up.

"It happened at my best friend's wedding. Aiden was a family member. We were all terribly upset."

Judy sighed. "He was a wonderful doctor. I was horrified to hear he'd been poisoned."

My curiosity was piqued. "Had he ever treated you?"

"Twice. I needed a biopsy a few years ago and more recently I had my gallbladder removed. Dr. Harrington was always kind and explained everything well. He was a skillful surgeon."

"Were you ever treated by Dr. Gannon?" I asked.

"No. Why do you ask?"

"Just curious," I said. "I met him and a few other people from the practice at the wake and the memorial service."

"A friend recommended Dr. Gannon. I saw him once. I found him rather abrupt and was glad that my next appointment was with Dr. Harrington. I asked him to perform my surgery, and he said no problem."

"Vera, the office manager, seemed very sociable," I said.

"She sure is!" Judy agreed eagerly. "She's warm and friendly and is great at keeping patients calm."

"I imagine that's a good asset for a surgery practice," Julia said.

"Oh, it is," Judy said. "By my second appointment, I knew I needed surgery and was a bundle of nerves sitting there in the waiting room. Vera noticed and came over to chat with me. She reassured me that Dr. Harrington was an excellent surgeon and everything would turn out all right. And it did."

"What about Nurse Gwen?" I asked. "She was really broken up over Aiden's death."

"I never met her," Judy answered. "There was a nurse named Debbie and two nurse practitioners, I believe. Gwen must have started working there after my surgery."

Minutes later I helped Aunt Harriet clear the table. Shortly after that, we all began to leave and there was a flurry of goodbyes. Julia and I made tentative plans to get together for a double date one Saturday evening. Aunt Harriet handed me a platter of leftovers for Dylan and me to enjoy the following evening.

Dylan and I had started walking to the car when a small hand tugged at my skirt. I bent down to talk to Tacey.

"Have you seen Miss Evelyn lately?" she asked in a whisper.

"I sure have. She's fine."

"Tell her now I can write my street address," Tacey said proudly.

"I certainly will," I promised.

Riding home, I told Dylan what Judy had said about Nick Gannon and Vera.

Dylan laughed. "So, Dr. Nick doesn't have a great bedside manner, and Vera is every patient's favorite. Personality won't reveal if either or both is involved in fraud or a two-time murderer. Samuel Franklin Devine, the shrewdest art thief I ever knew, came across as the nicest, friendliest guy you'd ever want to meet."

"Oh."

"Just sayin'."

Chapter
Twenty-Eight

A ngela called me that evening to tell me that John had grilled
Miles for hours that afternoon.

"On the Fourth of July?"

"You of all people should know that murder investigations
don't respect holidays."

"Speaking of which, how was your holiday?" I asked.

"Sad. We spent the afternoon at Aunt Marie and Uncle Vinnie's. No barbecuing. They brought in trays of food from a local
Italian restaurant. Poor Uncle Dominic couldn't stop crying. The
wake is tomorrow afternoon and evening."

"How did you find out about Miles?" I asked.

"He'd been invited to my aunt and uncle's. I'd only met Miles
a few times when he was married to Roxy, but it turns out he was
a big family favorite. Up until the divorce, of course. Then he
became the lowest of the low. That all changed when word got
out he was trying to woo Roxy back. Uncle Dominic and most
everyone else opened their arms and welcomed him back into the
fold."

"Do I detect a note of cynicism?" I asked.

"You bet," Ange said. "Aunt Marie insists that Miles is a wheeler-dealer. Always figuring out ways to make himself look good. But she stands alone."

"Do you think he really wanted to get back together with Roxy?"

"Who knows? It could have been an act."

"But why kill her?" I asked.

"If Miles is the possessive type, he could have killed Aiden, thinking Aiden was treading where he had no right to. After that, he took care of Roxy for betraying him. Or Roxy wisely decided not to go back to him and he didn't like being refused."

"But they were divorced!" I protested.

"No matter," Angela said. "Some possessive men think they own their wives, whether or not they're still together."

"And Miles was running around."

"Makes no difference," Angela said.

"That is, *if* Miles is the possessive type," I said.

"The thing is, Miles admits Roxy came to see him the night she died in that car crash. He insists she was perfectly fine—sober and alive—when she left his office."

"Then he has an alibi. Someone must have seen her leave."

"His last patient canceled so he told his nurse to go home. He stayed to do paperwork."

"Why did Roxy go to his office?" I asked.

"Miles said she was excited about something but wouldn't say what it was. Only that she was getting her head on straight and the pieces were falling into place."

"That's weird. And similar to what she said to Donna. "

"It gets weirder. She threw her arms around Miles and kissed him, then said that was so he wouldn't forget her."

"Wow!"

"Miles said for a minute or two he couldn't speak. Roxy was halfway out the door when he called to her, 'Does that mean you'll take me back?'"

"And Roxy's answer?"

"She said she'd think about it."

* * *

So, who killed Aiden and Roxy? I mulled over the question as I went to sleep that night and the following morning as I drove to work. Nothing came to mind, so it was time to approach the murder investigation from another angle: Aiden's medical practice.

Who was involved in sending out fraudulent bills to health insurers? Since Gwen had only come to work in the office the past year, I doubted that she was involved in the scheme. I'd talk to her and find out what she knew and who she suspected.

I dialed Gwen's number. It rang and rang. Disappointed, I left a message to call me and went downstairs to check on the two programs in progress—a chair yoga class with a new instructor and a craft lesson using seashells. Both were running smoothly.

Evelyn joined me as I walked upstairs. "Quiet day," she observed.

"It is. Lots of people are on vacation or enjoying the lovely weather."

Evelyn grinned. "Speaking of which, aren't your father and his significant other coming to visit this weekend?"

"They are."

"I bet you can't wait to meet Meredith."

"Uh huh. Did you know that Dylan's known her for years?"

"Yes, since you've mentioned it a few times."

I let out a huff of air. "Maybe I have, but with my father and Dylan working for the same company, knowing people I don't know—sometimes I feel left out."

"Carrie, those two men love you—" Evelyn stopped abruptly. "More than I can say."

I smiled sheepishly. "I know. At least, I think I know."

"When are they arriving?"

"Late Saturday afternoon. They'll stay at the cottage with us until they fly back to Atlanta on Monday."

* * *

That afternoon, I was in Sally's office chatting about the new retractable patio awning she and Bob had recently installed, when my cell phone played its jingle. It was Gwen.

"Excuse me," I said and stepped outside.

Good thing I did. Gwen was frantic. "Carrie, I'm so glad you called! I would have called you anyway as soon as—as soon as . . ."

She burst into tears before she'd managed to finish her sentence.

"Gwen, what is it? Were you fired?"

"No, it's worse." She started to bawl.

The sound was so loud, patrons stared at me as I hurried to my office, glad that neither of my assistants was working today. "What happened? Where are you?"

After several sniffing sounds, Gwen managed to get herself under control. "I'm a few blocks from the library."

"Oh."

"I know it's an imposition and I have no right to ask, but could I come to the library now? I need to talk to you."

I hesitated. My office would give us some privacy, but this was a workplace and a colleague or a patron might stop by. I glanced at my watch, saw it was almost four o'clock. Too late for lunch and too early for dinner.

"The Cozy Corner Café's close by and should be empty now," I said. "I could meet you there in a few minutes."

"Thank you, Carrie! I really appreciate this. I'm looking up the address on my phone right now."

As soon as we disconnected I sent Sally a text, telling her I was leaving the building for the day but would be back in an hour or so to pick up Smoky Joe.

* * *

Gwen was waiting for me outside the Cozy Corner Café. Inside, the place was practically deserted, as I'd expected. Joe, the manager, waved and said to sit anywhere we liked.

"Let's sit here." I pointed to the booth in the far corner. When we were seated facing each other, I observed that Gwen seemed to have settled down since we'd spoken on the phone earlier. She offered me a shy smile.

"I'm afraid you always see me at my worst. You must think I'm a mental case when in fact I'm usually calm and collected."

"Important traits in a nurse," I said.

"So Aiden often told me."

Joe came over and dropped two menus on the table.

"I'll just have coffee," I said.

"Me too. And a blueberry muffin, if you have one," Gwen said. "Lightly toasted."

"Sure do. Coming right up, soon as I put on a fresh pot of coffee."

Our orders in, I gave my full attention to Gwen. "What got you so upset?"

She bit her lip, which had begun to tremble. "I just spent an hour at the police station. Someone called me at work this morning and asked me to go there so I did."

"To talk about Aiden?"

Gwen nodded. "And Roxy. They'd questioned me about Aiden right after he died, but this time it was different. More intense."

"I suppose they found out about you and Aiden," I said, figuring John must have gotten that information from Aiden's phone.

She leaned over the table and eyed me intently. "Did you tell them?"

"Of course not. You told me that in confidence."

"Sorry, Carrie. I didn't think you'd do something like that." Was that a waspish tone I heard? I suddenly wondered if I was being played.

"These days the police have a way of checking every aspect of our lives—from CCTV in stores to phone records. And don't forget they interviewed everyone in your office."

"Vera must have said something." Gwen made a scoffing sound. "People will do anything to turn an investigation away from themselves."

"Why would the police suspect Vera of killing Aiden?" I asked "Didn't she like him?"

"Vera liked him all right, though I did hear them arguing a few times."

"About what?"

"Just office stuff. I didn't pay much attention. Besides, they always stopped when they saw me coming."

Joe delivered Gwen's lightly toasted blueberry muffin. "Be back in a jiffy with your coffee."

Gwen took her time buttering a small piece of muffin, then set it down on her plate. "Carrie, I'm frightened. I can tell Lieutenant Mathers thinks I murdered Roxy. But I didn't. I swear."

"What makes you say that? I'm sure he's questioning a lot of people. In fact, I know of two . . ." *Oh no! TMI.*

"Who?" The word shot out of her mouth like an order.

"I'd rather not say."

"Oh!" Gwen blinked, and I feared the waterworks were back.

To make up for my blunt refusal, I asked, "Did you tell Lieutenant Mathers what Donna said to Aiden—about killing anyone who tried to change her lifestyle?"

She shook her head. "I decided not to since I have no proof she said it. Mathers would think I made it up to get him off my case. And now it's too late."

"Tell me, Gwen, why do you think Lieutenant Mathers likes you for Roxy's murder?"

For a moment she said nothing. Then she seemed to sink into herself. "They found the note I sent her. It was stupid, I know. But she was stopping by the office nearly every day, and it was getting annoying."

"What did the note say?"

Gwen shrugged. "Something like 'stay away from Aiden if you know what's good for you.'"

"Wow!"

"As I said, she was being annoying." Gwen finally bit into her muffin. "Aiden and I had so little time together, and here was Roxy, taking up his lunch hours."

"Did Aiden mind?"

"Of course, but he was too kind to send Roxy on her way. I tried to explain that he was letting her cut into our time, but he said that when he divorced Donna we'd have all the time in the world to be together. Right now Roxy was distraught and needed his support."

"So you're saying when Roxy first started to come around to the office, Aiden had no idea she was in love with him?"

"Men," she said with a wave of her hand. "I figured it out immediately and told him, but he laughed it off. Aiden thought he could convince her to go back to that runaround Miles. I told him that wasn't possible. Roxy had fixed her sights on him. It was only when she came right out and propositioned him that he read her the riot act."

I stared at Gwen's cold demeanor, so different from the weeping lover who had shown up at Aiden's wake and memorial service. "So what you're telling me is you were in love with Aiden and resented the support he was giving Roxy. He wouldn't take your advice so you sent her a note."

She huffed dismissively "You make me sound so . . . calculating."

I *make you sound calculating?* "What I don't get is, the last time we talked you told me that things weren't that serious between you and Aiden. You weren't ready to marry him."

"I said that so you wouldn't think I was desperate enough to do something dumb."

"Like send Roxy a 'keep away' note," I murmured.

"Exactly. Aiden and I managed to go to the cabin a few times, but we would have been able to go more often if Roxy hadn't kept coming around."

I looked at Gwen. "What exactly do you want me to do?"

Her eyes were fixed on the table. "I've heard that you've helped solve a few murders around here."

I remained silent.

"And that Lieutenant Mathers is a good friend of yours."

"He is."

"I was hoping you could tell him that I didn't kill Roxy. And of course I didn't kill Aiden. I loved him."

So you keep on saying. I stood. "When I see Lieutenant Mathers I'll tell him exactly what you said."

It was only after I left the café that I realized I'd forgotten to ask Gwen what she knew about the medical fraud.

Chapter
Twenty-Nine

What an idiot I'd been, falling for Gwen Swithers' sweet-lonesome-girl act! She was nothing but a scheming con-niver. She must have intuited that Aiden was having marital problems and made a play for him. Of course Roxy was a detriment to her plan! And she'd had the nerve to ask me to tell John Mathers that she was a good person who would never kill anyone!

I glanced at my watch, surprised to discover that my meeting with Gwen had taken less than half an hour. Since it wasn't even four thirty, I decided that now would be a good time to stock up for my father and Meredith's visit.

The Gourmet Market was relatively empty. I figured we'd eat at home one evening, and since I had no idea what Meredith liked, I wanted to provide a variety of choices. I quickly selected an array of salads, sliced turkey, roast beef, and several cheeses as well as a platter of lobster mac and cheese, grilled veggies, and the Gourmet Market's special shrimp dish. I added a few appetizers and two desserts.

I stopped at the library to pick up Smoky Joe, then headed for home. I called Mrs. C, who cleaned Dylan's house and the cot-tage, to make sure she'd remembered to put fresh linens on the bed in the guest room. She told me rather huffily that of course she hadn't forgotten. In fact, she'd taken care of it first thing this morning. And she'd even moved my laptop to my bedroom.

As Dylan and I drove home later that night after a yummy pizza dinner, I was still smarting from the way Nurse Gwen had played me until I'd finally caught on to her act.

"I can't believe how wrong I was about her!" I groused. "I'm usually so good at reading people."

Dylan patted my leg. "Babe, don't be hard on yourself. Your Miss Swithers sounds like a con artist. Meaning she's had years of practice. While you're used to taking people at face value."

"To think I fell for her 'poor me' act. So upset about Aiden's dying. She was probably crying over her lost chance of becoming a rich doctor's wife."

"Maybe she really did love him," Dylan said.

"Fat chance. She sensed that his marriage was on the rocks and decided to go after him."

Dylan shrugged. "It's possible. Aiden was vulnerable."

"And she sent Roxy that letter in an attempt to get rid of the competition. Hmmm." I thought a minute. "I wonder if she tried pulling something like this where she came from. Only she failed and *that's* the reason she moved on."

"A very good hypothesis," Dylan said, "and I could easily have Rosalind check out her background except . . ."

"Except John's coming over later so I can tell him exactly what Gwen told me. Then *he* can follow up on Nurse Gwen."

Dylan laughed. "You're finally learning when to leave police work to the police."

"Which I wouldn't mind if the police ever filled me in on their end."

I reached for Dylan's hand and we drove the rest of the way in companionable silence. Soon we were turning onto the Avery road. Dylan pulled into the semicircular entranceway in front of his stately home.

"Would you like to come in? I want to drop off some stuff and collect a few things to bring over to your place."

"No. I'll wait out here."

"Okay. Be back in a few."

I stared at the manor: a beautiful house filled with fine, old-fashioned furniture that his parents had probably selected with a decorator when Dylan was very young. Angela had once asked me if I'd like to live here and I'd told her I wouldn't. I much preferred the informal, cozy atmosphere of my cottage. It suddenly occurred to me I had no idea how attached Dylan was to the home he'd lived in most of his life.

And now isn't the time to think about it, I told myself.

Dylan returned a few minutes later carrying an overnight bag and a case of wine. "We're running low on our wine supply at the cottage. Good thing I have a few bottles of the stuff your dad likes."

"What does Meredith like to drink?"

"I'm not sure. I think white wine—like you."

At the cottage, I fed Smoky Joe some treats, then joined Dylan in the living room to watch TV. It was a quarter to nine and John had said he'd be over around nine.

At a quarter past he called to say he was running late. "Would you rather stop by the precinct tomorrow?" he asked.

"Tonight's better. My dad's flying in for the weekend. He's bringing his girlfriend. I suppose I should say woman friend."

John chuckled. "So Jim Singleton's got himself a woman. Must be serious if he's introducing her to the family."

"Dylan says Meredith's nice. He knows her from work."

"Be sure to give your dad my best. Not many men can turn their lives around like he did."

"I will."

"I'll get to your place as soon as I can."

John was out of breath when he finally arrived at a quarter to ten and headed straight for the bathroom.

"Want some coffee?" I called after him.

"Love some."

"Would you like coffee?" I asked Dylan.

"No, thanks."

I brewed a small pot of coffee and waited for John in the kitchen. He dropped into a chair and rubbed his eyes.

"Want anything to eat?"

John nodded. "That would be nice. I never stopped for dinner."

I brought out some deli meat and cheese and toasted a roll, the kind I knew he liked.

Dylan strolled into the kitchen while John was munching away. "I didn't hear any conversation so I figured you guys were eating."

"John is. Would you like something?"

"Ice cream."

I put out two small bowls and two spoons for Dylan and me while he got the containers of chocolate and pistachio ice cream from the freezer. I let him scoop his own portion since, according to Dylan, I never got the amount right, then took my own.

"I'll leave you guys to it," Dylan said, departing with his bowl of ice cream.

When John had finished eating, he studied me, considerably more alert than when he'd arrived. "Shall we get started?"

"Okay."

"Did you call Gwendolyn Swithers or did she call you?"

Starting off with a tough one. "Er—I called her."

"Why?"

"The truth?"

"Of course the truth. That's why I'm here."

This wasn't going quite as I'd imagined. "After finding what looked to be Aiden's discovery of fraudulent claims, I wondered who was responsible for them."

"Did it ever occur to you that Aiden might have been involved in the scheme?"

My eyes widened. "No. Of course not. Donna said he seemed preoccupied the nights he spent in his home office."

John shrugged. "Maybe he felt he was getting in too deep and wanted out."

I made a scoffing sound. "And mentioned it to his partner, which got him killed?"

"Maybe. We don't know who's involved," John said with exaggerated patience. "Just like we don't know if there was fraud or if it's still going on. All. Police. Work."

Duly chastened, I nodded.

John grinned, looking pleased with himself. "Getting back to Ms. Swithers, did you contact her hoping she could tell you who was involved in the medical fraud?"

"Yes. She might have discovered it on her own. Or, since she was so close to Aiden, he might have confided his suspicions to her—" I frowned. "If he wasn't involved, as I'm pretty sure he wasn't."

"Go on."

"Gwen sounded frantic when she called me back—my earlier call had gone to voice mail—and wanted us to meet. The few times I'd seen her she came across as gentle. Kind of a lost soul. At Aiden's memorial, she'd mentioned she had no one to talk to, so I gave her my cell number. She called and we met for breakfast one morning."

John nodded.

"Today she was upset because she was afraid you thought she'd killed Roxy because of the note she'd sent her."

I drew a deep breath. "Well, that note didn't sit well with me, either. It revealed a side of Gwen I didn't much like. The more we talked the more I realized she wasn't the innocent girl who just happened to fall in love with her kind and sympathetic boss. I think she'd set her sights on marrying a doctor for the prestige and the money."

John exhaled loudly. "Then why would she murder him?"

"I have no idea. Maybe Aiden dumped her and that made her angry. Today's agenda was to get me to believe she'd only written the note because Roxy's visits to the office cut into the time she had with Aiden. I was supposed to convince you that she wasn't capable of killing Roxy."

John leaned back in his chair and stretched out his long legs. "Carrie, I appreciate your telling me all this. Finding out how a suspect's mind works is helpful, and, from what you say, Gwen Swithers is a schemer. But I need evidence to crack these two homicides."

* * *

The rain that greeted us on Saturday morning reflected my glum mood. John had poured a cold shower of reality over what I'd so proudly offered up regarding Gwen's true character. Going after Aiden for money and position was cold, but with him out of the picture, what possible reason could she have for killing Roxy?

Roxy was a loose cannon. And she was crazy in love with Aiden. Maybe she'd managed to learn some of Gwen's secrets and threatened to share them. Then Gwen might have risked losing Aiden and her job as well.

Gwen had access to drugs. But all this was supposition. It didn't prove that Gwen murdered Roxy. Just as the health care fraud and abuse in Aiden's medical practice might have nothing to do with either murder. I was beginning to appreciate the painstaking, tedious hours the police had to put in before they gathered enough evidence to charge a murderer.

Dylan was wise enough to see I didn't feel much like talking, so after suggesting that we go to the gym after breakfast, he buried his nose in the newspaper.

By the time we left for Parson's Gym, I was feeling more like myself. "The sun's come out," I observed, peering up at the sky.

"Anything special you'd like to do with your dad and Meredith this weekend?"

I shrugged. "I don't have anything particular in mind. I'm just so happy to see Jim. And I want to get to know Meredith. I have a feeling she means a lot to my father."

"She's a nice lady. I'm sure you'll like her," Dylan said.

Of course. Since you and Jim both do. "I figured we'd have dinner in one evening and take them to a nice restaurant on the water the other."

Dylan grinned. "My thoughts exactly. You'll be happy to know I managed to get us reservations at the Sea Maiden tonight."

"Oh."

"You don't want to eat there? I thought you loved their food."

"I do. It's just that we usually discuss where we'll be going before making plans."

Dylan glanced at me. "Sorry, babe. Jim mentioned he'd love to eat in a seafood restaurant when they were here so I called the Sea Maiden soon as I got off the phone. I think that was Thursday."

"You spoke to my father and didn't tell me?"

"Yes. We talk occasionally. We're work colleagues, remember? There are matters we need to discuss."

"I know that but . . ." I released a giant sigh. "You, Jim, and Meredith have this connection. You've all worked together at one time or another. To tell the truth, I feel kind of left out."

Dylan burst out laughing.

"What's so funny!" I demanded.

"You. Why do you think they're coming? To see me?"

"Well . . ."

"Your father wants you to meet the woman he loves. As for me and Jim, we only connected because of you. My take is you should be happy that your significant other and your father get along and have become good friends."

Dylan turned into the strip mall where the gym was located and parked. "You, Miss Carolinda Singleton, are the linchpin. The person who links us together."

"Oh." I felt my ears grow warm with embarrassment. "And how many times have I told you—that's *not* my name any longer."

Chapter Thirty

The gym appeared to be crowded to capacity, probably because of the rainy weather. We'd arrived just in time for me to make a stretch and yoga class while Dylan worked out on the machines.

"Hi, Billy," I called out to the good-looking personal trainer whose family murders I'd recently helped solve.

Billy Harper paused from adjusting a weights machine for a middle-aged woman to grin and wave at us.

"I simply must find someone for him," I murmured to Dylan.

"Are you considering replacing investigating with matchmaking?" he asked.

"It's an idea," I said as I headed to class.

* * *

An hour later, feeling relaxed and at peace, I sat down in the small entrance area to wait for Dylan. I quickly closed my mouth, which had fallen open when he exited the large workout room chatting with none other than Dr. Miles Forlano, Roxy's ex. They were in the middle of a conversation about exercise routines and had come to a standstill. I jumped to my feet and joined them.

Dylan slipped his arm around me. "There you are. I hope I haven't kept you waiting too long."

"Not at all."

"Carrie, this is Miles. Dr. Miles Forlano. Miles, my girlfriend, Carrie Singleton."

"Hello. Nice to actually meet you," I said, extending my hand.

"Hello, Carrie." Miles looked puzzled as we shook hands. "*Actually* meet me?"

"I saw you at Aiden's wake and memorial service. I understand the two of you were very close."

"We were." Miles sighed. "Were you a patient of Aiden's?"

"No. Angela Vecchio—er, Prisco—is my best friend. Dylan and I were at her wedding. Aiden died right in front of us."

Miles grimaced. "That must have been awful. I still reach for the phone to give him a call, then I remember he's gone. Well, nice meeting you both."

He started to move away when I quickly said, "And I'm very sorry about Roxy."

Miles turned pale. "The funeral's Tuesday. I don't know how I'll get through it. Her dying on top of Aiden's murder is . . ." He closed his eyes to blink back tears.

So he had no idea that Roxy's crash wasn't an accident. Unless he'd caused it. "I wonder if the two deaths are somehow connected," I said.

"I can't imagine who would have it in for Aiden, but Roxy's accident could have been avoided."

"What do you mean?" Dylan asked.

Miles exhaled loudly. "She stopped by my office that night. She was in a strangely agitated mood. When I saw how hyper she was, I should have insisted on driving her home."

This was exactly what Angela had told me. Unless Miles was an amazing actor, I believed him. I put my hand on his arm. "I'm so sorry."

"I kissed her and told her I'd never stopped loving her. At least she knew that before she died."

"Do you think she'd been drinking?"

Miles shook his head. "I don't think so. She just seemed hyper. I shouldn't have let her go off like that. It was dark out and she wasn't the most careful driver."

"Don't blame yourself, Miles. From what you've told us, it sounds like Roxy was heading somewhere after seeing you."

"I got that impression, but she refused to explain. And there was no convincing Roxy of anything when she got that way."

"At least she died knowing that you loved her."

"There's that," he said sadly and walked toward the door.

"So nobody knows where Roxy was going after she stopped at Miles's office," I said as we exited the gym.

"Looks that way," Dylan said. "If Miles is telling the truth."

"He seems very shaken up by Roxy's death. And Aiden's."

"I agree, but grief genuine or bogus—is no proof of innocence."

When we reached the car, I turned to Dylan. "What a coincidence—Aiden's best friend showing up at the gym when we were here. I had no idea you knew Miles."

"I didn't. I heard one of the personal trainers call him by name and remembered what you'd told me about him."

I burst out laughing. "You sly dog! What did you talk about when you first starting chatting?"

"You heard. Our exercise routines. Not one word about the murders."

"How come?"

Dylan grinned. "Thought I'd leave that for you."

* * *

My father had insisted that we were not to pick up him and Meredith at the airport so I found myself pacing the floor, wine glass in hand, as I waited for them to arrive. Their knock came a little after four o'clock—not at all the kind of entrance my father had made back in December when, after not seeing each other for years, he'd broken into my cottage at three thirty in the morning, wanting me to set up a meeting with his partner in crime, the local jeweler in town.

Dylan went to open the door, and I flew into my father's arms. I breathed in his familiar scent and hugged him tight.

"I've missed you so much!" I said, not letting go and realizing how true it was.

"I've missed you, too, Caro."

When I finally released him, he took the hand of the woman at his side. "Caro, Meredith. Meredith, Caro."

I extended my hand to the well-dressed, stately woman who stood almost as tall as Jim. My handsome father was close to sixty, and his full head of brown hair had just enough gray to make him look debonair. Meredith wore her salt and pepper–colored hair in a short, stylish cut. She appeared to be about ten years younger than Jim. Her lovely gray eyes expressed both intelligence and warmth.

"At last we meet!" she said. "I've heard so much about you, Carrie."

"You have?"

"Are you kidding?" Meredith cast a fond glance at Jim. "Your dad talks about you all the time."

I turned to my father, who was already in an animated discussion with Dylan about some case one of them was working on. Hard to believe that once Dylan had been hired to retrieve the gems my father had stolen. But it had all ended well when he and Mac had brought Jim into their company to make use of his "inside" knowledge. The arrangement had turned out better than anyone could have imagined, and the two most important men in my life—aside from Uncle Bosco—had forged a close friendship.

"Jim, you promised. No shop talk," Meredith said.

"My bad," Dylan said, hugging her. "Good to see you, Merry."

My father and Dylan brought the luggage into the guest room, then the four of us settled in the living room where we chatted over wine, cheese, and crackers. I learned that my father and Merry, as she asked me to call her, were flying to Colorado on Monday to visit her daughter, and then on to California to see her son and his family.

"You could always stop in Hollywood and visit Mom and Tom while you're in California," I teased.

"I believe I already did my good deed where your mother's concerned," Jim said.

"You certainly did." I chuckled at the memory. My mother and Tom had been here while Tom had a role in a movie being filmed in Clover Ridge. When Jim heard they were having marital problems he arrived on the scene to offer his ex-wife emotional support.

My father and Merry exchanged amused glances, which told me all I needed to know about their relationship.

A little after five, my father yawned and said he'd love to take a quick nap. And Merry wanted to take a shower. After they left,

Dylan helped me bring the glasses and leftover cheese to the kitchen.

"So, what do you think of Merry?" he asked.

"She seems nice," I said. "What's more important, my father looks happy."

*　*　*

As soon as we arrived at the Sea Maiden, a hostess beckoned us past the throng of diners waiting to be seated. We followed her through the main room buzzing with chatter, then through a passageway leading to smaller rooms for private parties. She opened the door to one of the rooms and invited us inside.

"This is lovely!" I said, staring out the floor-to-ceiling window that faced the Sound. "I never knew they had private rooms like this!"

We sat down at the round table covered with a crisp white cloth and silver utensils. Weren't the tables in the room we'd just walked through covered with paper—the easier to dispose of? The place settings had been arranged so that all four of us could gaze out at the sunset. I sat between Dylan and my father. Our hostess placed a menu before each of us, then lowered her head to converse in low tones with my father.

I looked at Dylan, who turned up his palms and shrugged, claiming total ignorance. Which made him look guilty as hell. Something was going down!

Finally, our hostess smiled at each of us in turn. "Welcome to the Sea Maiden. Enjoy your dinner." And with that, she left.

"Such a beautiful restaurant," Merry murmured. She smiled at Dylan. "Thank you for coming up with such a wonderful choice."

Dylan acknowledged her appreciation with a nod of his head. "My pleasure."

"And on such short notice, too," I said sarcastically. He must have made these reservations weeks ago.

He was saved from having to answer by the arrival of a waiter bearing a magnum of champagne and four flutes. He set the glasses on the small table in the corner and uncorked the champagne with a flourish and filled the flutes, which he then placed before us.

Is what I think is happening actually happening?

My father stood and cleared his throat. He reached out his hand to Merry, who clasped it in both of hers. "I am very happy to be here with the three most important people in my life." He beamed at Merry. "Meredith, my love; Carrie, my dearest child; and Dylan, my good friend."

I stared at my father. I'd never seen him so overjoyed. So happy. He beamed at me. "Carrie, Merry and I want to share our good news with you and Dylan. We were very lucky to find each other and fall in love, and—we're getting married!"

He raised his glass to Merry.

"To Meredith and Jim!" Dylan raised his flute of champagne.

"To Meredith and Jim," I echoed.

We all clinked glasses and sipped. That is, they sipped. I gulped down most of my drink. Stunned, I stood and hugged my father. "I'm so happy for you."

"You're not upset?" he whispered in my ear.

"Of course not," I whispered back. "I'm glad you found the right person to share your life."

"I am so lucky," he whispered.

"So is she."

Dylan stepped back from hugging Merry so I could embrace her.

"Congratulations!" I said.

Merry squeezed me tight. "I hope you're really pleased about this," she said.

"I really am. I want my dad to be happy, and it seems he is because you're in his life."

"He was worried you'd be upset."

I rolled my eyes. "I'm not losing a father, I'm gaining a stepmother."

My father came to stand between Merry and me and put an arm around each of us. "It means the world to me you feel that way."

We all ordered two-pound lobsters to celebrate, along with the Sea Maiden's signature salad, corn on the cob, and a bottle of Chardonnay. I sipped my refill of champagne, then turned to Dylan.

"You knew about this." It wasn't a question.

"I suspected as much when Jim called a few weeks ago, telling me to find a special restaurant with a private room. He asked me to keep it under wraps, so I did."

"So you were caught in the middle," I said.

"Yes, and I hope it's the last time."

I leaned over to kiss him. "It was for a good cause."

I hadn't appreciated the strain of anxiety Jim and Merry were under—worried about my reaction to their wedding plans—until I saw how openly joyous they were afterward with each other.

"When do you plan to get married?" I asked.

"After we visit my kids, we'll fly back to Atlanta and have a simple ceremony, perhaps Labor Day weekend," Merry said. "We're still making plans."

I turned to Dylan. "Maybe we'll fly down for the occasion."

"I'd love to, if that's what they want," Dylan said.

"We'd love it," Merry said. "We didn't want to put any pressure on you or my kids, making you feel that you had to come to an out-of-town wedding."

Our waiter arrived with a large bowl of salad and four salad plates. Merry looked at me. "Will you do the honors?"

"Why don't you?"

"My pleasure." Merry looked pleased as she deftly portioned out salad and passed the plates around.

When our lobsters arrived, all conversation faded away as we set about cracking shells and eating, but over dessert—we shared generous portions of chocolate fudge cake and key lime pie—and coffee I asked Merry about her children.

"My daughter Lianne lives in Denver, where she works for a local television station. Kevin and his family live outside of LA. He and his wife are both therapists and have a three-year-old daughter."

"I'd love to meet them some time," I said.

"I'm sure they'd love to meet you, too," Merry said. "Your dad tells me you've helped solve several mysteries."

I laughed. "I don't know about several, but life is never dull in Clover Ridge."

Jim must have caught the tail end of our discussion because he looked up to ask, "Caro, any new developments regarding the homicides in Angela's family?"

Merry looked stunned. "I had no idea you were currently involved in ongoing cases."

"Merry, my father is the master of omission. I suppose he didn't want to frighten you on your first visit to Clover Ridge."

Jim had the grace to look sheepish. "Something like that."

I gave Merry an abbreviated account of Aiden's death at Angela and Steve's wedding and Roxy's fatal car crash. I finished up by saying, "Several suspects but no evidence pointing to anyone in particular at the moment."

My father nodded. "So, if I have it right, the perp could be a family member—Aiden's wife comes to mind. She sounds pretty coldhearted to me—or someone he worked with. Nurse Gwen partner Nick, or Vera the business manager—or all three of them."

"Exactly," I said. "Of course, Angela's brother Tommy could have poisoned Aiden, though there are no indications he had anything against Roxy."

"That you know of," my father interjected.

"That we know of," I repeated. "Or if maybe Aiden and Roxy were murdered by two different killers for unconnected reasons. Nothing conclusive."

My father reached over to rest his hand on my shoulder. "You've been here before with other investigations. I have confidence that something will break soon."

"Jim, please don't encourage her!" Dylan said. "John Mathers has the investigation well in hand."

"Right. Except If I remember correctly, the time I was involved in a murder case here in Clover Ridge, it was Carrie who broke the case wide open."

Chapter
Thirty-One

I awoke Sunday morning to discover that Dylan and my father had gone out earlier to buy fresh bagels and all the trimmings. Breakfast turned out to be an all hands on deck kind of meal, with each of us doing our bit: I set the table, Merry made a large pot of coffee, Dylan made a pepper and onion frittata, and Jim had us laughing nonstop with stories I'd never heard before. I didn't say much, nor did I feel I had to. I was totally happy in a quiet sort of way. I was with family. *My* family, where I belonged.

When we had a minute to ourselves after breakfast, I asked Jim if he'd like to share his good news with Aunt Harriet and Uncle Bosco.

"Sure, honey. I'd like Merry to meet them. They're good people and I appreciate all they've done for you."

Surprised, since my father was never big on spending time with relatives, I called my aunt and uncle to invite them over for Sunday dinner.

"So Jim's in town with his fiancée," Aunt Harriet said. "Of course we're happy to come for dinner. I'll bring an apple pie. I happen to have one in the freezer."

"Shall we say six thirty?"

"See you then!" Aunt Harriet trilled.

An hour later, my father, Merry, Dylan and I climbed into Dylan's car and drove up Route 7. We stopped in Kent, where we wandered in and out of stores and galleries. In one gallery, Dylan and my father started to talk about a painting that reminded them of a piece of stolen artwork Dylan had found and returned to its owner. That led to more shop talk. Merry and I grinned at each other and moved on to a women's clothing store, leaving them outside gabbing away.

I enjoyed Merry's company. She didn't have the need to babble to make her presence known. She spoke when she had something to say. And she was a good listener.

Not like my mother suddenly came to mind. Immediately followed by a pang of guilt that I was being disloyal. I had no business comparing Merry to my mother, who was self-absorbed and manipulative but loved me in her own way. Merry and my mother were as different as any two women could be.

Or was I feeling disloyal because I was completely at ease with Merry—not obliged to watch what I said for fear of upsetting her or risk being criticized? I shook my head to chase away my disquieting thoughts. As much as I was all for it, acquiring a stepmother was going to take some getting used to.

The four of us shared a pizza for lunch, then headed for home. We made a planned stop at a juried craft fair that I was looking forward to. I was glad to have Merry at my side when I couldn't decide between two candle holders. She bought a few for her daughter and a silver bracelet for her little granddaughter.

"I bet you can't wait to see her," I said.

Her face lit up. "I love chatting with Francie on FaceTime, but spending real time with her is something else entirely."

We arrived back at the cottage a little past four. My father said he needed a short nap and Merry said she could use one, too. I giggled as they disappeared into the guest room.

Dylan slipped an arm around me. "The happy couple. Who would have thought those two would get together?"

"My dad is remarrying," I said in awe.

Dylan kissed me. "I think I could use a little nap myself."

I grinned. "Now that you mention it . . ."

*   *   *

Aunt Harriet and Uncle Bosco arrived bearing champagne along with a small chocolate fudge cake as well as the promised apple pie. Jim introduced Merry, and she was embraced and brought into the fold.

"Welcome to the family," Aunt Harriet said.

Dylan opened the champagne and filled the flutes. We drank to Jim and Merry and I brought out a few appetizers for us to nibble on. I hadn't realized I'd been a bit anxious about my father and Uncle Bosco getting together until I saw them talking in quiet tones in the den. There were times during the seven months I'd lived with my aunt and uncle before moving to the cottage that Uncle Bosco had shaken his head, bemoaning his nephew's wasting away his life when he should have been putting his good brain to positive use.

The evening ended too soon, and before I knew it, Monday morning had arrived and my father and Merry were wheeling their suitcases into the hall. They planned to leave for the airport in an hour for their flight to Colorado. I was going to miss them. I'd gotten used to having them around. Even Smoky Joe was agitated and showed it by weaving between everyone's legs.

Dylan had said his goodbyes earlier before leaving for work. From the doorway, I watched my father stow the suitcases in their rented car. When he came back inside, I dissolved in tears.

"I hate to see you go," I blubbered as I hugged him and Merry.

Merry patted my back. "You'll come visit us soon—you and Dylan."

I nodded as I sniffed. "We'll try to make it to the wedding."

It was time I left for the library. I put Smoky Joe in his carrier and moved to open the door.

"I'll walk you out," Jim offered.

We walked slowly to my car. "I'm so happy for you, Dad. I really like Merry."

My father exhaled. "You have no idea how glad I am—on both accounts. This marriage thing came up suddenly, and I wasn't sure how it was going to sit with you."

"Well, it sits with me just fine. You've become an upstanding member of society."

"I had you as my model," he said softly.

We hugged as best we could with the carrier in my arms.

"Talk to you soon," Jim said as I slid into the driver's seat.

"Don't forget to set the alarm before you leave."

My father, the former thief, laughed. "Will do."

* * *

The week passed quietly and uneventfully. My library friends were thrilled to learn that Jim had met someone he loved and soon they would be married. When I told Angela the news Monday morning in the parking lot, she gave me a knowing smile. "I hope this gives you a push in the right direction."

"Angela!" I said warningly.

"Just sayin' as your BBF," she declared and dashed ahead of me.

As soon as I entered my office, Evelyn appeared and echoed Angela's sentiment in her own Evelyn-like way. "Carrie, dear, your father's wonderful news can't but get you thinking about your own situation."

"I love Dylan," I said. Why did it come out sounding defensive?

"I know you do," Evelyn said soothingly. "Which is why it's only natural to consider your next step."

"Why do I have to? I like things exactly as they are. I wish you and Angela would stop trying to prod me into doing something I'm not ready for." I glared at her. "Besides, I haven't been asked."

"Well, maybe if you showed—"

I covered my ears and turned away. Evelyn took the hint and disappeared.

The truth of the matter was I was scared. Yes, Angela and Steve were deliriously happy. But they were newlyweds. They hadn't had to deal with children and money problems, sickness and whatever else came along that required attention and drained people. My father and Meredith were marrying at an older age with no problems to speak of—that I knew of.

But what about a couple like Donna and Aiden? I assumed they'd been madly in love when they married. They had two adorable children, a beautiful home, and a comfortable lifestyle. Aiden had a career, and I supposed Donna had opted to be a stay-at-home mom. In a few years they had grown apart. They both had taken lovers and, if Gwen was to be believed, Aiden was thinking about divorce.

My parents had loved each other once. Was it the responsibility of providing for a family that had driven my father to a life of crime? He'd stayed away even when he wasn't in prison, and left my mother, a woman who wasn't maternal in the least, to raise my brother and me. They divorced and now they each had partners they loved.

Another thing was, I didn't know if I'd be able to cope if Dylan and I were married and I had to deal with something really awful. Sure, I was handling things well now. I'd been trained for my job and I had wonderful colleagues who supported me. Living with Aunt Harriet and Uncle Bosco had given me the necessary confidence to make friends and form a loving relationship with Dylan. But for so many years before that I'd been adrift. Who was to say that if something I couldn't handle befell me that I wouldn't revert to the person I once was—someone who moved to a new town every year or two, never setting down roots or forming close friendships.

Of course there were good marriages. I was surrounded by them: Randy and Julia, Aunt Harriet and Uncle Bosco, even John and Sylvia Mathers—if I wanted to continue to fixate on the subject, which I most certainly did not!

*　*　*

Monday evening I called my mother to give her the news that my father was remarrying. There was a long pause. "I must say, that's about the last thing I ever expected Jim Singleton to do."

"Dad's changed a lot these past few years."

My mother made a scoffing sound. "At least he's given up his thieving ways. What's his fiancée like?"

"Nice. Pleasant," I said noncommittally. The last thing I wanted to do was rile up her competitive streak.

"Good luck to her. She's welcome to him."

"How's Tom?" I asked quickly.

"Doing exceedingly well." My mother rhapsodized about the two epic acting roles for which Tom was being considered. I was very fond of her husband and glad that his acting career had taken off.

* * *

With the excitement of my father's upcoming marriage and an unexpected flood of calls and emails from people wanting to give a program or class in the fall, I hadn't had much time to think about the two murders, much less do any sleuthing. And to be honest, my last meeting with John had dampened my enthusiasm for investigating. Still, the two victims were members of Angela's family, and Rosemary had asked me to do what I could to find their murderer.

Angela attended Roxy's funeral on Tuesday afternoon—a graveside service for family members only. She called me that evening to give me a detailed rundown of who was in attendance.

"Tommy was there, of course. I've never seen him so upset. He was really broken up. I had no idea he and Roxy were that close."

"That is surprising," I said. Or was he putting on an act? Since my wake-up call regarding Gwen's character, I'd decided I was too trusting. And someone like Tommy was clearly capable of violence.

"Miles was there. I tried to talk to him and Donna, but they stuck like two bookends to Uncle Dominic, who didn't stop crying. They finally managed to coax him away from the gravesite."

"Was anyone from Aiden's medical office there?" I asked.

"No. Why would any of them show up?"

"Just wondering. They say the murderer often attends his victim's funeral."

"We don't know that anyone in that office killed Roxy. Why would they?"

"I'm just trying to keep an open mind. Was John there?"

"No. But I overheard Uncle Vinnie tell my father that they managed to get the autopsy results as well as the preliminary toxicology report."

"And?" I prompted.

"Good thing my hearing is excellent because Uncle Vinnie suddenly lowered his voice. The autopsy showed that Roxy must have banged her head on the windshield before the airbag even opened."

"Meaning she fell asleep or was knocked unconscious before the car crashed. And the tox report?"

"There was evidence of a strong narcotic in her blood system. Which was suspicious. Roxy got drunk often enough, but she never took drugs."

"So her death is definitely being treated as a homicide."

"Looks that way."

*　*　*

When Evelyn made an appearance the following morning, I told her about Roxy's funeral and what Angela had overheard.

"No big surprise there," she said. Today Evelyn was wearing a sleeveless, salmon-colored dress and matching sandals.

"You look very pretty. Are you going somewhere later?"

"Thank you, Carrie. As a matter of fact, I am."

Ever since I'd met Evelyn, I'd been curious about her "life" when she wasn't stopping by to visit me. But any time I tried to find out more about her time spent elsewhere, she blew me off. "Where are you going?"

"To a festive event. A celebration, if you must know."

"You have parties in that other place when you're not here?"

Evelyn dismissed my question with a wave of her hand. "Of course. Parties. Meetings. Matters to resolve. None of which I can discuss with you."

"I just wondered—"

"Let's focus on what's important, Carrie. Finding the person or persons who murdered Aiden and Roxy."

Foiled again. I pursed my lips. "How I'd love to, but frankly, I don't see what more I can do."

Evelyn made a scoffing sound. "I'm surprised at you—giving up so quickly. You must have some ideas regarding this case."

"Of course I do! I wonder about Nurse Gwen, now that I know she's a phony. Gwen has access to drugs. So does Miles. And Nick Gannon, who was unhappy with Aiden and is probably scamming Medicare and insurance companies."

I stood suddenly, making Evelyn jump out of my path. "And let's not forget Tommy Vecchio. He had a gripe against Aiden. Angela said he was upset at Roxy's funeral, but with his hair-trigger temper, maybe he was crying crocodile tears. Who knows what he might have had against his cousin?" I jutted my face forward. "He might have had a reason to murder Roxy, a reason I'm not privy to!"

I was shouting now and I didn't care. "But these are only possibilities. Suspicions. What we need is evidence, Evelyn. Proof that someone poisoned Aiden and drugged Roxy. Anything else is irrelevant. John made that very clear to me Friday night after I'd shared what I'd learned about Gwen."

Evelyn smiled sweetly, but her sympathy wasn't for me. "Carrie, it's time you learned to show some compassion for your elders."

Had I offended her unknowingly? "What are you talking about?"

"Sometimes you have to look beyond a person's words to realize that he's upset. Poor John must be discouraged by his lack of results in solving these murders. He's worn down and sleep-deprived and was hoping to get something solid from you.

"When that didn't happen, you received a large dose of his disappointment in getting nowhere with this case. Carrie, dear, you have to know he respects you as a sleuth and appreciates every piece of information you've ever given him."

I tilted my head from side to side. "It's possible you're right."

Evelyn grinned. "You know I'm right. I'm sure he regrets having given your last offering such short shrift and would be more amenable than usual about sharing information. Now might be a good time to call him and casually ask what's new in the case?"

My mouth fell open in surprise. "Why, Evelyn, how devious of you."

She shrugged. "Even better if you can think of another reason to call him. One that has nothing to do with the murders?"

I thought a minute. "I could call him to tell him that Jim's getting married. John's rather fond of my father."

"There it is!" Evelyn said, looking very pleased with herself. "Now I must go or I'll be late for my fancy shindig."

"You're sure you won't tell me—" But she was gone.

Chapter
Thirty-Two

John was at the precinct and sounded glad to hear my voice. "Carrie, I've been meaning to call to congratulate you. I heard Jimbo is planning to tie the knot."

"He is. I met his fiancée this weekend. Who told you?"

"Your uncle. Why? Is it a secret? Bosco didn't seem to think it was."

"It's not. I was just wondering . . ."

John laughed. "You know how word gets out about every little thing in this town. Not that getting married is a little thing."

"The wedding will be in Atlanta in a month or two. Nothing big or fancy. Dylan and I may go down to help celebrate."

"Is that so? Speaking of weddings, how's your significant other?"

"John!"

He burst out laughing. "Sorry, kiddo. Couldn't resist."

"I was wondering—is there anything new regarding the two murders that you can share with me?"

"Well, I did talk to Miss Gwen Swithers after what you told me. Got her to admit she wasn't madly in love with Dr. Harrington. In fact, she even admitted that things hadn't turned out the way she'd planned."

My pulse quickened. "What do you mean?"

"It seems he caught on to her motives. They argued, and when Gwen asked Aiden if he still wanted to marry her he said he didn't want to rush into anything."

"Really? She never told me that!"

"Things started to unravel when Roxy told Aiden about the note Gwen had sent, warning her off. When Aiden asked Gwen why she'd sent it, she made the mistake of denying that she had. After that, Aiden cooled their relationship."

I thought a bit. "Then Gwen did have a motive to kill both Aiden and Roxy. And she has access to drugs."

John exhaled loudly. "Motive, opportunity, but no proof."

"Dylan and I ran into Roxy's ex-husband at the gym on Saturday morning. Miles told us he saw Roxy the evening she died."

"I know. The problem is, we have no idea where she went after she left his office."

"No security cameras?"

"We're checking. So far, nada."

We chatted a bit more, then ended the call. So Gwen was a suspect after all. But as John said—no evidence. No proof. Just lots of suspects with a variety of motives.

*　*　*

Mayor Tripp called me Friday midmorning. "Hello, Carrie. How are you?"

"Fine, Al," I said carefully, though my mind was racing. I'd forgotten all about his campaign to get me on the town council, and I'd yet to come up with a good reason to say no. "Everything's good."

Trish glanced at me. She knew how reluctant I was to fall in with his plans.

"We're enjoying a lovely summer," Al said. "And congratulations, by the way. I hear your dad is getting married."

"Yes, he is. Thank you." Uncle Bosco sure was spreading the word far and wide.

"Have you given any thought to taking Jeannette's seat on the council?"

"Sorry, I've been so busy, I haven't had a chance to give it the attention it deserves."

"That's quite all right. I just had a thought. The council members are meeting for brunch tomorrow at the new Waffles and Eggs place near the mall. It's just an informal affair, but I thought you might like to join us so you could meet the people you'd be working with. They can fill you in on the way we deal with various issues—how we go about ruling on policies and zoning matters and the like."

"They're okay with this?" I asked.

"They sure are. In fact, Jeannette was the one who suggested it, and the others all agreed." He laughed. "So you see, you'd be working with people who'd be welcoming you into the group."

"How nice," I said, meaning it. When I'd come to work at the library as head of programs and events, the reference librarian at the time, who also happened to be Evelyn's niece, resented that I'd gotten the job instead of her and had done her best to make my life miserable.

"I know it's short notice, but if you're available tomorrow— we're meeting at eleven—this could help you make your decision. And if you decide against joining us, I promise not to pressure you any further."

Oddly enough, brunch at eleven would fit right in with my Saturday plans. Since I wasn't working tomorrow and Dylan needed to go in to the office to take care of some work, I'd told Angela I would go to a few furniture stores with her in the afternoon. Dinner tomorrow night was going to be takeout—or I should say take in—at Dylan's house. When I'd asked where we'd be getting the food, he said he wanted to surprise me.

And here was my chance to give Al's question the consideration it truly deserved. "Sure, Al. I'll be happy to come. I'm honored that the members have extended this invitation."

"Wonderful!" Al was jubilant. "I'll let the others know. Brunch is on us, of course."

* * *

I got up early Saturday morning and drank a mug of coffee while Dylan ate a light breakfast.

"I should be home around three thirty, four," he said as he kissed me goodbye. "I'll text you when I'm on my way." He gave Smoky Joe a final pat and left.

There was a new boutique shop close to Waffles and Eggs that I wanted to visit. Not that I was in desperate need of any particular article of clothing to complete my summer wardrobe, but clothes shopping was in my blood and—my pulse quickened at the thought—perhaps I'd be lucky enough to find just the right end-of-summer dress for Jim and Merry's wedding.

I parked and stood outside Trends to admire the dynamite washed-silk dress in muted blue and purple colors in one display window and the silky tunic over white leggings in the other. Classy.

Inside, the racks and shelves of T-shirts and shorts and other summer clothing were arranged for easy viewing. There wasn't a saleswoman in sight, so I began looking for items in my size. It was only ten o'clock. I had an entire hour to browse and try on clothing at my leisure.

"Carrie, dear! What a lovely surprise?"

I gave a start, then smiled when I recognized the pretty, diminutive, fifty-something woman approaching me with open arms.

"Leila! How wonderful to see you. But weren't you working in Trendy Elegance?" I'd met Leila Bevins during the winter when I was investigating a colleague's murder.

"This is our second store. I'm the manager here."

"Are you and Fred . . . ?"

Leila's expression turned starry-eyed. "We're married and very happy. And you?"

"Dylan and I are fine."

"I'm delighted. What can I help you with today?"

"I thought I'd look around at everything then focus on getting a dress for my father's wedding. He's getting married around Labor Day. It will be a small affair."

Leila gestured to the back of the store where the more dressy items were located. "Take your time. We have some wonderful sales going."

What appeared to be a mother-daughter pair entered the shop and Leila went to greet them. I checked out a rack of cropped pants and succeeded in pulling out a few pairs to try on.

I added a few tops I liked and disappeared with the items I'd selected into one of the small dressing rooms. I emerged some minutes later, triumphantly holding two tops and a pair of pants that fit well. I brought them up to the front of the store and asked the young woman at the register to set them aside for me.

More shoppers had arrived and the shop was growing crowded. I had enough time to check out the dresses and try on a few before brunch. Waffles and Eggs was only a few doors away.

"Hello! Fancy meeting you here!"

For a moment, I stared at the short, plump woman in the colorful spaghetti-strapped dress, her hair piled high in a messy knot atop her head, as I tried to place her.

"Hello, Vera. Sorry I didn't recognize you at first."

She chuckled good naturedly. "People sometimes don't when I wear my hair up. We met at poor Aiden's wake and again at his memorial service."

"Yes. You're the office manager of his practice—his and Dr. Gannon's."

"I am." Vera shook her head in dismay. "Things haven't settled down since our terrible loss." She lowered her voice. "And we've had even more unpleasantness this past week."

I stepped closer. "Really? What happened?"

Vera pursed her lips and lowered her voice even more. "We had to let Gwen go."

"Oh."

"I shouldn't be telling tales out of school, but soon it will be public knowledge. Just the other day I caught her helping herself to the petty cash, which isn't so petty—let me tell you."

"Did you call the police?"

"Of course." Vera sighed deeply. "This is a serious matter. You think you know someone and then they go ahead and pull something so contemptible. And in an office in mourning."

I shook my head in commiseration. "I had my own eye-opening experience with Gwen. Did you know she'd sent a threatening note to Roxy Forlano?"

Vera's eyes widened. "To Aiden's friend? That poor girl who died in a car crash?"

"Uh huh."

Vera grinned knowingly. "I told Nick that Gwen got her claws into Aiden. Of course she didn't like Miss Roxy coming in to see him whenever she felt like." She cocked her head. "How did you find out?"

"Gwen told me. She knows I'm good friends with Lieutenant Mathers and wanted me to put in a good word for her—what an honorable person she is."

We both laughed.

"Who knows what else that girl is capable of," Vera said.

I glanced at my watch. It was a quarter to eleven. I had just enough time to pay for my new purchases and be on time for my brunch with the council members. I'd have to shop for a dress for my father's wedding another day.

Chapter
Thirty-Three

The interior of Waffles and Eggs was cheery and bright. Sunshine poured into the restaurant through large windows set in oak-paneled walls adorned with colorful posters. I'd no sooner stepped inside when Al called out to me.

"Carrie, over here!"

I walked past occupied tables and booths and headed to the round table for six in the rear of the room.

Al was beaming as he approached to escort me the last ten feet—as if I were his special project, which I supposed I was.

He bussed my cheek and led me to the table. "Carrie, you already know Jeannette Rivers. And this is Sean Powell and Reggie Williams."

"Hi, Jeannette. Nice to meet you, Sean and Reggie."

Jeannette often came to the library to attend art and history programs. I'd googled Sean and Reggie as well as Babette Fisher, who had yet to make an appearance. The two men and I shook hands, then I sat down between Al and Jeannette. I couldn't help but notice I was by far the youngest person at the table, one of the reasons Al wanted me on the council.

"It's so nice to see you, Carrie," Jeannette said. "I hope you're enjoying the good weather."

284

She was an attractive, no-nonsense, petite blonde with bright blue eyes that missed nothing. She and her husband owned a successful real estate company specializing in upscale homes. Sean Powell owned the construction company that had won the bid to convert the building next to the library into our new addition. An excellent tennis player, he appeared to be in excellent shape for a man in his early seventies. Reggie, a handsome black man some fifteen years younger than Sean, was an executive in a PR company that had branches in Greenwich and Manhattan.

"We're delighted you were able to join us on such short notice." Reggie shot me a grin that gave me the feeling he was the designated "get Carrie" hook. Well, sure, since he dealt in PR.

"My pleasure," I returned, hoping my smile was half as dazzling as his.

Our waitress arrived with a full carafe of coffee. After she filled our mugs, she took our orders. I decided to go all out and have waffles with strawberries, blueberries, and whipped cream.

Knowing Jeannette and her husband loved to travel, I asked if they were going on any trips later this summer.

"We're taking our kids and their families on a river cruise next month."

As she began mentioning the towns on the Rhine they'd be visiting, the three men engaged in an animated conversation. I couldn't make out what the subject was, but two things were clear: one, they were resuming a previous conversation, and two, they were at odds regarding the matter. When their voices grew louder, Jeannette and I turned to look at them, as did a few people at nearby tables.

"I thought we'd agreed no business today," she said.

"We did," Al said.

He, Sean, and Reggie nodded like three little boys being reprimanded.

"You can discuss the Seabrook property at the next meeting," Jeannette said.

Just then a woman rushed up to our table. Her straggly fair hair formed an unkempt halo about her face, and she wore a shapeless, wrinkled linen dress that almost reached her ankles. She was out of breath from hurrying.

"Sorry, everyone. I had to make a few stops, then my car refused to start. I ended up having to call the service station."

Al leaped to his feet. "No worries, Babette. Sit down and meet Carrie Singleton. We sincerely hope Carrie will agree to be Jeannette's replacement."

"Hello, Carrie Singleton. I'm honored to finally meet you— our own Nancy Drew!"

My face grew warm with embarrassment.

Al shook his finger at Babette. "You've made your grand entrance. Now please sit down and catch your breath. The waitress will be over in minute to take your order."

Babette smiled like a little girl caught with her hand in the cookie jar. "Of course. I do apologize." She turned to me. "And I really am glad to meet you, Carrie. I've heard you're doing wonderful things at the library."

"Thank you," I said, reaching across the table to shake her outstretched hand. "I'm glad to meet you, too."

Googling Babette, I'd discovered she was divorced and in her late forties like Al. She taught art at the local high school and had had several art shows in galleries around the country.

Our waitress came to take Babette's order, which was very similar to mine. She returned minutes later with our food. As I ate, I chatted with the council members. I learned that Sean's college-aged grandson was spending the summer in

Spain—taking courses in Valencia—and that Sean and his wife would be visiting him there next week. Babette was flying to Mexico to spend two weeks in San Miguel de Allende to paint, and Reggie would be driving his youngest daughter to college in late August.

Eventually, the table grew silent. Al nodded to me. "Carrie, we're so glad you could join us today. I thought it would be nice if everyone shared a little bit about him or herself.

"As you know, I'm a lawyer. I'm married and have two daughters, and I've been mayor of Clover Ridge almost four years now."

The others spoke briefly about their professions and families. When they'd finished, Al turned to me. "Your turn, Carrie."

I looked at the waiting faces, suddenly tongue-tied. "I didn't realize I'd be making a speech today."

Al waved his hand. "Not a speech, Carrie. Just a few words, if you will."

"Of course. I'm Carrie Singleton and I'm the head of programs and events at the Clover Ridge Library. I used to visit Clover Ridge when I was little and stay at the Singleton Farm, which my family owned for generations." I looked at Al. "I'm not sure what else to say."

"How about the part you played in helping to establish Haven House for the homeless?" Al said.

I returned my attention to the others. "I was on the committee that helped make Haven House a reality. Now I see to it that the library sends them books, movies, and magazines that we've culled from our collections."

Al chuckled. "As well as playing a big role in removing the criminal element that set up Haven House."

"I suppose." I didn't like talking about the criminal cases I'd helped solve with people I hardly knew. It might not be rational or even fair, but whenever strangers raised the subject, I felt like I was being asked to provide a cheap, vicarious thrill.

"And you did help bring a few murderers to justice," Babette said.

"I did," I said firmly, hoping that was the end of it.

Thank goodness Al sensed that I had no intention of going into details. "Carrie is a wonderful addition to our community, which is why I thought she would be the perfect replacement for Jeannette."

"And she's young," Babette quipped. "I hope she comes on board so I'll no longer be viewed as the baby of the group."

They all laughed, a sign of the good camaraderie they all shared. A plus if I were seriously considering joining them.

Reggie smiled. "Perhaps Carrie has some questions she'd like to ask us."

"Thanks, Reggie. I do have questions, and the most pressing one is: you have to vote and make policy decisions on so many different issues affecting the entire town. How can you make these decisions when you don't have the technical background—let's say regarding construction, financial matters, education? I'm sure you read reports, but often the real information or problems are hidden between the lines."

A silence fell. *Have I hit a nerve?* I wondered.

Sean nodded. "An excellent point. One thing we do is we turn to the expert in our group in that particular field. The five of us here—six, if we include you—have been trained in different areas of expertise. And we reach out to get the opinions of others in the field."

"I'd like to add that we make a point of really listening to each other when we don't have the same take regarding a particular project," Jeannette said.

"Do things ever get contentious?" I asked.

That brought chuckles and smiles and a few eye rolls. I already knew they didn't always agree. What group of people did?

I asked a few more questions and received the responses I more or less expected. Finally, Al said, "I think that's enough Q and A for now. We don't want Carrie to feel she's being interviewed for a job."

Which was exactly what I'd just been through. I shrugged. No matter. I wasn't after the job, anyway.

"I, for one, think Carrie is one smart cookie and I'd love to have her join us on the council," Reggie said.

The others nodded and murmured their agreement.

Sean glanced at his watch. "How time flies. It's a quarter to one. Gotta go. I told Pat I'd be home by one."

He picked up the bill on the table, glanced at it, then reached for his wallet and handed Al a few bills. "This should cover it."

"And then some," Al said.

"Nice to meet you, Carrie," Sean said. "Talk to you all later," he said to the others and left.

Minutes later, we were all getting ready to leave. I was meeting Angela outside the department store in the mall at one, and had just enough time to stop at the ladies' room to make it on time. I thanked everyone for inviting me to their brunch. Before I could move, Al put a hand on my shoulder.

"Do you have a minute?"

"Just one. I'm meeting a friend." I looked at the receding backs of the others making their way to the exit. I knew what was coming.

Al grinned, looking very pleased with himself. "They loved you, Carrie. Every one of them."

"That's very nice, Al, but—"

"All I'm saying is, please consider it seriously and get back to me ASAP."

* * *

"So, did you tell Al you're willing to become one of our Town Dignitaries?" Angela asked with mock enthusiasm. We were riding up the department store's escalator on our way to the furniture section.

"No, and I can't decide what to do. The council members were all there. They seem nice enough, though of course they were on their best behavior. Who knows how badly they carry on when they don't agree."

"The question is, do you want to be on the council?" Angela asked as we stepped onto firm ground and walked past a dining room display. "It's a whole new experience with lots of responsibility. You'd be helping to make some important town decisions."

I bit my lip. "The thought of that intimidates me. Who am I to weigh in on town decisions in areas I know nothing about? It's not something I ever considered doing."

"Which doesn't mean it's a bad idea. Al thinks you'd be a good addition to the council. And frankly, so do I."

I stared at Angela. "You do? Why?"

"For one thing, it would be good for the library. And the council needs young blood. Sean Powell doesn't look it, but he's close to seventy-five."

I laughed. "Babette Fisher said she's tired of being considered the baby of the group."

"And she's no baby," Angela quipped.

"Do you know her?"

"She was my art teacher in high school." Angela grinned. "At the time, she'd just gotten divorced and there were rumors that she and one of the social studies teachers were dating."

"So?"

"So nothing. It's the kind of thing high school kids notice and like to gossip about. Good, we're in living rooms. Just what I want."

We wandered through living room setups. Occasionally, Angela picked up a vase or a small statue, studied it at arm's length, then set it down again.

"Guess who I ran into this morning while shopping at Trends?" I said.

"Who?"

"Vera Ghent, Aiden's office manager."

"Oh?" Angela frowned as she eyed a large modern glass platter. "What did she have to say?"

"They fired Nurse Gwen. Vera caught her helping herself to petty cash."

"Really?" Angela gave me her full attention. "I hope they reported it to the police."

"Vera said they did. Not that that means Gwen killed Aiden and Roxy."

Angela released a deep sigh. "I wonder if we'll ever find out who killed them. The police don't seem to have any leads. No fingerprints. No DNA. No eye witnesses. No signs of anyone buying thallium. It leaves me wondering if one of my relatives is the killer—and that includes my brother. Not my favorite person, but it would destroy my parents if it turned out he killed Aiden for not investing in his movie of all things. And who knows why he would murder Roxy."

I put my arm around her. "I'm sorry, Ange. Maybe some piece of evidence will turn up when we least expect it."

"You're right." Angela thrust back her shoulders. "Anyway, I don't plan to spend the afternoon moping. Look, there's a display of crystal pieces and another of ceramics. I'm sure to find something."

But nothing in either section pleased her.

"What exactly are you looking for?" I asked.

"A few decorative objects to add to our place that will give it some pizzazz." She made a face. "These are all so ordinary."

"Sally mentioned a store that sells mostly imports. I'm pretty sure it's in the strip of shops just past the other end of the mall. She bought a beautiful Chinese fish bowl there that was very reasonable."

"Mmm, that sounds more like it." Angela glanced at her wristwatch. "Shall we walk over?"

"Tell you what—I'll get my car and meet you there. I have a few errands to run on the way home and this will save me time."

"Sure. See you in a few."

I exited the mall and crossed to the parking lot, which was filled with many more vehicles than had been there an hour ago. I opened my car door and was about to step inside when the sound of laughter caught my attention. Two lanes over, a man and a woman were walking away from the stores. They both looked familiar.

Of course they did! I recognized Vera Ghent and Dr. Nick Gannon. They worked together, but what were they doing at the mall on their day off? Laughing together and—did he just put his arm around her shoulders and kiss her cheek?

They stopped in front of a black Lexus for an animated discussion. Again Nick kissed Vera's cheek. She slid into the driver's seat. Nick walked around the car, put the shopping bag he'd been carrying into the back seat, then got into the seat beside her.

Vera and Nick! They struck me as two little kids up to some mischief. I pushed the button of my ignition and decided to investigate. Probably a waste of time, but I was intrigued. I'd had little opportunity to learn much about either of them since I wasn't planning on having surgery any time soon, and a visit to their office would only have exposed me as a snoop. I certainly wasn't planning to *do* anything—simply follow them a while to see where that led me. Could be Vera was just going to drop Nick off at home. Whatever, it was my only chance to find out more about them.

I watched Vera back out of her parking spot and I did the same. She didn't seem to be in a big hurry, so I waited for her to turn into the lane that exited the mall and fell into line a few cars behind. Two lights later she turned right and I did, too. My brain buzzed with questions. Why were they together? What were they doing at the mall? Shopping, perhaps, but I sensed they hadn't been on a simple shopping expedition.

I texted Angela that something had come up and I wouldn't be meeting her. I paused, then quickly added, "Don't worry. I won't do anything stupid."

Now why did I add that? I asked myself. By trying to reassure Angela, I had probably only succeeded in making her wonder what I was up to. I was so lost in my thoughts, I almost missed seeing the Lexus make a left turn.

The narrow two-lane road was bordered by trees and bushes growing wild, with an occasional house in view. Soon the terrain turned hilly. Now that there were no cars between us, I fell back so Vera wouldn't realize I was following them.

Did Nick or Vera live along this road? I caught glimpses of water and realized I was driving by a small lake where Dylan had gone swimming and boating when he was young. The houses I passed were bungalows and summer cabins. Cabins!

Gwen had said the cabin Aiden had taken her to was near a lake right outside of town. Maybe that's where they were heading. I grinned. Maybe I was about to get some answers to the mysteries surrounding the two murders.

Chapter
Thirty-Four

I dropped back even more as the road snaked from side to side, making wide esses. When it straightened out again, I felt a moment of panic because Vera's car was nowhere in sight. I sped up in time to watch the tail end of the Lexus disappear on a right-hand turn. They must have arrived at the cabin.

The rutted driveway sloped downhill about fifty feet, cutting through foliage only slightly less dense than the woods I'd been passing, Vera pulled onto a leveled-off cleared piece of land next to a red sports car. A few feet away stood a brown-shingled, weather-beaten cabin.

I edged a few feet past the driveway and parked on the side of the road. I closed the car door behind me as quietly as I could and inched back to the driveway, just in time to see the cabin door shut behind Vera and Nick.

Was I really going down there to spy on them? The cabin's two windows facing the road were about three feet above ground and partly covered by bushes. My pulse quickened at the thought of finally getting to hear what they had to say to each other. Here was my chance to find out.

I'll be careful, I promised myself. *Careful and cautious*, I instructed myself as I edged down the driveway, keeping as close to the bushes as I could without getting scratched.

I crouched down between the first window and a sprawling blueberry bush and peered inside. Gauzy curtains covered the glass, but they were sheer enough for good visibility. I was looking into the kitchen. The fridge and stove stood against the wall to my left, and the sink was below the window. Through a doorway to the right I caught a glimpse of a larger room.

Nick unloaded containers of food from the package he'd carried inside onto the small kitchen table. He retrieved a bottle of wine from the pint-size fridge and two glasses from an open shelf. He sat down and smiled at Vera as she emerged from the other room, where she'd probably gone to use the bathroom. She plopped down in the other chair. There were only two kitchen chairs, but then this was a lovers' nest. A hideaway for two, though despite the two kisses Nick had bestowed on Vera's cheek in the parking lot, surely they'd come here to discuss their medical scam and not to indulge in some hanky-panky.

They chatted as they ate and sipped wine—about setting up interviews to hire a new nurse and a few patients' medical conditions. The tone was friendly and congenial, as you'd expect from two people who had been working together for years. When they finished eating, Vera gathered up the debris and tossed it in a plastic garbage pail under the sink.

Were they leaving? If so, I'd better take off before they saw me. What a total waste of time! I swallowed my disappointment. I wasn't going to find out anything about their criminal activity, much less hear a confession that they'd murdered Aiden and Roxy.

But my curiosity got the better of me and I decided to remain a little longer. Good thing I did because instead of leaving the cabin, they picked up their wine glasses, Nick grabbed the bottle, and they went into the other room. I positioned myself in front of the other window and found myself peering into a sitting room-bedroom. A loveseat set off by two end tables sat against the wall facing me, and a king-sized bed jutted out from the adjacent wall. In the far corner was a door leading to a tiny bathroom.

I was very much relieved when Vera and Nick settled themselves on the loveseat and placed the glasses and wine bottle on the side tables. But why on earth had they moved to that room? I hoped they weren't planning to make use of the bed. I mean, Vera was at least fifteen years older than Nick. He was a good-looking guy in his early forties who took pride in his appearance, while Vera was blowsy and unkempt, and that was being kind. Her hair was like a bird's nest, and her choice of clothing made her look shorter and dumpier still.

I sensed the change in Nick even before he opened his mouth. It was as though sitting in this room allowed him to speak his mind. He reached for his wine glass and downed its contents. Then he turned to Vera.

"I'm relieved you didn't bump off poor Gwen."

Vera cocked her head, her eyes wide with false innocence. "Whatever do you mean?"

"Admit it, Vera. You wanted to get rid of her."

Vera sipped her wine and leaned back against the sofa. "I did. She's too nosy by far. I think she figured out a thing or two but had no proof to do anything about it. She's the type who wouldn't think twice about blackmailing us."

"And so you told the police that she stole from us? Wasn't that risky?"

Vera shrugged. "Not as risky as another death. That was sure to bring them sniffing around the office. Not that they'd find anything. As for Gwen, with her record I knew she'd keep her mouth shut and disappear." She scoffed. "The girl's a grifter with an RN degree."

My mouth fell open. So Vera had framed Gwen to get rid of her. Because of the medical fraud? The murders? And Gwen had a police record? I jerked away from the window as Nick got to his feet. He covered his face in his hands, then shook his head as though to chase away his thoughts.

"At least Gwen's alive. But why did you have to . . . do what you did to Roxy?"

Vera looked up at him. "Did you forget how she stormed into the office that night, accusing you of killing Aiden because you were jealous our patients preferred him to you?"

Nick turned up his palms. "That was ridiculous. I was glad they loved Aiden. The more they loved him, the more money we made."

"That wasn't the point," Vera said sharply. "Roxy was trouble. A loose cannon. Saying you killed Aiden would bring the cops to our door."

"I suppose, but did you have to kill her?"

"Sweetheart, I didn't kill Roxy. I merely agreed with her that you murdered Aiden and offered to give her something to calm her nerves."

"What did you really give her? You told me she thought it was something mild she'd taken before."

Vera shrugged. "It was a fast-acting barbiturate. She drove off into the night. Is it my fault her car crashed and the poor girl died?"

I stared, frozen in shock. Was this the same compassionate woman I'd spoken to at Aiden's wake? At his memorial service?

Nick bowed his head. "And Aiden? Was it really necessary to do that to him? He was my partner. We didn't always agree but—"

"He found out about our private enterprise and would have turned us in." Vera smiled. "We couldn't have that. We discussed it, remember?"

"No, *you* discussed it."

"We wanted to expand, add another office, but Aiden was against it."

"He wanted out of our partnership," Nick mumbled.

"And we couldn't have that." Vera opened her arms. "Come to Mama, Nicky boy, and forget all this unpleasantness."

Unpleasantness? I stared transfixed as Nick sat down and gazed into her eyes. Vera took his face in her hands. "Mama will work her magic and erase all the sad thoughts from your mind."

A minute later they were kissing passionately, their arms wrapped around each other like the final scene of a forties movie.

"Ugh!" I gasped in horror, then gasped in shock when I realized they'd heard me. Nick ran to the cabin door as I jumped to my feet and raced to the driveway.

"Don't let her get away!" Vera yelled.

I made a mad dash for my car, watching where I stepped and praying I wouldn't trip and break my ankle on that rutted driveway.

Nick was gaining on me. I heard him pant, felt his hot breath on my neck. He let out a cry as he stumbled and fell. Yay! I ran faster, watching my feet, careful not to step in a hole or under a tree root. I made it to my car, flung open the door, but he'd regained his footing and yanked me from the car.

"It's you!" Nick said. "What are you doing, spying on us?"

"I—" I shut up, realizing whatever I said wouldn't help the situation.

We stood there, his hand clasped around my upper arm. For a moment it seemed that he didn't know what to do with me.

"Please let me go."

"Bring her here!" Vera shouted from the bottom of the driveway.

Nick's grip tightened as he marched me down the driveway and into the cabin. I had a sense of déjà vu. I'd just been watching these two people and now I was their prisoner. What an idiot I was, giving myself away like that!

Nick shoved me down on the loveseat and stood aside as Vera inched closer. I trembled in fear, knowing she was a murderer.

"So," she said smiling down at me, "another nosy snoop. By now you must know what happens to nosy snoops."

"If anything happens to me, the cops will be on you in a flash," I said, my voice quavering.

"I don't think so, missy. I hear the cops like Aiden's BFF, Dr. Forlano, for both murders." She laughed. "No one will be surprised to learn he decided to murder you too. Especially when word gets out that you and Miles were seeing each other behind your boyfriend's back—until you had second thoughts. Being the possessive type, he couldn't bear for you to leave him."

"Miles? That's absurd. No one would believe that."

Vera shrugged into her fake innocence look. "Really? I think they will when the gossip spreads around town in a day or two."

What a spiteful woman. I had the sudden urge to kick her.

Vera stepped back and glanced at Nick. "Enough chitchat. Nicky dear, it's your turn. Take care of Miss Nosy over here."

Nick's eyes slid from side to side. "You mean tie her up? I doubt there's any rope in the cabin."

"I mean kill her. Shut her up for good."

The state of fear I'd been in since Nick had grabbed me heightened. Frozen in place, I couldn't move. But I had to move if I wanted to get out of here alive.

"How?" Nick said. He sounded scared, but I couldn't count on that.

"Everything we've worked for is ruined if you don't take care of her," Vera said.

"But I can't just kill her with my bare hands," Nick said.

"Your precious surgeon's hands," Vera jeered. "They're strong enough." She glanced at the bed. "If you're squeamish, use a pillow to smother her."

"I don't think we need to do this, Vera."

I looked around for a weapon—anything. And then I saw it.

"I'll get a pillow for you," Vera said.

As she started for the bed, I reached for the bottle of wine, grabbed the neck and swung with all my might. Vera went down like a ko'd boxer.

"What did you do to her?" Nick demanded.

He stared at me and I stared right back. He must have seen the fury in my eyes or realized I was now holding a broken wine bottle with jagged edges because he turned his attention to his beloved, who lay sprawled out on the floor, moaning softly.

I raced to my car, glad that the door had been left open and started up the engine. I spun the car around and sped toward town as if the Headless Horseman was chasing me. Luckily the road remained deserted.

When I realized that Nick wasn't coming after me, I calmed down enough to call the precinct. Gracie Venditto, the police-woman who usually dispatched the calls, answered.

"Gracie, it's Carrie Singleton," I said between gasps.

"What's wrong?"

"Tell John that Aiden's partner Nick Gannon and their office manager killed Aiden and Roxy. I just escaped from them."

"Are you all right?"

"Yes."

"Thank God. Where are you? Where are they?"

"I'm heading back to town. I'll come straight to the precinct. They're—"

A red sports car came speeding up behind me. Nick's car! Was he going to ram me into the side of the road? I stomped on the pedal to accelerate. A moment later he swerved around me, deter-mined to escape.

"Carrie! Are you there?"

"Yes. They just flew past me in Nick's red sports car."

"I'll tell John."

Shaken, I pulled over to the side of the road. Vera and Nick were on the run and I was safe. *Extremely* lucky to be safe, I reminded myself, after having done the stupidest thing—tailing them like a nineteenth-century nincompoop of a heroine. Though they never would have seen me if I hadn't given myself away.

Laughter welled up in my chest as the image of Nick and Vera in a clinch flashed across my brain. It dawned on me that Vera wanted Nick to kill me because she couldn't do it—at least not in a straightforward, cold-blooded way. And neither could he. I was laughing hysterically now, though there was nothing funny about it. I began to sob. Deep, heaving sobs that shook my shoulders and had me gasping for breath.

When the jingle of my cell phone sounded, I pressed the phone icon on my steering wheel. Dylan's worried voice came through.

"Are you okay?"

"I am. Just shaken—but how did you know?"

"John called. He's put out a BOLO and got the state troopers involved. You're to go straight home—or the hospital if you need medical attention."

"I don't need medical attention, though Vera might. I hit her over the head with a wine bottle."

"Oh, Carrie."

I heard the love, exasperation, and disapproval in his voice and was ashamed.

"I know. I had no business following them. I'm sorry I upset you after saying I wouldn't take unnecessary risks, but the chance to learn what they were up to was impossible to ignore. And nothing would have happened if I hadn't—"

"Stop!"

I shut up.

"Take a few deep breaths and drive carefully. I'll meet you at home."

Chapter Thirty-Five

I petted Smoky Joe absentmindedly as I watched Dylan, his cell phone pressed to his ear, and tried to make out his conversation with John. After a few "uh huhs" and "I'll tell hers," he ended the call and came to sit beside me on my living room sofa.

"They caught them!" Dylan laughed. "They were on their way to Vera's house to pick up her cat and all the cash she had stashed there."

I bent down to kiss the top of Smoky Joe's head. "I hope they find a good home for the kitty."

"John said Nick started talking as soon as their car was pulled over. He'll be busy booking them and taking their statements for the next few hours so he'd like you to stop by the precinct tomorrow morning to give your statement."

"Good. I'm not feeling up to doing it today." I reached for my wine glass and sipped. Dylan had just opened one of his better red wines when John had called. "In fact, I'm glad we're staying in tonight."

Dylan's face took on a pensive expression. "That little adventure really knocked you for a loop. Maybe we'd better eat here instead of at my place."

I turned to him, surprised at the fuss he was making over this your place-my place business. We did, in fact, spend most of our time here at the cottage, which I preferred since it was much cozier. Maybe Dylan wanted us to spend more time at the manor, which was so much more formal. Still, it was his home . . .

"Dylan, I'm fine. Really. Just a bit wiped out. I'll be happy to come to your place tonight."

He smiled. "Great. I'll pick you up at seven thirty."

"I can drive over."

"Nope. I'll pick you up."

"All right." I yawned. "And in the meantime, I'm taking a nap."

Dylan left. I got up to feed Smoky Joe some treats when my cell phone jingled. It was Angela.

"Are you all right?" she asked.

"Yeah. Just exhausted."

"Dylan told me a bit about what went down. I wish I'd been there with you."

"Me, too. That Vera turned out to be one scary witch. She was behind everything—the medical fraud, killing Aiden and Roxy."

"And Nick went along with it?"

"She had him bewitched with some kind of love spell. John has them in custody now." I yawned. "I need to get some sleep."

* * *

A few hours later I was humming and feeling peppy after my nap. I showered and, since Dylan was making a big deal about this mysterious takeout dinner at his place, I decided to put on a dress I hadn't yet worn this summer. I spritzed on perfume, fixed my hair, dabbed on lipstick and eye makeup, then turned on the TV to watch until Dylan arrived.

The local station was full of the arrest of Dr. Nick Gannon and Vera Ghent, who had been charged with the murders of Dr. Aiden Harrington and Roseanne Forlano. There were news bites of patients expressing their shock and disbelief, except for one elderly woman who insisted she wasn't surprised because there was something about Dr. Gannon she didn't quite like. No one had a bad word to say about Vera.

Dylan arrived at seven thirty on the dot. He wore a short-sleeved blue shirt and well-pressed white Bermuda shorts. He smelled heavenly from a new aftershave.

"Hmm, you look and smell delicious," I said when we'd finished kissing.

"And you look dynamite," he said.

He'd had his car washed, I noticed when I stepped into the black BMW.

"Are we eating outside?" I asked as we entered the large house. The AC was running, and all the drapes and curtains were drawn back, letting in the early evening light.

"Nope. I thought we'd eat inside tonight."

I followed him into the dining room, startled to see the table covered in a linen cloth and adorned with a vase full of pink and purple flowers and a pair of tall candles in elegant holders flickering at the far end.

"Oh, how beautiful!" *And how unlike Dylan.* I spotted the two place settings of Dylan's mother's Villeroy and Boch dinnerware side by side "What's the occasion?"

"A nice meal for us."

"Can I—?"

"No. Have a seat."

He pulled out a chair and I sat down at one of the place settings while Dylan disappeared inside the kitchen. A minute later he reappeared, a goblet of wine in each hand. He sat down and turned to me. "To us!"

We clinked glasses and sipped. "Wonderful wine," I said.

Dylan winked. "It has a very high rating."

He left again and returned a minute later with a tray bearing two dishes with six oysters on the half-shell, a warm loaf of bread, and a dish of butter.

I ate my first oyster and bit into my buttered bread. "This is delicious!"

"So glad you like it."

"Where did you get these oysters?"

"Good, aren't they?"

I got his message to stop asking questions and savored my remaining five oysters.

Dylan removed my empty dish and returned with salad bowls filled with baby greens, tiny tomatoes, and beets. The dressing was flavorful and light.

"Coming up is one of your favorites!" he announced, removing our empty plates.

I burst out laughing when he brought out jumbo-sized lobster rolls. "Thank you for my favorite summer dish. Lobster without the struggle."

"Don't I know it."

The lobster was tender and tasty, as was the roll. It took some effort, but I managed to eat every last bit. "I think I've reached my capacity."

Dylan raised his eyebrows. "Really? I have dessert, of course, but that can wait."

I put my hand on his. "Wait for what? I've enjoyed your special dinner, but what gives? What's going on?"

My mouth fell open as Dylan moved back his chair and sank to one knee. "Carrie Carolinda Singleton, I'm madly in love with you."

For the second time that day, I froze.

"It started back in October when you came by to rent the cottage. You didn't remember me, but I recognized you immediately—Jordan's little sister all grown up. Seeing you brought back memories of the only time I was ever really happy—until recently."

You seemed so grim that morning. So uptight. So different from how you are now. I tried to say the words, but they refused to emerge.

"You were like a wounded bird learning to fly, but you healed and you soared." Dylan took my hand. "You're smart and brave and loving and loyal, and I can't imagine not spending the rest of my life with you."

His smile was tender as he asked, "Carrie Singleton, will you marry me?"

I swallowed. I was awash in emotions—happiness, excitement, and anxiety. "I love you, Dylan, and of course I *want* to marry you. But . . ."

"But *what?*" Dylan sprang to his feet, frightened like I'd never seen him.

"I'm going to need time to get used to the idea."

"All right," he said slowly. "Anything else?"

I shuddered as I looked around me. "Dylan, I don't know how to put this, but I don't want to live in this house."

"Neither do I."

"You don't?"

Dylan sat and took my hands in his. "Are you kidding? This is my parents' house. Stuffy and formal, just like they were. We'll find our own house."

"Then I say yes, yes, yes!"

We kissed for what seemed like minutes.

"Oh, I almost forgot," Dylan said when we came up for air. He reached inside his shirt pocket and drew out a beautiful diamond ring with baguettes on the side and slipped it on my finger.

*   *   *

Back at the cottage, I spent the evening making phone calls to share my good news with the people I loved best in the world. My father was overjoyed. He already knew what Dylan had planned. Uncle Bosco and Aunt Harriet, Angela and Steve, John and Sylvia were all thrilled for me but not at all surprised. Cousin Julia said she was throwing me an engagement party. Sally and Marion and Fran were very happy to hear my good news. So were Trish and Susan.

So was my mother, who burst out crying when I told her. When she could speak, she said, "You must let me help plan your wedding, Carrie."

"Well, okay, but that's a long way off," I said.

"You mean you haven't even talked about dates?"

"Mom, I just got engaged."

"But you must have some idea—"

"Gotta go. Talk to you soon."

At eleven o'clock, Dylan and I finally ate the dessert he'd bought—a chocolate-pecan pie with real whipped cream. He insisted on opening a bottle of champagne, though I'd had more than enough alcohol that day. "To celebrate our engagement."

"All right."

He leaned over to kiss my cheek. "So agreeable. That's what I love about you."

We both burst out laughing.

* * *

Sunday morning Dylan and I woke up early. He offered to go to the precinct with me, but I told him to go work out. I hummed as I drove to the station for my debriefing, as I thought of it.

Gracie came out from behind her station to hug me and congratulate me on my engagement. Danny joined us a minute later. News sure traveled fast in Clover Ridge.

John came out and embraced me in a bear hug. "Sylvia and I are so happy for you guys," he whispered in my ear.

In his office, I answered his questions, most of which had to do with what I'd heard Nick and Vera say to each other. When we were done, John said, "You know you had no business following them to that cabin."

"I know, but they wouldn't have known I was there if I hadn't given myself away."

"Sign of an amateur," John said.

"I know."

Aunt Harriet and Uncle Bosco insisted that we come for dinner that evening. We said we would. It turned out to be a barbecue, and Aunt Harriet managed to snag my cousins Randy and Julia and the children, John and Sylvia, and Angela and Steve for the occasion.

"You're getting married, Cousin Carrie," little Tacey said to me when we had a minute alone.

"I am."

"Can I be your flower girl?"

I hugged her. "Of course. Who else would I have?"

"Does Miss Evelyn know?"

"I'll tell her tomorrow."

* * *

Monday morning, I kissed Dylan goodbye, put Smoky Joe in his carrier, and set out for the library. I accepted everyone's hugs and good wishes, and showed off my ring. I couldn't wait to tell Evelyn my good news.

I was too late. She'd overheard everyone talking about it on her way to my office.

"So, Miss Singleton, I understand you're engaged," she said when she appeared.

"Sure looks that way," I said.

"I'm so happy for you, Carrie. You'll make a fine wife and mother."

"Hey, easy on the mother bit."

"All in good time," she agreed. "Now let me see that sparkler on your finger."

I held up my left hand and my new ring.

"Stunning," Evelyn declared.

"Dylan's agreed to let me get used to being engaged and not rush anything."

"Dylan is one smart fella," Evelyn said.

"He's the love of my life," I murmured. A minute later, I said, "And the murders have been solved. John has Vera and Nick Gannon in custody, and they've admitted to everything, including Bradley Forbes's role over at the insurance company."

"And you're responsible for it all. Why don't you tell me how it all came about?" Evelyn said, her tone somber.

How does she know about my dumb behavior? How does she find out everything?

"All right. I followed them from the mall. Not the smartest, I agree, but they were oblivious to me. Until I gasped at seeing then in a clinch. It really . . ."

"Shocked you?" Evelyn asked quietly.

"It did," I admitted. "Nick and Vera aren't your typical couple."

"Carrie, dear, when will you learn that love takes many forms. Has many faces?"

"I don't know. I'm trying."

"Good girl. And what have you decided about the town council?"

I stared at her. "How did you know about *that*?"

Evelyn turned over her palms and shrugged. "One hears many things in the library."

There she was—mysterious as always. "I think I'm going to do it," I said, surprising myself.

Evelyn smiled. "I think that's a wise decision. Clover Ridge is going to need your support."

I laughed. "So now you're clairvoyant and see the future?"

"Not clairvoyant, but like the new library addition, I think Clover Ridge is in for many changes. And you're the person who can facilitate things."

"Really?" I said.

But she'd already disappeared.

Acknowledgments

My many thanks, as always, to the wonderful people at Crooked Lane Books—I love working with you all! My appreciation goes to:

My editor, Faith Black Ross, who knows how to turn a manuscript into a good read.

Melissa Rechter, Madeline Rathle, and Rebecca Nelson for staying on top of every situation and for being responsive to every question I send their way.

My cover designers Cheryl Griesbach and Stanley Martucci, who create covers that are total knockouts.

David Heath, my copy editor, for his help in making my book an easy, accurate read.

Luci Zahray, "The Poison Lady," for helping me find just the right poison for my poor victim.

And my dear friends and fellow mystery writers and Plothatchers—Janet Bolin, Peg Cochran, Krista Davis, Kaye George, Daryl Gerber, and Janet Koch—who never fail to come up with suggestions and support when their assistance is needed.

Marilyn/Allison